NO ONE LIKE YOU

NO ONE LIKE YOU

by
Dana Pride

Everlasting Publishing
Yakima, Washington
USA

No One Like You
by
Dana Pride

Cover Art by
Jahla Brown

Library of Congress Control Number
2007902946

ISBN: 978-0-9778083-6-6

First Edition
Everlasting Publishing
P.O. Box 1061
Yakima, WA 98907
USA

I would like to thank God,
Who makes all things possible;

and

I would like to thank everyone
who encouraged me while
I was writing this book.

Dana Pride

Dedicated to my family...

*and to everyone who has
ever truly been in love.*

Part 1

SARA

CHAPTER 1
APRIL 1970

Sara Lewis looked at the clock on the wall for the fiftieth time, wondering if it had stopped. How could it be only 6:00? She still had two more hours until the end of her shift, and she had already finished all of her work. The men's suits in her area were in order, every bit of dust had been removed from every shelf and corner, and since she hadn't had a customer in hours, she had already counted the money in the cash register.

She decided to rearrange the ties on the table again. As she was contemplating which one to put on the top of the little pyramid she had made, suddenly she felt tingly all down her head, neck and back. The hair stood up straight on her arms. She felt a presence in the room before she heard the voices of people coming from the elevator. Her head seemed like it was too light for her body, about to float away. She swayed, then she caught her balance by grabbing the edge of the table. She turned to see who – or what – had entered the room.

A group of five young men seemed to roll into the room, bouncing from one display to another, laughing and joking with each other. They looked as if they may be brothers, all with dark hair and dark eyes and tan skin. Sara immediately locked eyes with one of them, drawn to him by a supernatural force. She leaned against the table so she wouldn't collapse, unable to look away from this distinctive man. As the group came closer to her, she could hear them speaking a different language. Sara realized she had lost her words; she did not know what to say to them, she could not think of words in English. In some part of her mind she knew she had a job to do, but she couldn't make herself move or speak. Her own will to act had been captured, as she stared at the man with the black shiny hair like a lion's mane.

"Ingleezi," one of the men said to the others, as they approached her.

"Do you work here?" one man asked her.

"Of course she does," said the man who had entranced her, leaning close to her so he could read her name tag. She felt her strength leave her, as the top of her head began to feel so tingly it was becoming numb. Her brain was already numb. "This is Sara," he told his companions.

"Good evening, Miss Sara," said one of the other men. "We are here to pick up our suits for a wedding. Alameddine?"

Sara knew she was expected to respond. She tried to snap herself out of her daze. These men were speaking to her and waiting for her to act.

"Are we in the right department?" the tallest man asked.

"Are we speaking in English?" another asked, and they all laughed, all except the one who had caused her to lose control of her mind and body. He stayed in complete control of himself while keeping his eyes directly on her.

"Sara, I would like to introduce myself to you. I am Sammy Samson," he said politely, speaking with a British accent. The others had some other kind of foreign accent. "This is my cousin, Hassan, and these are his nephews, Essom, Imad and Jihad. We were told by our friend, who is getting married next week, to pick up our suits here for his wedding."

"Don't be afraid of us because we are bloody foreigners," Hassan told her.

Sara managed to smile at them as she remembered how to speak. "No, I'm not afraid," she said, then immediately regretted that those were the words she had spoken. "What can I do to help you?" she asked, attempting to regain control of herself and the situation.

"Suits, for a wedding?" Sammy reminded her. He smiled kindly at her and she felt her insides melting. His deep brown eyes were tugging at her pounding heart.

"Oh, yes, of course," Sara answered, finally able to move,

reluctant to take her eyes off him. She forced her feet to take her to the holding area where the suits were kept. She concentrated on each step. As she reached for the receipt to confirm the name, she noticed that her hands were shaking. She felt faint, and fell against the wall.

Breathe, breathe, she told herself. What is wrong with me, she wondered. Who is this guy, this Sammy Samson, and what is he doing to me?

She transferred the suits to a rolling rack and brought them out to where the men were waiting. She kept her eyes on the rack so she could keep her composure.

"Do you need to try them on?" she asked, brushing at the suits with her hands, in an attempt to do something besides stare at Sammy Samson.

"Yes we do, Miss Sara," Hassan said. His nephews laughed. She felt Sammy looking at her.

"The dressing rooms are over there," Sara said, pointing.

"How do we know which one is which?" Imad asked. "They all look the same."

"Of course they look the same, Mr. Brilliant," Essom said. "They are for the wedding, they have to look the same."

"The only difference is the sizes," Sara said, noting that all five men were of various sizes. Hassan was the tallest, well over six feet, Sammy was the second tallest, and Imad was the shortest. The other two were about the same height, but Jihad was very thin. They all had black, curly hair and dark brown eyes, but they did not look alike. They examined the suits and each chose one. They took their suits to the dressing rooms. Sara watched them go, and just a second later, Sammy emerged and strode over to her.

"Tomorrow is my birthday," he said. "Would you like to go to dinner with me, and help me celebrate?"

"I – we – I –" Sara stammered.

"I will be 24 tomorrow," he said. "That's something worth celebrating, don't you agree?"

Although Sara was 19, she had never yet been on a date. She didn't know how to respond to this first invitation.

"I can't," she said. She hoped he didn't see that the hair on her arms was extending, reaching towards him.

"Is it because I'm a foreigner?" Sammy asked.

"No—" Sara began.

"Because I'm not really a foreigner. My parents came to the United States from Lebanon, and I was born here in Seattle," he explained.

"You don't sound like a Seattle-ite," Sara said.

"I went to school in England," he said, as if that explained everything. "So, what time do you get off work tomorrow?"

"I'm sorry, but I really can't go out with you," she said, daring to glimpse at his eyes, his piercing eyes, the eyes that could see inside of her.

Sammy stood solidly facing her without speaking, as if he were reading and memorizing her. Sara wondered if he could hear the deafening pounding of her heart.

"Not tomorrow," he finally said. He smiled at her. "We will go out another time." He returned to the dressing room as Sara flopped down in a nearby chair.

She had wanted so badly to say yes, she would go out with Sammy Samson to celebrate his birthday, but she had so many reasons why she had to say no to him. She had never been on a date. He was over 21, and she was only 19. According to store policy, she wasn't allowed to date customers. She had just met him! She didn't know him, and he hadn't met her dad. She couldn't ever go out with a guy until after he had met her dad, and she wasn't ready to introduce them yet. How could she introduce her dad to Sammy, a man she had just met, who wanted to take her on a date?

She also had her Christian standards to consider. Was he a Christian? She could not date a man who was not a Christian, and she could not date a man that she would not consider marrying; which meant that she couldn't date someone she just met until she knew more about him and he had passed her Basic Standards Test. She wasn't like so many girls she knew who dated a variety of men to 'try them out' to see if they liked them, or if they were compatible. Sara would have to know a guy first, he would have to be her friend,

4

and then possibly they would graduate to dating, if their relationship moved in that direction.

Sara smiled to herself. She had her whole dating strategy planned in her mind, but she had never been on a date; and now, the moment she had met an interesting man, she had lost her senses and her ability to function in his presence, except to tell him no, she couldn't go on a date with him.

"Hey, Kid, about time to close up!" The shrill voice of Sara's supervisor, Kelly Garby, brought Sara back to the present. She glanced at the clock and was surprised to see it was nearly 8:00.

"I have customers in the dressing rooms," Sara said.

"I'll get them out for you," Kelly said, heading across the floor.

"No, they're trying on suits for a wedding," Sara said, then lowering her voice, "already paid."

"Well, have you reconciled your cash?" Kelly asked.

"Yes, I have," Sara said.

"I want to get out of here on time," Kelly said. "I'm meeting Harvey at the Oasis Lounge, so get these guys out of here as quick as you can." She marched out of the department.

Kelly Garby was not an easy person to please nor to like. She was demanding and rude, and rumor had it that she had only gotten the job of floor supervisor because she was dating Harvey Maggers, one of the store supervisors. Kelly didn't really do anything except to tell Sara and three of the other salesgirls on the floor when it was time to close. Sara knew Kelly was only 19 – their birthdays were just days apart – but Kelly had no problem passing for 21. She looked much older than 19, with her ironed-straight hair and caked-on makeup. Sara had known Kelly since the seventh grade when they had been in school together, but apparently Kelly didn't remember Sara. Kelly had been sent by her parents to St. Elizabeth's School for Girls in an effort to reform her, but her truancy and constant breaking of the rules had caused her to be expelled before her six month trial period had ended. Sara and her friends at St. Elizabeth's had been shocked by Kelly's behavior.

The men emerged from the dressing rooms in their suits, examining each other. They had been transformed from ordinary guys

5

in jeans to dashing young men in matching black suits with bright blue ties.

"What do you think?" Essom asked, as they approached Sara.

"They look very nice on you," Sara responded.

"Yet the question is, do we look good in them?" Sammy asked. His cousins laughed.

Sara was afraid of how she might answer, but was saved from her unknown words when Hassan spoke.

"Perfect fit, Miss Sara," he said. "Thank you very much."

"It doesn't look like you'll need any alterations," Sara managed to say.

Sammy's eyes bored into Sara's. "Why alter something that is perfect?" he asked, causing Sara's heart to resume its thunderous pounding.

"We'll take them now," Hassan said.

"I can put them into suit bags for you," Sara said.

"No, that's okay, we'll wear them now," Essom said. They all laughed.

"Are you sure?" Sara asked, avoiding looking at Sammy.

"Yes, Miss Sara. Maybe you can just give us a couple of bags to carry our other clothes," Hassan suggested.

"Oh, yes, of course," Sara answered, fumbling behind the counter for some bags. *Think, think, concentrate,* she told herself. *What should I be thinking?* she answered herself. *Customers, courtesy, composure,* she thought, but she couldn't relate those things to this situation.

As Sammy reached to take the bags from her, his fingers brushed lightly against hers, sending an electrifying jolt through her entire body and leaving her completely numb for several seconds. She felt him continue to look at her as he handed the bags to his companions, who carried the bags toward the dressing rooms.

"I felt it too," he said softly. The deep, quiet tone of his voice sent Sara's heart down to her stomach and then up to her head. She held the counter to keep her balance. She looked up to see him gazing into her eyes. "There is no one like you," he said.

"Sammy, are you coming?" one of the men called across the room.

"You won't go out with me for my birthday tomorrow because we just met," he said, keeping his voice low, "so meet me on Saturday at noon at the Space Needle. Don't break my heart."

Before Sara could answer, he was gone, they were all gone, and she was left in the quiet of the store as it had been before they had arrived. However, the atmosphere had changed. She felt as if she had just been dreaming, the images fading as she awakened, being transported from one reality to another. Now she was at work, closing her section, moving automatically.

"You get on out of here, Kid," Kelly's harsh voice barked. "I'm in a hurry," she said, as she removed the cash drawer.

"Everything is in order," Sara said, feeling strange in this familiar environment.

"It better be, or it's your neck," Kelly said.

Sara picked up her rain coat and walked to the elevator.

"Sara, are you okay?"

Sara turned and saw Janet Quipporwhill, who worked in the next department, looking at her with a strange expression on her face.

"I'm fine, thank you."

"Then why are you standing here?"

"I'm going home," Sara said, wondering why Janet was questioning her.

"Don't you think you need to push the button?"

"Button?"

"Sara, what's gotten into you?"

"Nothing, I'm fine," Sara insisted. She wondered if Sammy's presence could be seen on her face, as it had taken over her whole body.

"How long are you going to stand here?"

"What do you mean? I'm waiting for the elevator."

"Then maybe you should push the button, the ELEVATOR button."

"Oh, yeah, sure," she said, reaching to push the button.

"Did Kelly say something to you?" Janet asked.

"Um, no, I don't think so," Sara said, trying to remember if Kelly had said anything to her.

"Then what is wrong with you?" Janet asked, truly concerned. Janet was one of the nicest people Sara knew. She cared about others more than herself. When Kelly had become their supervisor, Janet had encouraged Sara after each of Kelly's verbal attacks.

"Nothing is wrong with me, I just need to get home," Sara said.

"Is your dad alright?" Janet asked.

"Yes, he's fine," Sara answered.

"Well, it must be something," Janet said.

"He is," Sara said without thinking.

"Your dad?"

"What about my dad?"

"Is he something?"

"What are you talking about?"

"What am I talking about?"

"Yeah, I'm not following you."

"You better get home and get some rest. Do you work tomorrow?"

"Yes... no... I forget."

"Maybe we should check the schedule," Janet asked.

"No, I mean, yes, I do work tomorrow."

"Is that before or after your doctor's appointment?"

"What doctor's appointment?"

"The one you need to figure out what is wrong with you."

CHAPTER 2

Sara let herself into the house and wondered if her dad would notice that she was a completely different person than she had been when she had gone to work; then she remembered he was at a meeting at the church. Her father was the pastor of a small church, and they lived in the parsonage next door to the church. The church and house were both made of stone, so Sara had always thought of their house as a little castle.

She wandered dreamily around the house, trying to think if she should be doing something. Everything seemed to be in order, so she went into her tiny room and sat on the bed with her Bible. She knew the answer she needed was in the Bible, but she couldn't formulate the question. She tried to be logical. She had just met a man. She could see his face as clearly as if he were standing in front of her; then she couldn't remember what he looked like. She could hear his voice, speaking to her soul; his words evaporated. She felt intensely alive, yet she was numb throughout her body.

She was going crazy, that's what it was. She had always been a logical thinking person, and now suddenly she was forgetful and out of her mind. She tried to remember the bus ride home. Had she even ridden the bus? She must have ridden it, because if she had walked from downtown Seattle all the way up Capitol Hill, she would have known. Still, she couldn't remember standing at the bus stop, boarding the bus, paying the driver or walking the four blocks home. All she could remember was Sammy Samson.

She knew she couldn't trust her feelings, because feelings changed. Only the Word of God did not change. What did the Word of God say? She opened her Bible, silently asking God for guidance, since she had no idea what she was seeking. Her eyes fell upon a scripture in Proverbs, chapter 19, verse 21.

"There are many devices in a man's heart; nevertheless, the counsel of the LORD, that shall stand."

That was her answer. She had to depend on God. She knew that. She could not trust her own feelings.

Sara couldn't stop thinking about Sammy. He wasn't the first guy to be interested in her, but he was the first guy who had captured her with his very presence. Just for something to do, she unbraided her long hair and began to brush it, her hands moving automatically. She braided her hair again without thinking. She sat on her bed, telling herself to trust God, to concentrate on Him and His Word. She always talked to her dad about everything, but she wasn't ready to tell him about this new experience yet. She wondered if her mom had felt this when she had met her dad. Her mom had told her that for every woman, God had made one specific, special man, and that Sara would know who he was when she met him. Her dad had preached about 'when a man finds a wife he finds a good thing,' inferring that in God's plan, it was the man's job to find a wife. It was not a woman's job to find a husband, so Sara had never thought about looking for a boyfriend. She trusted that when the time was right, God would send the right man to her: but how would she know, if she couldn't trust her feelings?

What was she thinking, anyway? She had just met a man, that's all, nothing more. Sara had met a man. Sara had met Sammy Samson. She made a note on her calendar, 'Met S,' and turned off her light. She stared into the darkness, trying not to think about him.

She heard her dad's key in the front door and decided to pretend she was asleep so she wouldn't have to have a conversation about Sammy. Her dad knew her so well, he would know something had changed about her. She wouldn't be able to contain her new and strange feelings and she wasn't ready to share them yet. Her dad came into her room and he stood there for a moment. She knew he was praying for her, then she heard him go to the kitchen.

She hadn't even gone into the kitchen this evening. Now he would know something had happened to Sara – she always fixed something for him to eat on Thursday evenings because he had meetings at church and he was hungry when he came home. She closed her eyes, trying to think of an excuse, and drifted off to sleep.

CHAPTER 3

Sara walked nervously through Seattle Center toward the Space Needle on Saturday, just before noon. This was the first time she had ever met a man, which wasn't really a date, it was more of an appointment. Why was she doing this? Who was this man who made her heart pound? She glanced from side to side, feeling unseen eyes upon her. What she was doing was not a secret. She hadn't told anyone where she was going... she knew she could trust Sammy. She was being drawn to him by a force beyond her control.

She made her way through the carnival booths, past the food stands and saw the gigantic base of the Space Needle ahead of her. She took a deep breath, deciding that she was going to be calm and cool, logical and sensible. As she approached the enclosed area, she had the fleeting thought that Sammy might not be there. If that were the case, she would not wait for him. She would simply make a loop around the Space Needle and return to the bus stop and go home. The thought had no sooner entered her mind when she felt the heat, the tingling going from her head to her feet, the presence of Sammy. She didn't see him; suddenly he was standing beside her.

"Good afternoon, Beautiful," he spoke into her ear, giving her the shivers.

"Hi," she managed to squeak.

"Let's go up," he said.

"Up?" she asked, not sure what he meant.

"In the Space Needle. Have you been up before?"

"Yeah, when the World's Fair was here, I went with my parents."

"Well, that was awhile ago. I'm sure you'll find it much more exciting now." Sara silently agreed; she was already extremely thrilled, just being near Sammy.

Sammy paid for tickets for them to go to the top of the Space Needle, and they stepped into a crowded elevator. Sara felt the rush of the bullet-shaped elevator as it rose. She wanted to say something, wanted him to say something, but they didn't speak until they reached the observation deck.

"Here we are," Sammy announced as they stepped outside. The wind was blowing up here, compounding the dizzy feeling Sara already had from being near Sammy. He gently held her elbow to stabilize her.

"You're not afraid of heights, are you?" he asked.

"Well, actually, a little," she said. "When I look down, I get a tingly feeling in my feet, and I imagine myself falling, then I feel dizzy, like I'm losing my balance."

"Then don't look down."

"What's the point of coming up here if we are not going to look down?"

"I mean, don't look straight down. Look out, look at the water, look at the beauty of the city and hills around us."

She leaned on Sammy in an attempt to keep herself steady. She knew they were safe, even at this height, with the guard rail surrounding the observation deck. Sammy slowly guided her to one of the telescopes, inserted a quarter, and focused it on Queen Anne Hill.

"Look over there," he said.

"Where?"

"Right there. Do you see that?"

"That castle?"

"Yes, I call it Queen Anne Castle."

"How could I not see it? It's huge."

"I'm going to buy it some day."

"Why?"

"I want us to live there."

13

"What would we do in a big house like that?"

"In Queen Anne Castle, we will raise our children and live happily ever after."

"Do you know how much it would cost, if it were for sale?"

"It doesn't matter. I'm going to make lots of money. We're going to be rich."

"What do you do?"

"I'm an artist."

"How are you going to make that much money?"

"I'm a musician and a singer. Did you hear that the Beatles broke up yesterday? That leaves an opening in the rock and roll world, an opening for our band."

"You're in a band?"

"Yes. Grand. Have you heard of us?"

"Grand?"

"That's our name."

"Just Grand?"

"Hey, great name for an album. We could name our second album that. 'Just Grand.' Do you have any paper in your purse?"

"I might, let me check."

"You need to always carry paper and a pen so we don't lose any ideas. Always be ready, always be prepared."

"Here's a note pad."

"Good, take this down. 'Just Grand.' 'Grand Avenue.' '100 Grand.' Those are some of our future album titles."

"Have you written any songs yet?" she asked as she wrote everything he just said.

"Oh, yes, Darling, I have written more than 300 songs already, and the other members write songs, too."

"So... who are the other members? Those guys you were with the other night?"

"No, those are my cousins. They don't know anything about

music, except they like to listen to it. They can't sing, they're not musicians."

"So who's in your band?"

"We are four, including myself. Dale is our guitar player – he is fantastic, the best guitar player that has ever been born – and then we have Jake Jacobi , master of the romantic bass, and Luke Maybee plays drums. We all sing, and I play around on the piano a bit."

"So, do you perform, or do you just practice together?"

"We have been playing at the colleges and at the University. I would like for you to come and watch us. You can be my special guest."

"I would like that." What was she saying? Her dad would not approve; but she wanted to go.

"In two weeks, we will be playing at the University again."

"That sounds wonderful."

"Let's go inside and get something to eat."

Sara had never eaten in the Space Needle, but she had heard that the restaurant rotated once an hour, so diners could get a full view of the city from its highest building. They took the elevator to the dining level. Sammy spoke to the waitress, who ushered them to a table by the window.

"Do you eat here often?" Sara asked.

"Only with you," he answered, causing Sara to blush.

"This is my first time," she said.

"Would you like something to drink?" the waiter asked.

"Two root beers," Sammy answered. "You do like root beer, don't you?" he asked Sara, after the waiter had left.

"Yes, how did you know?" Sara asked. Root beer was her favorite kind of pop.

"You don't look like a Coca-Cola type of girl."

"I don't like Coke."

"I don't either... and I don't think you are over 21, are you?"

"I'll be 20 on my birthday," she said.

"I turned 24 yesterday."

"Yesterday was really your birthday?"

"Of course! What did you think, I was just using that as a pick-up line?"

"I wasn't sure."

"I will never use a line on you, my Dear," Sammy said. He looked deeply into her eyes, and she knew he meant it. "I'm not like that. So, you're afraid of heights. Of what else are you afraid?"

"Nothing, really," she answered.

"Nothing, really, but what?" he asked. How did he know there was something else?

"Well, it's not important," she said.

"It is to me," he said. "Everything about you is important to me."

"It's so silly, really," she said.

"I'm sure it's not, if it's a fear."

"Well, it's such a weird fear, like, it's never going to happen."

"You have made me so curious, Darling. What is it?"

"Well... you know those drain things they have in the street?"

"Drain things?"

"On the side of the street, so the water can drain into them when it rains?"

"Oh, yes, I know what you mean. You are afraid of them?"

"No, I'm not afraid of them, but I just have an unusual fear that I am going to drop my keys in one and I won't be able to get them."

"Has this ever happened to you?"

"No."

"Has this ever happened to anyone you know?"

"No."

"Then it is not a logical fear."

"Fear is not always logical, but really, it's not a fear, it's just a... just a... fear."

"Well, let's think through this. What would happen if you lost your keys and you couldn't retrieve them?"

"Nothing. I mean, I would have to get new keys."

"How many keys do you have?"

"Two."

"Just two?"

"Yes, one to the front door of our house and one to the back door."

"Just two keys."

"Yes."

"Does anybody else have copies of these keys?"

"Yes, my dad does, and several people that he trusts."

"When will you give me a copy of your keys?"

"Well, actually, I live with my dad. They are his."

"Oh, then it's no problem. If your keys suddenly become irretrievable, they are easily replaceable."

"I guess so."

"So your fear..."

"It's unnatural, I know, but it's still there."

"You have now dealt with it. Your fear no longer has power over you."

"It never had power over me."

"Then you are free."

"I know, you're right. So, if I can ask, what are you afraid of?"

"I am not afraid of anything, my Dear."

"Not anything?"

"No, I have no fear. When you trust God, you have no fear. Surely you know the scripture that says, 'perfect love casteth out all fear,' don't you?"

"Yes, but fear isn't always rational."

"I am."

"You are what?"

"Always rational."

"Always?"

"Call me Mr. Level-Headed, if you like."

"I'd rather just call you Sammy."

"Sara, I have been seeking you all of my life, and now I have found you."

"Seeking me? Why?" What did he see in her? He was so outgoing, so dynamic, so confident; she was just an ordinary girl who could not look away from him.

"You are so special," he told her, as if reading her mind.

"I'm just..." she didn't know how to finish.

"You are just the most special girl in the world," he said.

"Me? No, I'm not," she protested, smiling.

"You are to me," he said, drilling into her heart with his deep brown eyes, "and I would go as far as to say that you are the most special person in the world to your parents. Wouldn't you say so?"

"To my father, yes, -- my mother died a long time ago."

"Oh, I am so sorry, I didn't know," he said tenderly, gently touching her hand.

"No, it's okay, you didn't know," she said.

"If you don't mind me asking, how did she die?" he asked. "You don't have to tell me, I mean, if it is too painful."

"No, that's okay, she died six years ago," Sara said softly. "She was hit by a car while crossing the street. The car came flying around the corner and she didn't hear it."

"Is that why you don't drive?"

"No... but how do you know I don't drive?"

"I saw you come from the bus stop."

"Do you have a car?"

"Oh, no, my Dear, I have no interest in driving. I don't need to drive. Everyone I know has a car. I can get a ride any time, anywhere."

"Isn't that a little inconvenient, finding someone else to drive you?"

"Our drummer, Luke, who is also my roommate, loves to drive, and he'll take me wherever I want to go."

"What if he's not available? I mean, doesn't he have a life of his own?"

"Yes, of course, but in Seattle, who needs a car? I can take a cab or ride the bus. One day, I will have a chauffer to drive me."

Sara couldn't picture Sammy riding the bus. She nodded.

"And you are an only child?" he asked.

"Yes."

"It must be especially hard on your father, with your mother gone. My father depends on my mother every hour of every day."

"I'm sure it is hard for him, but he is very strong," she said, not wanting to reveal much about her family at this time. "So, what did you do for your birthday?"

"My family had a party for me, and all my cousins were there. Then I wrote a song for you. Actually, I wrote three songs for you."

"You wrote three songs for me? But you just met me."

"Finally!"

"Do your parents live in Seattle?"

"In Bothell. My two sisters and my brother live with them."

"Are they younger?"

"Yes, I am the oldest, then my brother, Nadim, then my two sisters, Layla and Lena."

"Why did you go to school in England?"

"My father is an ambassador to Lebanon, so he put me in a boarding school just outside of London. He didn't want me to be kidnapped."

"Did your brother and sisters go to boarding school, too?"

"No, they lived at the embassy with my parents. Terrorists generally want to kidnap the firstborn son, so my father thought it was safer for me to be away at school."

"So, what was that like? I mean, didn't you miss your family?"

"Of course, but a boy has to do what his parents decide is best, and I am glad, because I had opportunities to advance in my studies that I wouldn't have had if I were living at the embassy. I had an excellent piano teacher, and I was able to go to the highest level. Also I was able to explore art history and modern art in places that just don't exist in Lebanon or even over here."

"Did you go to college?"

"Yes, I graduated from the University of Washington. That's where I met the band. That's where it all began, five years ago. What about you? Are you going to college? I know you don't plan to work at Nordstrom all your life."

"I'm not sure about college, but maybe business college. I want to be an accountant or something. I like working with numbers."

"Ah, you are strong where I am weak, my Dear," he said. "I have no interest in numbers at all."

"You were just talking about making lots of money, being rich, so you must have some interest in numbers. I mean, you have to know what to do with it, how to invest, how to budget."

"That is why I have you, to take care of all that for me," he said.

"We just met two days ago."

"I know, that is why we met. Do you believe that for every man, God made one woman?"

"Yes…"

"So do I, and you are mine."

CHAPTER 4

Sammy rode the bus with Sara from Seattle Center to her bus stop. She was surprised when he boarded the bus with her, and again when he got off the bus with her and offered to walk her home. She wasn't sure how her dad would react to Sammy, or how Sammy would react to her dad, but she guessed this was the time to learn. She walked slowly, wanting to savor the moment, but also to delay the inevitable. She needed to explain to Sammy about her dad.

"You live in a beautiful area," Sammy remarked.

"Oh, yes, especially this time of year, with everything blooming."

"Who says trees can't be pink or yellow or purple? I see all of them right here. I remember when I was in the first grade and I painted a pink tree, my teacher threw away my painting and made me do it again, insisting that all trees are green."

"That's terrible!"

"No, that was wonderful. At that moment, he inspired me to become an artist, so I could show others the world through my eyes."

"Oh, that's good," she said, slowing her steps as they approached the church grounds.

"Don't tell me you live in a church?" he asked.

"No, we live next door, in the parsonage."

"Are you a good Catholic?"

"No, we are not Catholic; and Jesus says no one is good but God."

"Then why do you live in the parsonage?"

"My dad is the pastor of a church, a small church, that meets in the basement of the Catholic church. My dad started the church before

I was born, and the priest who lived in the parsonage wanted to move, so he asked if my dad and mom wanted to live here."

"I don't get it. Why do you meet in the basement of a Catholic church if you are not Catholic?"

"It's a long story," she said hesitantly.

"I have plenty of time for you, my Dear."

"Well, I guess it's not that long."

"I'm listening."

"My parents are – my dad is deaf," she said, watching to see Sammy's reaction. When he didn't react, she continued, "About 22 years ago when my parents first moved to Seattle, my dad wanted to organize a church for deaf people. He met the priest of this church at a church conference, and the priest offered to let the deaf church meet in the big room in the basement. I guess he figured they wouldn't make any noise and disturb the services that were being held upstairs."

"That is fascinating!"

"What?"

"I mean, how did your dad talk to the priest?"

"Oh, they used sign language. The priest's mother was deaf so he knew how to sign."

"You mean, talking with their hands?"

"Yes, that's how most deaf people communicate."

"I thought they could read lips."

"Sometimes they do, to some extent, but if they are totally deaf, it's easier for them to use sign language. If a person has a mustache, or doesn't really move his lips when he talks, or if he turns away from the deaf person, it makes it hard to read lips."

"But using their hands isn't really a language, is it? Aren't they just pointing and gesturing?"

"No, sign language is a real language."

"Can they really talk about anything with their hands?"

"I could ask you the same question. Weren't you speaking another language with your cousins at Nordstrom the other night?"

"Yes, we were speaking Arabic."

"Can you talk about anything in Arabic?"

"Well, yes, there is a word in Arabic for every word in English, well, almost."

"It's the same with sign language. There is a sign for every word, or for every phrase, anyway. Sometimes one sign can mean a whole phrase."

"That is amazing."

"Well, now that you know about my dad, I guess this would be a good time for you to meet him."

"I don't know how to do sign language."

"I'll interpret for you."

"You mean you can translate everything I say into sign language?"

"We call it interpreting."

"Can he talk? How will I know what he's saying?"

"My dad does not use his voice. I'll tell you what he's signing."

"Where did you learn to do that?"

"Sign language was my first language. My parents taught me to sign before I learned how to talk. I signed my first word when I was only three months old."

"What was your first word?"

"The first word I signed was 'mama,' before I could say anything." Sara showed him the sign for 'mama,' an open hand with her thumb tapping her chin. Sammy did it too.

"I just signed my first sign," he said, "and it was the same as your first sign."

"So, are you going to teach me a word in Arabic?" she asked.

"Yes, my first word, which was also 'mama.' I think that's more than a coincidence."

"How do you say it in Arabic?"

"Mama."

"Mama. I just said my first Arabic word."

23

"Very good! I love your accent!"

"Thank you. Now, let's go inside so you can meet my dad," she said.

"Wait! How can I talk to your father if you are not in the room?"

"You could write a note."

"He can read?"

"Of course! He reads all the time, the Bible, Bible study books, the newspaper. He reads both Seattle newspapers every day to keep up on the news – he can't hear the radio."

"How does he watch TV?"

"We don't have a TV."

"You don't have a TV? I thought everyone in this country had a TV."

"We don't."

"I don't have one either."

"You don't?"

"No, we don't have one in our apartment. We don't have time for television, we're practicing all the time. My parents have one, though."

They walked up the sidewalk to the front door, which was locked. "Dad must not be home," Sara said. "He never locks the door when he's home."

"It would not be proper for me to enter your father's house when he is not at home, so I must be on my way. I will miss you, my Dear, but I promise I will see you soon."

"Sammy," Sara said.

"I love the sound of my name coming from your mouth, my Dear Sara," he replied, almost causing her to forget what she was going to say. "What is it? Why do you call my name so sweetly?"

"I need to know, are you a Christian?" she asked.

"Of course! What else would I be?" he asked.

"Well, not everyone is a Christian," she said.

"It is important to you that I am a Christian," he said.

"Yes, it is, but I don't want you to just say you are a Christian if you aren't."

"My family is a Christian family. Most of the Lebanese are Christians. We celebrate Christmas and Easter, and my parents go to church."

"Do you go to church?"

"Probably not as often as I should, but yes, I do go. Sometimes I go to church with my family, and sometimes I go with Jake Jacobi. I believe in God, and I believe in His Son, Jesus. So doesn't that make me a Christian?"

"If you believe in your heart and confess with your mouth that Jesus is the Son of God and that God raised Him from the dead, you are saved."

"I confess that I believe He died on the cross for my sins, and He rose from the dead."

"Then you are saved."

"Does that mean we can go out together?"

"You have to meet my dad first."

"I would not dream of taking you anywhere without first securing your father's permission."

"I met you at Seattle Center without his permission."

"Ah, but you came of your own accord, and whether or not you told your father was in your hands, not mine. I did not take you there."

"You took me up in the Space Needle."

"I want to take you everywhere, as soon as I get your father's blessing. However, now I must go. Grand is practicing this evening, and although I savor every moment I spend with you, the band is depending on me to be there on time. Goodbye, my Darling. I will see you soon."

"Bye, Sammy," she said, letting herself in the house. She hurried to the window so she could watch him walk down the street. A car came around the corner, stopped beside him, the door opened, and he ducked into the car.

Sara was full, yet empty; full of excitement, full of questions, full of secrets she must not keep, secrets she needed to share with her dad; yet she was somehow unfulfilled, unsatisfied. She didn't know when she was going to see Sammy again, that was the problem. She felt like an open bottle that needed to be closed before the contents evaporated.

She fixed dinner for her dad while in a daze. Each movement was automatic, without thought, for her mind had left the property with Sammy. She couldn't think, so she just did what was expected of her while replaying the afternoon in her mind: Sammy's deep, romantic voice, his precise British pronunciation, his mannerisms, the way he tossed his black hair by flicking his head, the way his smile was always lingering when he looked at her and spoke to her, his eyes, which were able to see inside of her, his scent, which she could still smell, somehow, and especially the super-charged feeling she had when he was near her.

That evening, Sara was a whirlwind of emotions. She was so excited she couldn't contain herself, yet she was hesitant to let her dad know what was happening to her. She was afraid to admit to herself what was happening to her. She already knew she loved Sammy; she felt as if she had known him all of her life. She felt they were destined to be a couple. Again, she told herself this was not logical; but then, life was not always logical. God did things in unexpected ways, which weren't always logical, and these new feelings were not at all logical. Sara had never had feelings like this for a man; she had never met a man who had interested her. However, she knew that Sammy was the man that God had put in her life. Although they had just met two days ago, he had encompassed her being, and she knew she would never be able to imagine her life without him, or with any other man.

She had to talk to her dad about it; but how could she? What would she tell him? Her dad had very high expectations for her and he wanted only the very best for his daughter. At least she knew Sammy was a Christian, and wasn't that the most important characteristic a man had to have in order for her dad to approve of him?

Maybe her dad would be happy for her. She had always been obedient to him. She had always done everything she could to please him. She knew he loved her; so shouldn't he be happy about this relationship? Oh, how could he be happy about it? Sara had just met Sammy and he was causing Sara to go crazy. She couldn't concentrate on anything. No, she decided this was not the time to tell her dad about Sammy. She would wait until Monday, because her dad would be preparing his sermon for tomorrow and she knew he needed to stay in contact with God. Her dad didn't need her to bother him with something this trivial.

However, this wasn't trivial; this was a turning point in her life. She was no longer just Sara, the pastor's daughter, now she was Sara, connected to Sammy. She just needed time to think; but she could not think!

Her dad came into the kitchen where she was preparing the table for them.

"Could it be possible that you had lunch in the Space Needle today with a man, a long-haired hippie?" he asked.

He already knew about Sammy. Sara had momentarily forgotten that information traveled faster on the deaf grapevine than the news. Someone must have seen her with Sammy, and she had been too engrossed in him to notice anyone signing in the restaurant. Probably the entire deaf community of Seattle knew by now that she had been at the Space Needle today with a man. Normally, she would have been aware of any deaf person in the vicinity, but today was not a normal day. As far as she knew, she and Sammy had been the only two people in the restaurant.

"Yes, Daddy, but he's not a hippie," she began.

"Why didn't you tell me about him?" he asked. "Why are you keeping your boyfriend a secret?"

"He's not my boyfriend—"

"Is he a Christian?"

"Yes, he is."

"He has long hair."

"Daddy, Jesus had long hair."

"Don't try to make excuses for this man – what is his name?"

"Sammy Samson."

"How long have you been seeing him behind my back?"

"I haven't! We just met two days ago."

"Two days ago! You just met him and you went up in the Space

27

Needle with him, and didn't even bother to tell me about it?"

"We were planning to meet at Seattle Center to talk, to get to know each other."

"How well do you know each other now?"

"We just talked, that's all, and we had lunch together."

"And you left the restaurant together and got on the bus together, and where did you go?"

"He brought me home and he wanted to meet you, but you weren't here."

"I trust you did not let him in the house when I wasn't home."

"He respects me too much for that! He said goodbye outside, on the porch, when I told him you weren't here."

"Did he kiss you?"

"No!"

"He's a lot older than you, isn't he? How old is he?"

"Yesterday was his birthday, he just turned 24."

"He's too old for you."

"Daddy, you were seven years older than Mom."

"That was different, God rest her soul. Boys these days are a lot more mature at 24 than they were back in my day."

"Daddy, he is very respectful, and he's not like other guys."

"How do you know? How many other guys do you know?"

"I mean, you will like Sammy. He is very nice."

"I don't want anyone to take advantage of you, of your youth and your innocence."

"Daddy, you have always trusted me, and you have trusted my judgment."

"When it comes to matters of the heart, a person can be easily deceived. I suggest you talk to the Lord, seek Him and see what He has to say about it."

"I think God brought us together."

"Of course God brought you together! God is in control of

everything! But you have to be watchful and alert, to be sure it isn't a trick of the devil."

"Daddy! Just because a man is interested in me, it's not a trick of the devil."

"I didn't say that. I said you have to be sure. If this is what God has for you, you can be patient and wait on His plan."

"Yes, of course, Daddy. We are not rushing into anything."

"You already think you love him, don't you?"

Besides the deaf grapevine, her dad had an insight or discernment that came from God, always revealing her innermost thoughts. Sara had been foolish to think she could have kept a secret from him. She couldn't answer him.

"When you decide to get married, I can either walk you down the aisle or perform the ceremony, but whatever you do, I ask you, please, don't elope."

"Daddy, we just met! It's a little too early to even think about marriage."

"I hope you are not planning to move in with him, like so many young men and women are doing these days."

"No! I'm not!"

"They call it the new morality, but really, it's the same old immorality that has been going on for centuries. You have to call sin 'sin,' you can't give it some other name. And there is always a consequence to sin."

"I know, Daddy, but really, we are just getting to know each other."

"I can see that you are already emotionally involved with him. If his intentions are not pure, it would be better for you to not see him ever again, to suffer a little pain now instead of a complete heartbreak later."

"I think you are over-dramatizing it a little."

"A gallon of clean water can be polluted by just one drop of dirty water."

"I know."

"Where does he work?"

"He's an artist."

"An artist? How will he be able to support you?"

"Daddy, we haven't even talked about that."

"You better seek the Lord while you still have your wits about you. I just hope it's not too late."

CHAPTER 5

A week had passed and Sara hadn't heard anything from Sammy. She had been an emotional mess all week, longing for him, questioning his motives, wondering if he had had an accident, thinking maybe she had conjured him up in her mind. She was at work, keeping her area clean, thankful that she didn't have any customers, when suddenly she felt electrified. She knew Sammy was in the store.

"Hello, my Darling," he said, surprising her. How had he gotten so close to her without her noticing him on the floor? "I missed you."

"I missed you too," she said, without thinking. She consciously decided at that moment to remember to think when he was near her, especially before speaking to him.

"I was out of town, at the wedding," he explained. "I wanted to call you, but I don't have your phone number, and I didn't think it would be proper for me to call you at work."

"I appreciate that. We can't take personal calls here."

"Do you have a telephone at home?"

"Yes, we do, why wouldn't we?"

"With your father being deaf, I mean, did he get a phone just for you?"

"No, he uses it too. We have a TTY."

"A what?"

"It's a machine like a teletype machine. Deaf people type over the phone lines to other deaf people who have them."

"I never heard of such a thing," Sammy remarked. "That is so cool."

"Well, we have one," she said, feeling so comfortable around him. She saw Kelly coming from the elevator, reminding her that she was at work. "Act like you are a customer. My supervisor is coming."

Sammy turned to the display beside them and picked up a blue dress shirt.

"Do you have this in my size?" he asked, perfectly in character.

"I can help this one," Kelly growled, pushing her way over to Sammy and grinning at him.

"It's okay, I am taking care of him," Sara said.

"Back off, Chick, this one is mine," Kelly said, stepping in front of her.

"I believe the lady said she is taking care of me," Sammy said.

"She can't take care of you like I can," Kelly insisted. "What can I do for you?" She looked up at Sammy seductively, moving closer to him.

"Not a thing, ma'am," Sammy said, taking a step away from her.

"Sara doesn't know anything about men," Kelly said, smacking her gum. "She can't help you."

"She was doing a beautiful job before you came and interrupted us."

"Sara, if you need help with anything, I'll be right over there," Kelly said, keeping her eyes on Sammy.

"Thanks," Sara said meekly. Turning to Sammy, she asked, "What size did you say you needed?"

"Your size," he said softly, when Kelly was out of hearing range. Sara felt herself blush. "You are just the right size for me."

CHAPTER 6

Sara knew she was making a mistake. Every instinct told her she should not be going with Sammy to his apartment, but she didn't want to say no to his invitation. She wanted to go with him. She knew that adult things happened in adult apartments, but she felt like she could trust Sammy. He would not force her to do anything she didn't want to do; however, could she trust herself? What did she want to do? She just knew that she felt complete when she was with him.

Sara was riding with Sammy in the back seat of Luke Maybee's blue Mustang, the same car that had picked up Sammy in front of her house the day they met at Seattle Center. Today Sammy had met Sara when she got off work and he took her to the car where Luke and his girlfriend, Debbie, were waiting. Debbie was sitting close to Luke as he drove to their apartment near the University District. Luke had his arm around Debbie, he was driving fast and stopping quickly.

"Are you afraid?" Sammy asked. Sara didn't know if he meant afraid of the way Luke was driving or afraid of going to their apartment.

"No," she said tentatively.

"Luke is an excellent driver," Sammy said reassuringly.

"I can tell," she said, leaning to one side as they flew around a corner.

"Here we are," Luke said, as he turned into a driveway of an old house and slammed on the brakes. "Home, sweet home."

They got out of the car and Sammy led Sara up a back stairway to the upstairs of the house. He opened the door – it was not locked – and showed her into the apartment.

"Welcome to our humble abode," Sammy said, extending his

hand. "This is our living room, and over here our kitchen and dining area, and through there is the bedroom and bathroom. So there you have it."

"Now that Sammy has finally found you, we will leave you two alone to get acquainted," Luke said, pulling Debbie into the bedroom. "If you have to use the bathroom, please knock."

Sara looked around at the sparsely furnished apartment. The kitchen had a small table with three mismatched chairs, and the living room had an old sofa and one chair. Boxes and boxes of record albums surrounded a stereo with huge speakers. The walls were covered with beautiful paintings, and several easels held paintings in progress, with many rows of paintings on the floor, leaning against the walls.

"Let me show you something," Sammy said, looking through a group of paintings. He lifted one gently and placed it on an easel. "What do you think?"

Sara saw her reflection in the painting: her green eyes, her long blond hair, unbraided, falling softly across her shoulder. She slowly approached the painting and looked at it with wonder. Her expression and her very being were captured in the painting.

"You painted this?" she asked.

"I did."

"From memory?"

"Look at the date."

She leaned close to the painting and found his signature – one large 'S' with his first name above his last name. Under his name was the date.

"You painted this on October 4, 1966?" she asked.

"Ten-four, that was the date I completed it. It took me a couple of days."

"That was my 16th birthday," she said. "How did you paint a painting of me before we ever met?"

"From memory."

"But we hadn't met."

"You have always been in my memory," he said softly. "I have known you all my life. I just didn't find you until this month."

"Are you saying that you approached me because I look like this painting you made?"

"No, I painted you in anticipation of finding you. When I found you, I knew it was you. We were meant to be together. Even our birthdays are in tune with each other: mine is 4-10 and yours is 10-4. I'm an Aries and you're a Libra. We're compatible."

"I don't believe in astrology," Sara said.

"Neither do I," Sammy said quickly, "but God put us together, and He had a good reason to put us together."

Sara suddenly felt uncomfortable, and the feeling that she was making a mistake returned. She wondered what Sammy was expecting from her today.

"Would you like a glass of lemonade?" Sammy asked, going into the kitchen area.

"Yes, that would be nice."

Sammy opened the refrigerator, and Sara could see it was packed with food.

"We're fresh out of lemonade," Sammy said, "and out of every beverage, as a matter of fact. How about a glass of water?"

"Yes, thank you."

He brought her a glass of water and motioned for her to sit on the couch. He glanced at the bedroom door as Luke and Debbie burst into laughter.

"So, do you only have one bedroom?"

"Yes, I usually sleep out here. Don't worry, I did not coax you onto my bed. During the day, this is strictly a couch."

"I wasn't worried."

"Thank you for trusting me. I will always remain a gentleman in your presence."

"Thank you," Sara said, though she wasn't sure why.

"What kind of music do you like?" Sammy asked. "We have everything."

"I can see that," Sara said, as Sammy began to look through the albums.

"I know something you haven't heard," he said, going over to the stereo and turning some switches. A huge tape began to roll. He brought two sets of headphones to the couch and sat beside her. "This is a tape of our first album, and you'll be hearing some of these songs on the radio soon."

"Your band is going to be on the radio?"

"Yes, we are. Put these on and listen."

Sara put the headphones on her ears and began to listen to the most unusual and most beautiful music she had ever heard. Sammy put on the other set of headphones and leaned his head back on the couch.

"What instrument is that?" she asked, hearing an unfamiliar sound.

"That is the guitar."

"I didn't know a guitar could sound like that."

"Dale does fantastic things with the guitar. He can make it do things no one has ever heard."

Sara listened for a while longer and was amazed at the harmony of the vocals.

"Did you have a whole choir there when you made this tape? How many people are singing?" she asked.

"Just the four of us," Sammy replied.

"That is amazing! It sounds like at least 20 people are singing. How did you do that?"

"Our voices blend well. Listen to this part."

The voices went from her right ear to her left ear then back to her right ear, as if they were circling her head. An angelic voice then seemed to be covering her entire head, pouring in through the top of her brain.

"Whose voice is that?"

"Do you like it?"

"That voice is incredible. I love it. Who is singing?"

"That's my voice."

She listened for a few more minutes. "How did you do that? How can you sing two parts at one time?"

"Double track. We recorded my voice, then played it back while I recorded the second voice."

"You are singing into my right ear, and then into my left ear."

"Now comes the third ear."

"Third ear?"

"Just listen."

Surely enough, as she listened, Sammy's voice seemed to be entering her head from the top, as if she had a third ear. It didn't come in her left ear or her right ear, it was just inside her head.

"Did you write this song?"

"I wrote the lyrics and the piano, and then the guys each added their own parts. Listen to the bass coming up right here."

"The bass?"

"Yeah, the bass guitar."

As Sara listened, she heard music in a new way. She began to pay attention to each of the individual instruments.

"This is so different," she said.

"It is not your regular run-of-the-mill rock and roll," Sammy agreed.

"No, I mean, I haven't ever heard the instruments separated like this."

"What do you mean?"

"Before today, when I heard music, I just heard it all as a whole, one whole thing. I didn't notice that each instrument was playing its own tune. I just thought they were all together. Unless one instrument, like the piano, was playing by itself, I never heard the separation like this."

They listened for a few minutes and Sara was swept away by the beauty of the music and the captivating sound of Sammy's powerful voice on the tape.

"That is very interesting," Sammy said, nodding slowly. "I would like to hear music as you have heard it. The ultimate goal is to get the instruments to perfectly complement each other, so they all come together as one, the way you have heard it. I could never do that. I always hear each individual instrument. My ear follows each one through the song."

"Well, I don't really have an ear for music," Sara said. "Being raised in a deaf family, we didn't listen to music at all at home. We don't even have a radio or a record player."

"I hadn't thought of that," Sammy admitted. "So... I wonder if other people hear music the way you do, or the way I do?"

"Now I am beginning to hear it your way," Sara said. They listened to the rest of the tape without speaking, and Sara fell in love with the music and with Sammy's romantic voice. They removed their headphones. Sammy rewound the tape.

"Which song did you like best?" Sammy asked.

"That's hard to say," Sara said, "for two reasons. First, I like the whole thing, and secondly, it was hard to tell when one song ended and the next song began, the way they all flowed together, from one to another."

Sammy looked directly into her eyes and smiled. "That is exactly the effect we strove to achieve."

"I think it might have been the second song I really love, though, the one about being 'loving you from the beginning of time.' Did you write that one?"

"Yes, that is one of mine. I wrote the first five songs on the tape, Dale wrote the next three, Jake wrote one and Luke wrote the last song, the one with the drum solo."

"The last one was kind of funny, about dancing with dingoes."

"Luke is somewhat of a comedian."

As if responding to his name, Luke came out of the bedroom wearing a tiger stripe bathrobe. He let out a loud roar.

"What is that?" Sammy asked.

"I'm Tony the Tiger," Luke replied.

"No, I mean that smell," Sammy said, wrinkling his nose. "It smells like mosquito repellent."

Luke ignored the remark. "Ah, young lovers, don't let me interrupt anything," he said, heading to the kitchen area.

"We're just talking," Sammy said.

"Yeah, sure," Luke said, leaning into the refrigerator. "Are we out of beer?"

"If you finished it, we must be out, because I haven't had a bottle of beer in years."

"Yeah, you say that, but they keep disappearing from the fridge anyway."

"That's because you and your girlfriends drink them."

"That's no excuse! We need to keep track of these things."

"YOU need to keep track of these things. I have no interest in beer. It slows me down, and my mind moves too fast."

"Hey, do you guys want to use the bedroom now? We're finished in there."

"No, we're okay out here," Sammy said.

"Yeah, you wouldn't know what to do anyway," Luke said. "Hey, Sara, did you know you are Sammy's first girl he has brought up here?"

"First and only," Sammy corrected.

"Like I said, Sammy probably needs a few lessons."

"No, thank you, we are fine," Sammy insisted.

"Really, I can't stay much longer," Sara said.

"Luke, we'll need to take Sara home in a few minutes," Sammy said.

"No problemo! Gotcha covered," Luke said, returning to the bedroom.

"He was just joking around," Sammy explained.

"I thought you probably had a lot of girlfriends," Sara said.

"Why would you think that?"

"You're so..." Sara stopped and felt her face become hot. She couldn't tell him he was so handsome, so beautiful, so fascinating, and that she had been instantly attracted to him. "You're so kind and so outgoing."

"I was waiting until I found you."

"How did you know you would find me?"

"I have always known."

"How do you know – I mean, you painted a picture of someone who looks like me – but how do you know I'm the way you want me to be?"

"I painted *you*. I feel as if I have always know you. I accept you exactly the way you are. The first time I met you, I knew you were the one."

"How did you know I didn't have a boyfriend?"

"Did you?"

"No."

"I just knew, I have always known you. I knew you would be waiting for me."

"I didn't know that."

"We don't know everything. Some things have to be a surprise. When we are patient and wait, all things God has for us will come to us."

"I have to admit, I haven't had a boyfriend or even dated anyone before."

"I knew that," Sammy said softly, touching her hair. She was already electrified, and his hand so close to her face made her jump.

"Do you ever wear your hair down?" he asked.

"No, I keep it braided for work. It stays much neater that way."

A huge crashing sound came from the bedroom.

"Hey, Sammy, the curtain rod just fell again," Luke shouted.

"You have too many clothes!" Sammy said as he stood. He turned to Sara. "We'll take you home after we take care of this minor catastrophe."

"Me? What about you, Mr. Fashion King?" Luke yelled.

Debbie came into the living room and sat beside Sara on the couch.

"So, how is he?" Debbie asked.

"Pardon?"

"Sammy, how is he?"

"Fine, he's very nice, very polite."

"No, I mean, how is he in bed? I have always wondered, I mean, he looks so strong."

"Uh, we didn't—"

"Oh, yeah, sure. You don't have to cover up with me, I've known him almost two months, since Luke and I have been going out, and you're the first girl he's brought up here. Don't worry, I won't steal him from ya, I just wanna know what he's like."

"Like I said, he's very nice and polite."

"Are you one of those prudes or something? Or are you just afraid to talk about it?"

"Are you ready, Darling?" Sammy asked, as he came from the bedroom.

"Yes," Sara answered, glad to escape from the uncomfortable conversation.

"Hey, do you have a cigarette?" Debbie asked Sammy.

"No, I don't have one and I never will have one," Sammy told her. "Smoking is a filthy habit! It pollutes the air and gives a person the worst breath imaginable. You'd have to hate yourself and your body to want to defile yourself like that, to kill yourself – it's a slow, painful death – that way. I would never waste my money on cigarettes."

"Neither would I," Debbie said. "That's why I'm asking you for one."

"Come on, Baby, we're taking Sammy's girlfriend home," Luke said, coming into the room.

Sara felt her heart skip a beat when she heard herself called 'Sammy's girlfriend.' She floated down the steps and rode home in a daze of unreality.

"This is it, right up here," Sammy said, as they approached the church grounds.

"Oh, excuse me, you really are a prude," Debbie said loudly.

"Don't worry about her," Sammy said to Sara, after he helped her climb out of the car. "You will be around long after she's gone."

"What do you mean?"

"Luke never keeps a girlfriend for long, but you and I will always be together."

CHAPTER 7

All evening, Sara thought about what Sammy had said. She agreed that they seemed to be made for each other, and Sammy accepted her the way she was. However, she didn't know him very well. What if, as she got to know him better, she discovered he wasn't the man of her dreams? She felt whole when she was with him, and more alive than she had ever thought possible; but was she committed for the rest of her life to a man she had just met?

She tried to think logically, to weigh the pros and cons, the way she always did when she made an important decision. She had strong feelings for Sammy, to say the least, and he was a Christian. She was physically attracted to him, and he was polite and kind, and he treated her with respect. He hadn't even tried to kiss her yet. Was that a pro or a con? She wasn't sure if she was ready, so that was a pro. What were the cons? They were slipping from her mind, but she knew they were there... oh, yes, he seemed to think their relationship was permanent already, without giving her a chance to make a decision. Even at this early stage in their relationship, she felt that she could never get away from Sammy. She didn't want to get away from him, but what if she did? Okay, her mind was going in circles. The next thing was that her dad hadn't met him and hadn't given his approval, and that was very important to her. Then there was the question about his employment. She had seen some of his paintings, and they were magnificent, but was he making any money? How did he support himself? His band's music was good enough to be on the radio, but that was a big step, and it hadn't happened yet, so he wasn't making money that way.

She thought about the fact that she hadn't been struck by lightening or killed in a car accident; in fact, nothing bad had happened to her, even though she had gone to a man's apartment without telling her dad about it. Obviously, she couldn't tell her dad about going there, because he would say that an unmarried woman going to a man's apartment was 'the appearance of evil,' and the Bible taught Christians 'to abstain from the very appearance of evil.' She had been seen with Sammy at the Space Needle; she hoped she hadn't been seen with him going to his apartment.

The phone rang and the indicator light flashed. Sara's dad was in his study, so she went to answer it, thinking it was probably a member of the church congregation, since they were the only people who ever called. She lifted the receiver and listened for the TTY sounds but didn't hear any.

"Hello?" she said, getting ready to put the receiver on the TTY coupler.

"Hi, my beautiful one," Sammy said. At the sound of his voice, Sara melted into the chair by the phone. "Are you there?" he asked, when she didn't respond.

"Oh, yes, hi, Sammy," she sighed.

"I just called to tell you I miss you," he said.

"We were just together a couple of hours ago," she said.

"I know, but the more I am with you, the more I miss you when you are away from me."

"Sammy, I wanted to ask you something."

"Yes, Darling, ask me anything."

"I was just wondering, I mean…"

"What is it?"

"Do you… I know you are an artist, but do you have a job?"

"Of course, my Dear. Luke and I have a booth down at Pike Place Market, on the weekends."

"You do?"

"Yes, indeed. Our booth is called 'Out and Out.' We sell outrageous clothing and outstanding pieces of art."

"Really?"

"Do you doubt me?"

44

"No, but you never mentioned it before."

"You never asked. You have to come down and see us at work one day."

"Yes, I'll do that."

"Now, I don't want to keep you on the phone all night. Your father would not approve, although I wouldn't mind keeping you on the phone all night, just to hear the sound of your voice or your breathing in my ear."

Sara lost her words; she couldn't think of a proper response.

"Good night, my Dear, and we will pick you up at 5:00 on Saturday."

"Good night, Sammy," Sara said, hanging up the phone.

Saturday Grand was going to perform at the University and Sara hadn't yet told her dad about it. She felt bad enough that she hadn't told him she was going over to Sammy's apartment – but nothing bad had happened there, had it? She had been introduced to a whole new way of listening to music and Sammy had been a perfect gentleman. Still, she felt as if she were being deceptive by not telling her dad everything she was doing.

Pastor Lewis looked up from his Bible as Sara entered his study.

"Who was on the phone?" he asked.

"Sammy."

"I thought it might be Andrew. His mother is in the hospital. I'm expecting him to call. What did Sammy say?"

"He wants me to go to a concert with him at the University on Saturday," Sara signed, trying not to let the uncertainty show in her face.

"A concert? What for?"

"He's in a band, and they are playing at the U."

"I knew it! He's one of those hippie beatniks."

"No, he isn't, Daddy. You haven't met him yet."

"Are you planning to go with a man I haven't met?"

"No, you'll meet him before I go with him. You're always telling

45

me not to pre-judge people."

"Is he a foreigner?"

"No, Daddy, he was born in Seattle. His parents are from Lebanon, but he was born here."

"He's not one of those terrorists, is he?"

"No, Daddy! He is very nice. You are going to like him."

"I can't stop you from living your own life, but I wish I could stop you from making mistakes."

"Daddy, let me make my own decisions, and if I make mistakes, then I will learn from them," Sara said, trying to convince herself as much as she was trying to convince her dad.

"I pray that you will keep your eyes on the Lord and not be distracted by the first man who comes into your life."

"You have taught me well, and I'm not going to stray just because I met a man."

"I know it's a worldly saying that love is blind, so I pray that you will not be blinded by what you might think is love."

"Thank you. I won't, I promise. You know that I have always been logical and level-headed."

"A boy has not tried to lure you off the narrow path until now."

"He's not luring me off the narrow path! He's a Christian, I told you."

"I'll reserve my further comments until I meet him. When will I meet him?"

"On Saturday, before we go. He's going to pick me up at 5:00."

"He has a car?"

"No, his friend, Luke, the drummer in the band, will be taking us in his car."

"I suggest you seek the Lord while He may be found."

"I am, Daddy. I am seeking Him."

CHAPTER 8

On Saturday at exactly 5:00, Luke's car stopped at the sidewalk leading to the parsonage. Sara watched out her window as Sammy climbed out of the car and she felt her heartbeat increase as he approached the house. He rang the doorbell and the indicator light flashed. Sara and her dad answered the door together.

"Good evening," Sammy said. Sara interpreted in sign language for her dad.

"Tell him I said good evening," Sammy said. Sara interpreted every word he said.

"You can talk to him directly, and I will interpret," Sara explained, signing at the same time. "Come in," she voiced as her dad signed it. Sammy entered the tiny living room.

"Daddy, this is Sammy Samson, and Sammy, this is my dad, Pastor Lewis," Sara said and signed for the benefit of them both. "I will be voicing for my dad, and signing for you, so you two just have a conversation. When you hear me speak, I am voicing what my dad is signing."

"Tell him it's very nice to meet him," Sammy said.

"You can just talk directly to him, you tell him." Sara said.

"It's very nice to meet you, Pastor Lewis," Sammy said.

"It is nice to finally meet you, too."

"You have a lovely home."

"Thank you. Now, what are your intentions for my daughter?"

"Daddy!" Sara said and signed. "Sorry, I just stepped out of my role as interpreter, that was my word. Daddy, please." She gave him a pleading look.

"My intentions are to take Sara to our concert at the University, where she will enjoy a delightful evening of musical entertainment. I will bring her home by 2:00 a.m. when we are finished. Are you signing to him everything I am saying?"

Sara nodded.

"2:00 a.m. on Saturday night?" her dad asked. "We have church tomorrow."

"Yes, I am aware of that," Sammy said, "but by the time we finish and put away our equipment and get her home it will be nearly 2:00."

"She is going to be with you for nine hours on a date?"

"We have to set up and do a sound check and make sure everything is just right, and then we'll change into our stage clothes before the audience arrives. The concert starts at 9:00."

"What about dinner? Sara hasn't eaten."

"We will have something for her to eat. I believe we are bringing in some chicken tonight."

"Sara is my only daughter."

"I will take very good care of her, I promise."

"Sara, have a good time. Wake me up when you get home."

"Thank you so much, Pastor Lewis. It was my pleasure meeting you. I look forward to spending more time with you."

Sammy and Sara got into the car with Luke and Debbie and they drove to the University. Sammy seemed to be struggling to contain extreme excitement. They went in through the stage door of the auditorium where about fifteen people were setting up equipment.

"Hey, take it easy with that!" Luke shouted to a man who was setting up a drum. "That's not a toy!" Luke rushed over to the drums and began to rearrange them.

"I want you to meet the other members of the band," Sammy told Sara, leading her across the stage.

"This is Dale," Sammy said, "the best guitar player in the world. He's the one who made those guitar sounds you didn't recognize on that tape. Dale, meet Sara." Dale was very tall and thin, with long, curly, brown hair and smiling brown eyes. He was holding a purple electric guitar.

"Nice to meet you," Sara said.

"My pleasure, I am sure," Dale said, extending his hand.

"Jake!" Sammy shouted, and a very tan man with fuzzy hair came over to them.

"Jake, I want you to meet Sara," Sammy said. "Sara, this is Jacob Jacobi, the master of the romantic bass guitar."

"Very nice to meet you," Sara said.

"Man, you look just like the painting!" Jake said. "Sammy knew he was going to meet you three years ago, and he painted your picture."

"Yeah, I saw it."

"That's just eerie, man."

"I told you, I would keep searching until I found her," Sammy said. Dale and Jake went back to their instruments as Sammy guided Sara down the steps of the stage to a seat in the front row of the auditorium.

"This is going to take some time, so just relax and watch. One of our roadies will bring you something to eat in an hour or so. I want you to have the best seat in the house, especially when I sing the new song I wrote for you. We have only practiced it a few times, but we all agreed that we should perform it tonight. Oh, the restrooms are up that aisle and out the door and down the hall. Pray for me."

"I am," Sara said, settling into her seat. She watched Sammy jump up onto the stage and move energetically from person to person, until he finally sat at the piano. He played some scales, stopping on one key.

"Larry!" Sammy shouted. A young man scooted across the stage to the piano. "What do you call this?" Sammy tapped the piano key several times.

"Out of tune?" Larry asked.

"I can't play it like this," Sammy said, storming away from the piano and out one of the side doors. Larry opened the top of the piano and began working on it.

Sara watched as each of the musicians and their assistants set up the instruments, microphones, and enormous speakers, and pulled miles of cables across the stage. Larry finished with the piano and sat down and played each key, then he played a tune that Sara did not recognize. Sammy returned to the stage and took his place at the piano. His fingers glided over each key, up and down the scales. He played the piano portion of one of the songs Sara had heard on the tape at his apartment. Dale joined in with the guitar part, and they played several songs together. They stopped abruptly.

"Travis!" Sammy suddenly shouted. "Where is Travis? Get him down here right away!"

"Yeah, Sammy?" a guy said, running across the stage to where Sammy was.

"It's not loud enough," Sammy and Dale said together.

"What's not loud enough?"

"The piano," Sammy said.

"The guitar," Dale said. "We can barely hear ourselves play."

"They are plenty loud enough from the back," Travis said.

"I don't care how they sound from back there," Sammy said. "We have to be able to hear our instruments. We need more VOLUME."

"Any louder and you'll get feedback," Travis said.

"Just turn it up so we can hear it," Sammy insisted. He leaned into the microphone that had been placed at the piano.

"The aliens have arrived," he said, his voice loud and clear throughout the auditorium. "Travis, more volume on the mics too, if it's not too much trouble."

"You're the boss," Travis said.

Sammy sang a portion of a song that tested his entire vocal

range, from deep to high, and Sara felt all tingly and numb. She couldn't believe she was actually at a concert, much less the guest of one of the band members. Grand played several songs together, testing all the microphones, with many more volume adjustments suggested. Luke seemed to be a different person sitting at the drums, never missing a beat, with a very high and distinctive voice which harmonized well with the other voices.

A man brought Sara a box with a Kentucky Fried Chicken dinner. "You're Sammy's girl, so you probably want root beer instead of Coke, right?" he asked, handing her a cup and a straw.

"If it's not too much trouble."

"Anything for Sammy. Everything has to be perfect for him. He would never settle for a Coke girl."

As the man left, Sara took a sip – she was surprisingly thirsty – and discovered it was Coke and not root beer. She decided not to say anything, because Sammy was already emotionally charged. She ate a few bites of the chicken, roll, and mashed potatoes out of politeness, since she was too excited to have an appetite. As soon as she stopped eating, the same man appeared to remove her containers with the leftovers.

"They don't really allow food and drinks in here, but if we clean up, they don't say anything about it," he explained.

A little while later, the band disappeared from the stage and people began to flood into the auditorium. The seats beside Sara were instantly filled. She saw Debbie standing near one of the giant speakers on the stage, near the stage door. She looked angry. A security guard approached her and she shouted profanity at him. He grabbed her arm. She struggled to get away from him. Another security guard joined him and they led her through the stage door. The audience lights were dimmed, as the stage was lit with colorful lights.

"Hey, man, do you have a match?" a guy sitting beside Sara asked.

"No," she answered. "Smoking isn't allowed in here."

He laughed and asked the guy on the other side of Sara for a match, and he handed a lighter to him. The first guy pulled out what looked like a hand-rolled cigarette and lit it. A strange, sweet smell came from the smoke and drifted to Sara's face, and she coughed. A security guard appeared in front of them.

"There is definitely no smoking in here," he said, "and that is definitely illegal. Put it out right now, or it will definitely be confiscated, and you will definitely be thrown out of here."

"Yes, sir!" the guy said, giggling.

"This is the University, not a hippie love-in," the security guard said.

"All right, all right, man, take it easy."

"You take it easy, or you will definitely be put out of here."

"You can't put me out! I paid three bucks to get in here!"

"If you break the rules, I definitely CAN put you out of here, and I can even have you arrested."

"Okay! I get it, man. No smoking, no drinking, no food."

"Now you're talking," the security guard said. "I'll definitely have my eye on you," he said as walked away from them.

"What a bummer, man," the guy complained.

"Hey, man, we're here for the music," the guy next to him said. "I hear these guys are pretty good."

"SHHH! They're starting!" the first guy said.

A man stepped onto the stage and the general murmur of the crowd changed to shouts and cheers.

"Good evening, ladies and gentlemen," the man said into the microphone. Now Sara understood why the band wanted the sound to be so loud, so they could be heard above the noise of the crowd. Girls were screaming and guys were yelling.

"If I can have your attention, please, it is my pleasure to introduce to you, Seattle's own, Seattle's finest, Seattle's toast of the town, who made their debut right here on this stage three years ago, and will be releasing their first album next month: Let's have a warm welcome for Grand!"

The entire auditorium exploded in applause and whistles.

The stage lights focused on the band members and Grand began to play. The crowd hushed. Sara recognized the first two songs from the tape, then Grand played several songs she hadn't heard. Sammy's clear, strong voice floated throughout the auditorium, and Sara felt as if she were floating with it. They stopped playing for a few minutes while Sammy introduced the members of the band. Each introduction was met with cheers, screams, and thunderous applause. The band went into a fast-moving song and the audience clapped hands to the beat.

After Grand played a few more songs, Sammy stood in the middle of the stage and raised his hands as the fans yelled and screamed.

"This next song was written by Dale, and you will soon be hearing this one on the radio. Put your hands together for 'Vivid Love!'"

The crowd went wild as the band played another song Sara had heard on the tape. Then Grand played a love song Sammy had written, and followed it with a song that had a long guitar solo in the middle. The other members of the band left the stage as Dale made very unusual sounds on his guitar. The others returned dressed in different outfits, then they joined the song, one by one: the drums, the bass, and finally the piano. Then they began to sing. Sara was amazed that only four men were singing all the parts: the harmony was so tightly knit, they sounded like a huge choir. She was mesmerized during the entire concert.

All too soon, the performance ended after the third encore. Sara's head was pounding. Her ears were buzzing from the sudden quiet. The crowd left her sitting in the front row, trying to decide what to do. She waited in her seat for about fifteen minutes, then she went up to the stage door, which was now unguarded, and walked down a long hallway. She saw about 50 girls mobbing Luke. Another 25 girls were crowding around Sammy, laughing, crying, and grabbing at him, begging for his autograph. Sammy was talking and joking with the girls, and Sara saw that he was too busy for her. He had all those girls around him; he didn't need her to bother him or to hang around waiting for him. She turned to leave, deciding to take a cab home. Her dad had told her to always have cab fare in case she was stranded somewhere without a ride. She didn't feel upset or rejected. She just knew this was what she had to do. This was Sammy's life, not hers.

As she approached an exit door, she suddenly felt the charge she always felt when Sammy was near. An electric jolt shot through her, starting at her shoulder, where he touched her softly.

"Where are you going, my Darling?" Sammy asked. He must have broken through the crowd of girls and run down the long hallway to catch her. He gently turned her around to face him. He looked directly into her eyes.

"I saw how busy you were..." she began.

"I am never too busy for you, my sweet Sara."

"But all those girls..."

"Just fans, that's all they are. You are my girl. They are good for publicity, and it's part of my job to give autographs, but you are the only girl I need." He put one hand on each side of her face and tenderly kissed her on the lips. Sara was stunned.

"Forgive me, my Dear," he apologized. "I don't know what came over me. I just want you to know, you are mine and I don't need any other girls."

"Um... um... it's okay." She felt better than okay, but words had escaped her again.

"I wanted our first kiss to be special," he said.

"It was," she said truthfully.

"No, I mean, I wanted our first kiss to be on the roof of a tall building, or on a ferry boat crossing Puget Sound, or on top of Mt. Rainier or Mt. St. Helens, somewhere special, somewhere we would never forget. I had to stop myself from kissing you when we were at the top of the Space Needle. I didn't want to appear too eager... but I was."

"I'll never forget our first kiss," Sara assured him.

"Mark this date down in history, April 25, 1970. Or, no, it's actually April 26, it's past midnight."

"My first concert, my first kiss," Sara said, aware that they were being surrounded by girls. "I'll wait for you. I'm not going anywhere."

"Your place is beside me," he said.

For the next hour, Sammy signed autographs and asked each fan to buy a copy of their album when it was released. The girls were all acting so giddy, as if each one of them loved Sammy; and even though he hadn't said it to her yet, Sara knew she was the one he loved.

When Luke and Sammy gave Sara a ride home, a different girl was riding in the front seat with Luke. No mention was made of what had happened to Debbie.

CHAPTER 9

The next Saturday Sara didn't have to work, so she made her way to Pike Place Market to see the booth where Sammy and Luke sold their merchandise. She passed plenty of colorful fruit and vegetable stands, the famous fish market, and several craft booths before she felt Sammy's presence. Then she saw strings of flashing Christmas lights and the huge elegant sign that said 'Out and Out.'

Sammy, standing at the back of the booth with his arms crossed, watched Sara approach him, as Luke tried to entice customers to come to their booth. Sara smiled as she looked at the assortment of clothing they had on display.

"Is that a dingo?" Luke asked a young woman who was walking a dog. He spoke to her using an Australian accent.

"What?" she asked, clearly confused.

"Is that a dingo?" he repeated.

"A what?"

"A dingo. I asked if that's a dingo."

"This?"

"Yes, is that a dingo?"

"No, it's my dog."

"Your dog? Well, it looks like a dingo."

"No, it's a spaniel mix."

"Are you sure it's not a dingo?"

"I'm sure."

"I could have sworn it's a dingo."

"No, it isn't."

"It certainly resembles a dingo."

"What's a dingo?" she asked.

"Actually, I'm not sure. I just like to say 'dingo.'"

Sammy and Sara laughed heartily as Luke walked down the street with the woman and her dog.

"Good afternoon, my Dear," Sammy said, turning to Sara. "What can I help you find? Perhaps a hand embroidered blouse, or a tie-dyed pullover?"

"I found your booth. That was the first item on my list."

"What do you think of it?"

"I like it. Are these all your paintings?"

"Yes. We haven't sold any paintings yet, but they do attract customers."

"These are really good," she said, looking through the rows and rows of paintings. Some were realistic and others had a dreamlike quality.

"Why, I thank you for the compliment."

"No, really, they are really good."

"I went through a painting phase. An image would pop into my head and I'd paint it immediately, before it slipped away from me. Now I'm in a music phase. I do the same thing with songs."

"Where did you get all these clothes?"

"We find clothes on sale and decorate them."

"Who buys them from you?"

"Tourists, guys in bands, hippies."

"Do you sell a lot of clothes?"

"Enough to pay for the booth, and our rent."

"Maybe my dad would like this," she said, holding up a terry cloth bathrobe that had been tie-dyed.

"Do you think so?" Sammy asked.

"No. But I think it would look good on him."

"Oh, yes, indeed. The bathrobe makes the man."

Sara laughed. She admired Sammy's carefree life. He truly enjoyed working in the booth and playing in his band. He didn't seem to be worried about anything, and he was so enthusiastic about everything.

"Our demo tape was picked up by a record company," Sammy said.

"It was? What does that mean?"

"It means we have signed a contract with them, they are producing our first album, and we have committed to doing three more albums with them. Plus they gave us a big cash advance."

"That's great! Congratulations!"

"However, there is a down side to it."

"A down side?"

"For me, anyway. We are going to be traveling all summer to promote the album. We'll be out of town for at least three months, maybe six. Plus, they want us to go into the studio as soon as we can and record our second album. We have more than enough material already."

"How is that a down side?"

"I will have to be away from you."

"But this is your life, your career."

"You are part of my life too."

"I'll be here when you come home."

"You'll wait for me?"

"I don't have anywhere to go."

"You don't now, but something could come up. How long can you wait for me?"

"Until you come back."

"What if I'm gone for six months?"

"I'll wait."

"Nine months?"

"I'll wait."

"A year?"

"I'll wait."

"I can't ask you to wait more than a year."

"Why not?"

"That would be too long."

"You're the one who said we have forever."

"Could you wait for me forever?"

"Will I have to wait forever?"

"No. I'll come back as soon as I can."

"I'll be here."

"I want you to go to school."

"Why? I have a good job."

"I want you to take some classes so you can learn how to handle large amounts of money for me. When we start to make a lot of money, I want you to take care of my accounts for me. You are the only person I can trust."

"How do you know you can trust me?"

"Because I have always known you. I know I can trust you."

"Really, you haven't known me one whole month."

"Can I trust you?"

"Well, yeah, but…"

"But what? You just gave me your word."

"And you believe me, just like that?"

"I believe you, just like that. God put us together. You are strong where I am weak. You can take some classes. I'll pay for them. Just let me know how much you need."

"I can't ask you to do that."

"You're not asking, I'm telling you. We got a large advance from the record company, and I'm investing in you." He reached into his pocket and pulled out some money and offered it to her. "Is this enough? Will this cover your classes and books and everything?"

"Sammy..."

"I love the way you say my name."

"Sammy..."

"It sounds so sweet from your lips."

"I can't take this."

"You need to use it to take your classes. I need you to help me."

Sara looked at the amount he was offering her. It was more than twice as much as she would make working full time all summer at her current job. She could take classes and work part time.

"You shouldn't be carrying around this much cash," Sara said, glancing around to see if anyone was looking.

"I know, that's why I need you to take care of it for me."

"I really can't do this."

"Don't hesitate, it's yours. I have plenty more."

Sara reluctantly took it and wondered how she would explain this to her dad.

Luke came up the sidewalk and settled down in a folding chair in the booth.

"Her name is Erica," he said. "We're going out tonight."

"Man, we're playing tonight at SCC," Sammy reminded him.

"I know, I mean, after."

"What about Julie?" Sammy asked.

"We broke up. She was too clingy, man, a clinging vine, man, wrapped around my neck and strangling me. Hey, got any paper? I need to write that down, I can hear it now." Sara handed Luke a piece of paper and a pen, and he began to write quickly.

"Can you come to our concert tonight, Sara?" Sammy asked.

"I can't. I promised my dad I'd cut his hair."

"And that is going to take all night?"

"I can't be out all evening like I was last Saturday."

"We're going to have to do something about that," Sammy said. "I can't have my girl stuck at home on Saturday night. I need you there with me, in my corner."

"I'm in your corner, always praying for you."

"Thank you, I need that."

"What do you think of 'Bamba' for a song title?" Luke asked.

"Bamber?" Sammy asked.

"Not BamBER, Bamba."

"What does that mean?" Sara asked.

"Bamba, Bamba, you know, it just rolls off the tongue like something you want to sing."

"Like 'La Bamba?' That's a song," Sammy said.

"No! Not Bom-ba. Baaaam-ba."

"Bambi?"

"This is not Walt Disney here. Bamba."

"You write the song, we'll play it," Sammy promised.

"It's got to have a drum solo," Luke insisted.

"Of course! How could a song called 'Bamba' not have a drum solo?"

"I have to get going. My dad will be expecting me," Sara said.

"I would love to be expecting you," Sammy said.

"I'll see you soon," Sara said.

"I'll call you sooner," Sammy said.

Sara drifted home on a cloud, oblivious to her surroundings. Although Sammy had made no commitment to her, in fact, he hadn't even told her he loved her, she felt they were bound together by an unexplainable force. They were certainly attracted to each other, and the only time she felt complete was when he was in her presence. Now that they had been drawn together, she could not imagine her life without Sammy. She was torn: on one hand, they had just met a few weeks ago, and on the other hand, she wanted their relationship to become permanent, or sealed. Sammy spoke as if she were already his, but he hadn't given her a ring or even asked her what she wanted. Yet he knew what she wanted: he knew she wanted him as much as she knew he wanted her.

Now, she just had to get through the evening without letting her dad read her mind or recognize her emotions. If he did, she would have to find a way to tell him she was going to take bookkeeping and accounting classes at the business college this summer on a scholarship funded by Sammy.

CHAPTER 10
OCTOBER 1970

By August, Grand's first album, 'Grand Entrance,' had been released and two singles written by Dale, 'Vivid Love' and 'Cool Heat,' were already playing on the radio. Grand was in high demand and they played all summer at colleges and universities around the Pacific Northwest. Sammy saw Sara daily when he was in Seattle, but he was out of town most of the summer. He reminded her that they didn't need to be in a hurry, that they had plenty of time for their relationship to grow. Sara longed to spend more time with Sammy, but she was glad they were taking things slowly. They still hadn't had their second kiss. She took business classes and worked part time all summer. While doing her homework, she often found herself daydreaming about Sammy and she had to force herself to concentrate on what she was trying to learn. At the end of summer, Grand went into the studio to record their second album.

Sara's birthday fell on a Sunday that year. That afternoon, her dad was at a meeting with the deacons of the church and she was at home trying to decide what to fix for her birthday dinner. All of a sudden, she felt Sammy's presence an instant before the doorbell rang. She ran to answer it.

"I thought you were in Portland!" she said, hugging him.

"I was, but I came back to see you." He held her at arm's length and examined her, smiling.

"That is so sweet of you."

"I couldn't miss your birthday."

"You remembered."

"Of course, and I brought you a gift."

"You didn't have to do that."

"Open it."

Sara opened the beautifully wrapped package and pulled out an AM/FM radio.

"Thank you."

"Now you can hear the songs I write for you when they play on the radio."

"Thank you so much."

Just then the door opened and her dad entered to find them standing in the hallway.

"Good afternoon, Pastor Lewis," Sammy said, and Sara interpreted.

"Hi, Sammy," he said, noticing the box in Sara's hand. "What is this?"

"Sammy gave me a radio for my birthday," Sara explained.

"Why do you want one of those?"

"So I can listen to Sammy's songs on the radio."

"You can just listen to him talk."

"But it's not the same. He writes some really good songs."

"If you are going to listen to music, that is not the proper type of music."

"Daddy, Sammy writes love songs, and they are beautiful."

"If they are not songs of praise to the Lord, then it is a waste of your time. You don't need to fill up your mind with ungodly lyrics. The Bible tells us to sing to ourselves in Psalms and hymns and spiritual songs, not worldly, romantic songs. You start listening to that worldly music from the devil and the next thing you know, you are thinking impure thoughts, changing your attitude, becoming like the world, drifting away from God."

"Daddy, please."

"You are 20 years old today, old enough to make your own

decisions, but as long as you live under my roof, you live by my rules. An idle mind begets idol worship."

"Daddy, there are Christian stations on the radio."

"Do you intend to use the radio to listen to Christian stations?"

"Well, yeah, I can."

"In that case, you can keep it; but you need to watch what kind of spirits you let into our home. If the Lord tells me that you are allowing ungodly spirits to enter through the radio stations you hear, you will have to get rid of it."

"Sara, I would like to take you to dinner for your birthday," Sammy said.

"Can I go, Daddy? I haven't started fixing anything yet."

"Go ahead, it's your birthday."

"What about your dinner?"

"Go on! I'll fix some hot dogs," Pastor Lewis said.

Sara gave him a hug. "Thanks, Daddy." She knew he loved hot dogs.

"See you later, Pastor Lewis," Sammy said. "I'm going to have to learn sign language," he told Sara as they left the house. Sara saw an unfamiliar car waiting for them, a red Datsun with a wide white stripe.

"You remember my cousin, Hassan?" Sammy asked. "You met him at Nordstrom, the first time we met."

"Yes, I remember him, and he has three nephews, right?"

"Yes, he's driving us to their house for dinner," Sammy said, as he held the front seat forward. He followed her into the back seat. "They have prepared for you a traditional Lebanese dinner, for your birthday. Have you ever had Lebanese food?"

"I'm not sure."

"You are going to love it," Hassan assured her, as he carefully navigated the crowded Seattle streets.

Sara was thrilled to be sitting beside Sammy again, her heart pounding, her skin tingling.

"I missed you," Sammy whispered in her ear. Sara felt light-headed. "Hassan, turn on the radio," Sammy said.

As soon as Hassan switched on the radio, 'Vivid Love' began to play.

"How did you know this song was going to play now?" Sara asked.

"Haven't you been listening to the radio?" Hassan asked. "They play it all the time."

"No, I didn't have a radio until today," Sara said. She heard Sammy's vocals, pure and clear, and wondered how many girls across the Seattle area were falling in love with his beautiful voice. "Do they really play it that much?"

"Yeah, and they've started playing Luke's song, 'Grand Am,' too," Sammy said.

"When are they going to play one of your songs, Sammy?" Hassan asked.

"Probably our next single will be one of mine, but it's really up to our managers and the record company. We tell them which one we want to be released as a single, then they pick the one they think will sell the most records."

"Will it be another song from your first album? Because didn't you write just about all the rest of those songs?"

"It's up to the record company. I think they want to release one from our second album, to start promoting it. You know, we recorded enough material for a third album while we were in the studio."

"I believe it! You guys were in there 24 hours a day for more than a month," Hassan said.

"We were on a roll and we couldn't stop. We had to get everything just right."

"What's your second album going to be called?" Sara asked.

"We had a slight dispute over that," Sammy said. "We wanted to call it '100,' but our managers didn't like it. They said it will be confusing when they put it on the shelves in record stores, you know, because they put them in alphabetical order."

"I'm sure!" Hassan said. "That's the hassle?"

"That's what they said, *Abu-shabob*."

"What did you call him?" Sara asked.

"Oh, excuse me, it is kind of like a nickname," Sammy said. "It means, like, father of the *shabob*, eh, father of the guys, you might say."

"Here we are," Hassan said, as he pulled the car into a small garage under a house that sat on the side of a hill. They got out of the car and went up a long staircase to the small house. Sara was greeted by the scent of freshly baked bread as Hassan held the door open for her and Sammy.

"Welcome to the house of my cousins," Sammy said, as he showed her into the house. His cousins were speaking in Arabic as Sammy and Sara entered the living room.

"Excuse me, my cousins, you remember Sara?" They all stood to greet her.

"Hi, Sara, nice to see you again," Imad said.

"Sara, you remember Hassan's nephews, Imad, Jihad and Essom?"

"Yes, I do. Thank you for inviting me to your house."

"This is Imad's girlfriend, Pamela," Sammy said.

"Nice to meet you, Sara," Pamela said. She had beautiful, flowing, red hair and a wide, friendly smile.

"Nice meeting you, too," Sara said.

"Guys, I would like to ask you to respect the fact that Sara doesn't know Arabic, so please, speak only in English while she is here."

"Sure, not a problem," Imad said.

"Come, sit at the table," Essom said, showing her to the dining room. Although Sara's first impression had been that the house was small, inside it was actually quite roomy, with high ceilings and large rooms. The table was beautifully set. "We have

67

fixed a birthday dinner for you that you will not soon forget."

"Something smells really good," Sara said.

"Imad's bread," Jihad said. "He makes bread for us every day."

"Every day?" Sara asked. "You make bread every day?"

"Lebanese bread," Imad said. "We all have our duties at the house, and my duty is to make the bread every day. We each make a contribution to every meal." He brought a plate of flat bread, like thick tortillas, from the kitchen and set it on the table.

"We like to have bread and *hummus* with *tahini* with every meal," Sammy explained.

Hassan brought a tray of cut-up vegetables, including tomatoes, onions, cucumbers, celery and carrots, surrounding a thick, tan-colored dip. "Have you tried *hummus* with *tahini* before?" he asked.

"I don't think so," Sara said.

"You can dip the bread or any of these vegetables in the *hummus*," Sammy said.

"After we have blessed the table," Jihad reminded them. They sat down around the table. Sammy sat beside Sara. Hassan sat at the head of the table.

"Let us join hands," Hassan said. "Father in heaven, for this food we are about to receive, we thank You. Bless the hands that prepared it, and thank You for our special guest today. In Jesus' name we pray. Amen."

"Amen," the others said in unison, as they began to help themselves to the bread and vegetables.

"Oh, the *baba ganouche*," Hassan said, standing and going into the kitchen. "And the shish-kabob," he called.

"He's bringing the eggplant dip, the *baba ganouche*," Sammy explained. "Eh, *Shabob*, what is the English word for shish-kabob?"

"That is the English word," Essom said, "for *lahm meshwe*."

"Oh, I'm sorry, Sara, I am so used to calling them '*Shabob*,' I just broke my own rule. I forgot I was speaking in Arabic."

"It's okay," Sara said.

"Are you going to learn Arabic?" Pamela asked.

"I don't know," Sara said. "Do you know it?"

"I'm learning," Pamela answered. "I have a very good teacher," she said, leaning into Imad.

"I have a very good student," Imad said, and they began to kiss each other passionately.

Sammy cleared his throat. "Excuse me, young sweethearts, we have a guest at the table."

Imad and Pamela pulled apart slowly, looking into each others' eyes. Sara was very embarrassed and tried to occupy herself with some vegetables and the strange-tasting dip.

"Do you like it?" Jihad asked. "It's okay if you don't like it. Most Americans don't like *hummus bi-tahini*."

"It is different, but I like it," Sara said.

"She likes it, *Shabob!*" Sammy said.

"Do you eat here often?" Sara asked Sammy.

"They fix Lebanese dinners here every night, and I come over as often as I am able," Sammy said. "This food is so much better than the American food. This is just like my mother makes."

"Yeah, Sammy used to come every night to eat with us, until he got famous and started traveling with the band," Essom remarked.

"Speaking of your mother, when are they coming back?" Hassan asked.

"They'll be back for Christmas," Sammy said. "They are in Lebanon for a few months," he said to Sara.

"Have you ever been there?" Sara asked.

"Yes, but not in a long time. I plan to go with the band over there."

"Do they listen to that kind of music in the Middle East?"

"In the Middle East, no, but in Lebanon, yes," Sammy said. "Lebanon is the most modern country in the Middle East. They have all the Western styles and fashions there."

"Try some of this cheese," Jihad suggested. "Have you ever had boiled cheese?"

"Boiled cheese?" Sara asked. "How can you boil cheese? Won't it melt?"

"My mother sent this cheese from Lebanon," Hassan said, "and it's really hard, compared to the soft cheeses you have in America. It's also rather salty, so we boil it or fry it. Taste some."

"*Jibneh*," Pamela said. "That means cheese in Arabic."

Sara tasted it and found it to be extremely salty. The men laughed at her expression.

"It's different," she said.

"Now for my specialty," Essom said, bringing a large chicken on a platter to the table. "Garlic chicken." He served some to everyone.

"That looks really good," Sara said, her mouth watering.

"And don't forget the *tabbouleh* salad," Jihad said. He set a type of salad on the table that Sara did not recognize and he spooned a small amount into each salad bowl. "Parsley, tomatoes, *burghul*, a little lemon juice and olive oil and a few onions, all chopped very small, and salt and pepper, with a pinch of mint leaves."

"Bulgur, not *burghul*," Sammy corrected him.

"I always get mixed up, they are so similar," Jihad said, laughing.

"Bulgur in Arabic is *burghul*," Sammy explained. "It's easy to confuse them. Do you know bulgur?"

"I don't think I've heard of it," Sara said.

"Cracked wheat," Pamela said.

"Oh, yeah, okay, that seems, um, interesting," Sara said.

"Most Americans don't like *tabbouleh*," Imad said.

"You have to make it just right," Jihad said, "not too much lemon, and not too much *burghul*. And you have to use fresh parsley, if you want the nutritional benefits. Dried parsley tastes okay, but all the nourishment is long gone."

"It's pretty good," Sara said, after she had tasted it.

"Hey, Sammy, she likes it," Essom teased. "She passed the test! If you truly love a Lebanese man, you've got to love the food from his country."

Sara didn't know how to respond, so she tasted the garlic chicken, which was delicious.

"Sammy, how long are you going to be home?" Hassan asked.

"Actually, I'm not here now," Sammy said. "I'm flying back to Portland later tonight. Can you take me to the airport, *Abu-shabob?*"

"What time?"

"My flight is at 1:30 a.m. I just came to Seattle to celebrate Sara's 20th birthday."

"You're only 20?" Pamela asked.

"Yes, today."

"Oh, I didn't mean that you look older than 20, you really look like you're about 17, but I was just surprised that you are so young. I'm 26."

"You're 26?"

"Yeah, what did you think?"

"I thought you were about my age."

"Thank you, I love you," Pamela joked.

"I told you, you are my little girl," Imad said, starting another round of smooching at the table.

"Ahem!" Hassan said loudly. "Pamela made a contribution to the dinner tonight also."

"Mmmmm, yes," she said, pulling away from Imad. "I made a birthday cake for you."

"That's so sweet of you," Sara said.

"I love to bake cakes," she said, "and decorate them. So for every birthday or special occasion, I bake the cake." She got up from the table, kissing Imad as she stood, and went to get the cake from the kitchen. She returned with a beautifully decorated cake, with flowers and some writing in Arabic on it.

"What does it say?" Sara asked.

"It's your name, in Arabic."

"What's my name in Arabic?"

"It's still Sara, but this is the way they write it."

"It is very beautiful," Sara said.

"I think our written language is much more beautiful than English," Jihad said, cutting a piece of cake for Sara.

"It depends on who is doing the writing," Hassan said, and they all laughed.

"We have to sing 'Happy Birthday' to Sara," Sammy said, leading the song. The entire group sang with joy and enthusiasm.

"Sammy, what was your contribution to the meal?" Sara asked, when they had finished singing.

"You are my contribution," Sammy said. Sara blushed.

"Sammy doesn't cook," Hassan said, "so we make sure he gets fed."

"Is that really fair?" Sara asked. "I mean, you guys do all the work, and Sammy just comes and eats? Do you do the dishes, Sammy?"

The men exploded in laughter.

"Sammy wouldn't know how to begin to wash a dish," Jihad said.

"Yeah, Imad and I usually do that," Pamela said, gazing into Imad's eyes.

"Sammy doesn't have to do anything," Essom said. "He pays for the food."

The table fell silent. Sara felt the tension as they ate their cake without speaking.

"How about some traditional Lebanese music?" Essom asked, going over to the stereo.

"Hassan, we better get Sara home if you are going to get me to the airport on time," Sammy said.

"Yeah, sure, Sammy," Hassan said, clearing the table.

"Can I help you with anything?" Sara asked.

"No! You are the guest," Hassan insisted.

"Let's get ready to go," Sammy told her.

"Thank you all for everything," Sara said. "I really appreciate you having me to dinner, and everything was really good."

"We hope you will grace us with your presence again soon," Jihad said.

"Thank you, I would like that," Sara said, as Sammy steered her toward the door.

"My cousins, I thank you for a delightful evening," Sammy said, bowing. He opened the door for Sara and they went to the car, with Hassan following them.

"Sara," Sammy said, when they were comfortable in the back seat.

"Yes?" she asked, looking at him expectantly.

"I hope this is the best birthday you have ever had," he said softly. He wrapped his arms around her gave her a long kiss, so tenderly, on her lips.

Sara was tingling all over. She felt so good in his arms. When the kiss ended, she felt dizzy.

"Was it?" Sammy asked.

"Was it what?" Sara asked. "What was the question?"

"The best birthday you've ever had," he reminded her.

"Oh, yes," she said, then she added, "so far."

CHAPTER 11

Several days after her birthday, Sara was at work, daydreaming about Sammy. She hadn't had a customer in hours and had nothing else to do. She saw Janet at the edge of her section and she went to talk to her.

"Busy?" Sara asked, not looking directly at her, in case Kelly might be watching.

"Yeah, busy counting the minutes until my shift ends," Janet said. "One hundred eighty-nine."

"Balanced your till?"

"Yep."

"Me too," Sara said, straightening the already straightened clothing near her.

"How's your boyfriend?"

"He's not my boyfriend," Sara said defensively.

"Well, how is he? I heard he has a record out or something."

"He's fine, I guess."

"What, are you two breaking up?"

"No, he's just really busy."

"Oh, yeah, that was what my ex-boyfriend told me before he broke up with me."

"No, really, he took me to dinner for my birthday."

"Really? What did he give you for your birthday?"

"A radio."

"A radio? Guys can be so romantic, can't they?"

"Actually, it was sweet of him. I didn't have one before."

"You didn't have a radio? Are you kidding? Who doesn't have a radio in America? I suppose you're going to tell me you don't have a TV either?"

"No, we don't have a TV either."

"Step into the 70's, Sara! Everyone has a TV. Are you anti-American or something?"

"No."

"How did you watch the moon landing last year?"

"We didn't."

"You're not one of those religious freaks, are you?"

"No, but my dad is a pastor. We just don't have time for radio and TV. Besides, he's deaf."

"Your dad is deaf? Then how come you can hear?"

"His deafness wasn't genetic."

"Then how can he listen to the radio?"

"He can't, but I can."

"How do you talk to him? I mean, you can just say whatever you want, and he can't hear it."

"We communicate using sign language."

"You mean, gesturing and stuff with your hands?"

"Well, kind of, but it's a language."

"How do you know what he's saying?"

"I know sign language."

"I don't get it. Like, how do you know he's talking about a cat if he can't say 'cat'?"

"There is a sign for 'cat,' like this," Sara said, showing Janet the sign for cat.

"But how did you know that meant 'cat' if you didn't know English?"

"My parents taught me sign language before I knew English, so I learned what all the signs meant first. Then when I learned English, I learned how to translate from one language to the other."

"That is so far-out! I had no idea! You must be really smart!"

"Ladies, you are wasting company time," Kelly said harshly, appearing out of nowhere.

"We are all caught up," Janet told her.

"Are you back-talking me? Because I can get you fired for back-talking me."

"I was just informing you of our situation."

"You better watch it – what's your name again?"

"Janet."

"Yeah, Janet, and you, too, Blondie," Kelly said to Sara. "You both better watch it."

Sara suddenly felt Sammy's presence and returned quickly to her section as he stepped off the elevator.

"This one's mine," Kelly said, pushing past Sara to approach Sammy. "What can I do for you, sir?" Kelly asked him sweetly.

"You can't do anything for me, ma'am. I'm here to see Sara."

"She's not allowed to have visitors at work."

"I'm not visiting. I'm a customer."

"Oh, I remember you," she said, looking at him disapprovingly. "Sara is not allowed to date her customers. Store policy."

"If you will please excuse us, I would like to speak with Sara."

"Beat it, Buster! Like I said, employees are not allowed to wait on their friends, and they can't date the customers."

"Sara no longer works here," Sammy said. "Come on, Sara, let's get out of here. I have a new job for you. You'll be making more than your boss here by next week. Good day, ma'am. I suggest you check your manners before you get fired."

"Sara, you can't just leave like that," Kelly warned. "You'll never be able to work here again."

"She won't need to work here again," Sammy said.

"I'll give her a lousy reference!"

"She's already got the best reference she'll ever need."

Sammy grabbed Sara's hand.

"Gather your personal belongings and let's go."

"I just have to get my purse. It's in my locker over there."

"You better leave your locker key," Kelly shouted.

Sara got the key out of the cash register, where she always kept it, and removed her purse from the locker, as Kelly shouted obscenities at her and Sammy. Sara wasn't ready to leave her job like this, but she felt as if she had no choice.

"One last thing before I go," Sara said to Sammy.

"You better not go," Kelly said. "I'm warning you."

Sara made her way over to Janet's section and called out to her, "I hope to see you again some time. I'm quitting."

"Quitting?" Janet asked, coming over to Sara.

"Yes, apparently I have a better job waiting for me."

"Think about me if they have another opening," Janet said. She gave Sara a hug.

"You get back to work!" Kelly shouted at Janet. Janet glared at her without responding.

"Bye, Sara."

"Goodbye, Janet."

"Don't you have something to tell me?" Kelly asked Janet.

"I can't think of anything."

"You better watch it. I can get you fired, you know."

"I know."

Sara left them to join Sammy, who was waiting for her near the elevator. As soon as they were in the elevator and the doors had closed, Sara turned to Sammy.

"Sammy, I just quit my job."

"You don't need it."

"Yes, I do. I need to work."

"You don't need to work here. I have a better job for you, one that pays a lot more."

"What are you talking about?"

"Come with me."

They walked several blocks in silence until Sammy guided Sara into an office building. They climbed three flights of stairs and Sammy unlocked a door. He opened it to reveal a small office with a huge pile of mail and a telephone on the floor.

"What is this place?" Sara asked.

"This is your new office," Sammy said.

"My new office?"

"Yes. I leased it for a year. I need to you take care of my personal finances."

"Are these all your bills?"

"No, I also need you to respond to our fan mail. This is what we received this week. The record company sent it to us and I had it delivered here."

"There must be hundreds of letters here."

"More than a thousand. That's why I need you. I don't have time to deal with it, but I want everyone to have a personal response. We need to get our band's merchandise organized, some t-shirts and stickers, and I want you to type a quarterly newsletter for people who join our fan club. You can buy the furniture you need, desks, chairs, file cabinets, tables, cabinets, whatever you need. Here's some cash to get you started." He put a stack of $100 bills in her hand. "Now, come with me to the bank. I want to put you on my bank accounts."

"Sammy, I'm not—"

"The money is really starting to come in, and you are the only one I trust to handle my finances, Sara. I can't do it."

"What about one of your cousins?"

"They can't do it. They don't know anything about money. You do. You can do it. Say you will. I need you. You are the only one I trust."

She felt pressured to accept the job, especially since she had so suddenly left the job she had had for the past three years, the only job she had ever had. She was afraid of what her dad would say.

"You haven't mentioned my salary."

"You decide what that should be, when you see how much is in my accounts. What do accountants make? You should make at least twice that much. I don't want to underpay you, because this is going to be quite a big job for you. I'll need you to take care of all my bills for me, and to take care of my investments."

"I don't know how to do that."

"Take more classes. Hire someone to help you. If you need help with the fan club, by all means, hire someone to help you with that too. Give yourself a hundred dollar bonus today."

"One hundred dollars?" she asked, shocked.

"Okay, make it five hundred dollars. You deserve a raise. Be sure to pay yourself at least double – no, make it five times what you were making at the store. Five times your full-time salary, only I don't want you working full time. If you need to work more than 20 hours a week, hire someone to help you. Who ever decided a work week has to be 40 hours? That's too much."

He locked the office and handed the key to Sara. "Here's one more key for your key ring. Now, don't worry about dropping it down a storm drain. I have a copy too."

They left the building and walked a few blocks to Rainier Bank. When Sammy asked to speak to the manager, Mr. Lavricka, he appeared immediately.

"What can I do for you today, Mr. Samson?"

"This is my accountant, Sara Lewis, and I want to put her name on all my accounts. She will be taking care of my finances."

Mr. Lavricka eyed Sara suspiciously.

"ALL of your finances, Mr. Samson?"

"Yes. All of them. Can we get to the paperwork? I have a schedule to keep."

"Of course, come into my office." Mr. Lavricka took them to a beautifully furnished corner office on the second floor.

"Now, to which account do you want to add her name?"

"All of them."

"Miss Dunn, can you please bring me Mr. Sammy Samson's file for signature changes?" he said into the intercom.

"Yes, Mr. Lavricka," a voice replied. A moment later, a young lady appeared with a folder and placed it on Mr. Lavricka's desk.

"Thank you, Miss Dunn, that will be all."

"Miss Dunn, we are done," Sammy added, and Mr. Lavricka forced a laugh. Miss Dunn smiled at Sammy as she left the office.

"Have a seat, please," Mr. Lavricka said. "You'll need to sign here, Mr. Samson, and both of you need to sign here and here. I'll need your initials on this page, and sign here and here, both of you."

"Is that all of my accounts?" Sammy asked.

"Do you want to give her access to your safety deposit box and your savings bonds, and all of your savings accounts?"

"Yes, everything," Sammy said.

"All right, both of you need to sign here and here, and on each of these." He pointed to each place where they needed to sign. When they finished signing, Mr. Lavricka gathered all the papers together and placed them back in the folder.

"That should do it. Can I help you with anything else today, Mr. Samson?"

"Does Miss Lewis have full control of all my accounts now?"

"Yes, she does, but so do you. Do you need anything else today, Mr. Samson?"

"Yes, I would like a copy of the balance in all my accounts

for Miss Lewis," Sammy said.

"Miss Dunn," Mr. Lavricka said into the intercom, "please make a copy of all Mr. Samson's account balances for him to take with him today. Can I do anything else for you, Mr. Samson?"

"Yes, you can stop calling me Mr. Samson and just call me Sammy," he said.

"Whatever you say, Mr.— uh, Sammy."

As they left the bank, Sammy remarked, "I don't really trust that guy. If you find anything wrong with any of my accounts, switch banks. Everything I have is in your hands."

Sara was overwhelmed by the rapid occurrence of the events of the day, and the amount of money Sammy was putting in her control. She knew she was trustworthy, but why did he trust her with everything he had? Was this going to be more than she could handle?

Hassan was parked beside the bank, ready to take Sammy to the airport to catch a plane to Los Angeles, where he would be spending the next few weeks with Grand. Sara stood on the sidewalk and thought for about two minutes. Then she decided to go back to Nordstrom and talk to Janet.

"What are you doing here?" Janet asked, nervously watching for Kelly.

"I have a job for you," Sara said.

"Are you serious?"

"Yes, working for Grand."

"No kidding?"

"I'm serious."

"Really? Doing what?"

"Sammy just put me in charge of the fan club, and I need some help."

"Do they really have that many fans?"

"We have more than a thousand letters to answer already."

"Seriously?"

"I'm serious."

"Hey, Chick, you come crawling back, to beg for your job back?" Kelly's harsh voice resonated off the walls.

"No, I'm here to talk to Janet."

"You, of all people, should know that she can't wait on her friends, and she can't be visiting on her work time," Kelly said rudely.

"Is this a real deal?" Janet asked Sara quietly.

"More real than working here," Sara told her.

"Kelly," Janet said, pulling up her courage, "I'm quitting now. It's been nice – well, maybe nice isn't the word – it's been a job working for you. Goodbye."

"You can't just quit like that! I'll never give you a reference! Either of you! You are going to be sorry!" Kelly shouted.

"Kelly!" Harvey Maggers said. "Why are you shouting at our employees like that?"

"They both quit today," Kelly said.

"Well, then, you better be extra nice to them, so they will remain our customers. Come with me, Kelly. You need a lesson in customer relations. Good luck with your future endeavors, girls," Harvey said to Sara and Janet as they walked to the elevator.

Sara took Janet to the fan club office. Janet was so excited, she jumped up and down in their new workplace.

"Help me make a list of what we need," Sara said.

"First, we need paper and a pen to make a list," Janet said. "Then, how about a couple of desks and chairs and file cabinets and a typewriter and some paper and a crate of envelopes and a postage machine."

"What's a postage machine?"

"It's a thing you get from the post office so you can weigh mail and then stamp it, for bulk mailing. My aunt has one at her business."

"So you think we'll be mailing in bulk?" Sara asked,

attempting to stack the huge mountain of letters into some kind of order.

"So, how much are we making? At least minimum wage, I hope."

"I haven't figured it out yet, but you'll be well paid for your work, I can guarantee that. Sammy is very generous to his employees."

"I like it already!" Janet said. "When do we start?"

"Let's start tomorrow. I need to figure out how I'm going to tell my dad about everything that happened today."

"Why do you have to tell him?"

"I tell him everything. We're very close."

"Sara, there comes a time when a girl has to leave her family to pursue her dreams, her career, her own life."

"I know, but for me, that time has not yet come. I'm still Daddy's girl."

"Let's get an apartment together!"

"I'm not ready for that."

"Sure you are. You're 20 now. I'm 21. We need to get out on our own."

"Let's do one thing at a time. We'll get things in order here, then we can think about getting an apartment."

"Okay, I'll meet you here at 9:00 tomorrow morning?"

"Why so early? Let's come in at about 11:00 or so, after the morning traffic rush."

"It doesn't matter, I take the bus."

"Yeah, me too, but we only need to work part time to make a full-time salary here. Let's work from eleven to three."

"I can live with that."

"Tomorrow we'll look for the furniture and stuff we need. We can't get started until we have the proper furnishings."

"Sara," Janet said, twirling around in the office, "I'm going to love working with you."

CHAPTER 12
DECEMBER 1970

By December, Sara and Janet had the fan club office running smoothly. They kept up with the hundreds of letters that were sent to Grand monthly, and they had received a huge stock of Grand t-shirts and biographical folders to send to people who joined the fan club. Janet checked the post office box daily to collect fan mail and Sara started a separate bank account at a different bank just for the fan club money they were receiving. With the release of Grand's second album and their third and fourth singles being played on the radio, their fan club had already grown to more than 900 members.

Sara was becoming familiar with Sammy's finances as well. She was now writing checks for his rent and living expenses, and for his credit card, which he used while he traveled. It must have had an unlimited ceiling, because he spent so much; yet Sara was able to pay the full balance every month. Sammy had instructed her to send checks monthly to his cousins, to his parents, to his grandparents in Lebanon, and to her dad's church. When she read the quarterly statement and saw the huge deposits the record company had made into his account, she began to fathom just how large his empire was already growing to be.

A week before Christmas, Sara and Janet were sorting Grand's fan mail. Since many of the letters were addressed to Sammy, Sara took care of them, while Janet answered the letters addressed to the rest of the band members. Sammy had mentioned that the band didn't have time to read all the letters, which was why they had hired the girls to run their fan club. They saved all the letters and cards in boxes for the band members to read later. They received hundreds of Christmas cards after sending out a Christmas letter to all their fans which included a personal message from each of the band members and a preview of Grand's schedule for the next four months. Sara had been amazed when she had seen the full schedule of touring and recording, and she wondered how this could be humanly possible.

All of a sudden, Sara felt tingly and light-headed and she knew Sammy was in the vicinity.

"Sammy's here," she told Janet.

"Sammy? Really? He's coming here?" Janet hadn't met him yet and was quite impressed that Sara actually knew a famous person.

The door opened and Sammy entered the office.

"Sara, my Darling," he said, his eyes sparkling as he said her name. He kissed her on the cheek.

"Hi Sammy," she said, "I'd like you to meet—"

"Janet, of course," Sammy said, turning to Janet. "Sara has told me about you."

"Me? You... me?" Janet stammered. "You know my name?"

"Of course, Dear, you are a great help to my Sara, and I greatly appreciate you. I beg you, though, don't let her work too hard. You let me know if the work becomes overwhelming."

"Oh, yeah, sure, that's cool," she said.

"Sara, Darling, would you like to accompany me to a Christmas party tonight?"

"Tonight?" she repeated.

"Yes, it starts at 8:00, but we can arrive any time after that. It's a publicity party for Grand at the Hilton hotel."

"At the Hilton?" Janet said.

"Janet, you can come too," Sammy said, "if you don't mind keeping my driver company."

"Your driver?" Sara asked. "You have a driver now?"

"I hired Hassan to be my driver," Sammy said. "He drives me everywhere when I'm in Seattle. You'll love him, Janet. He's coming to the party too. Oh, did you think I meant you'd stay in the car with him all evening? Forgive me if I gave you the wrong impression."

"The whole band is going to be there?" Janet asked.

"I'm not sure about Jake. He doesn't like parties, but it would be beneficial if we are all there."

"I can't believe it," Janet asked.

"The band needs to know who's running the fan club," Sammy said. "They'll be stopping by here from time to time to autograph merchandise. Try to act cool. You're one of our staff."

"I am?" Janet asked.

Sara hadn't thought of that before and was feeling a little star-struck. She knew her dad wouldn't approve, but she was making her own decisions these days.

"Well, Darling, shall we pick you up at 9:00?" Sammy asked Sara.

"Yeah, that would be perfect," Sara said, then wondered why she had said that. It wouldn't be perfect for her to leave the house at that time. Her dad would be upset; and she had no idea what she would wear.

"Janet, we'll pick you up after we pick up Sara. By the way, don't wear our fan club t-shirts. This will be a formal affair, at the top of the Hilton. They are reserving the entire restaurant for us."

"Wow!" Janet said.

"Get used to it, Dear. This is just the first of many publicity parties we are planning. You'll want to get dressed up. This is going to be a gala affair."

"It really sounds like fun," Sara said.

"Fun? Ah, just part of the job. You girls need to take off early today, so you can go and get ready. As a matter of fact, why are you working on Friday, anyway? You shouldn't work more than four days a week."

"There's so much to do," Janet said.

"Besides, it's not like work, it's so fun," Sara said.

"You would make any work seem like fun, my Darling," Sammy said. "I'm off, Hassan is waiting for me in the car. We will see you both this evening." He touched Sara lightly on her hair and looked directly into her eyes, causing her to feel weak. She was glad she was sitting. "You're so beautiful. You know, you can let your hair down here. You don't have to keep it in that braid. This isn't Nordstrom, you know," he said quietly.

"Thanks, Sammy, I know. It stays out of the way better when I braid it."

"I'm sure it does. In any case, you look lovely. Adios, Compadres," he said as he went out the door.

"What's a Compadre?" Janet asked after he had gone.

"I'm not sure," Sara said.

"What are you going to wear tonight?"

"I don't know. It's a good thing we worked at Nordstrom. At least I have something to choose from."

"Me too. You're wearing a dress, right?"

"I almost always wear a dress."

"Oh, yeah, you do. Well, I mean, are you going to dress formal, or sexy, or both?"

"I think kind of formal. I don't really have anything sexy."

"Should we go get something new? We have time. I'd love to see Smelly Garbage's face if we walked into Nordstrom together and bought something really fantastic."

"Smelly Garbage?"

"Oh, that's right, you never knew her nickname. Sorry, I know you're a Christian. I didn't mean to offend you."

"It really isn't nice... but it is kind of funny."

"What do you think? Shall we go shopping?"

"No, I have lots of nice clothes already. I can find something to wear."

"But do you have something nice enough for this *gala* affair?"

"You're right. Let's go find something special," Sara agreed.

They closed the fan club office and walked to Nordstrom. Janet found a green silk dress and Sara found a beautiful blue, long gown with a wrap to go with it. They each bought a new pair of shoes and some special perfume. A new employee waited on them. They didn't see Kelly.

Sara arrived at home and when she opened the door, she smelled chicken frying. Her dad was in the kitchen. She laid her dress across the back of a chair and set her purse on the table so she could use both hands to sign.

"Hi Daddy," she said.

"Did you go shopping?"

"Yes, I bought a new dress."

"For the potluck tonight?"

Sara had forgotten about the Christmas potluck at the deaf social club, the Puget Sound Association for the Deaf. She had never missed the Christmas potluck in her entire life. This was one of the big social events of the deaf community in Seattle, and all of their friends, including all of their church members, would be there. Now she summoned the courage to tell her dad she wouldn't be going to the potluck.

"Daddy..."

"What is it?" he asked, reading the expression on her face. "Are you feeling sick?"

"No... I have other plans for tonight."

"Other plans? You have known about this all year. We always go to the Christmas potluck. Everyone is going to be there."

"I know, but Sammy asked me to go out with him tonight," she said. The chicken smelled so good, her stomach growled loudly. She was thankful her dad couldn't hear it.

"So you're going to drop everything, forget about the deaf community, because you got asked out by a boy?"

"No, Daddy, it's not like that."

"The way of a man seems right in his own eyes, but the end thereof is destruction," her dad said.

"Daddy, I just want to go out with Sammy tonight." She decided against telling her dad where they were planning to go and how late she would be leaving the house.

"You can go out with him any night, but the Christmas potluck only comes once a year."

"I know, but we made plans. I already told him I would go with him."

"You already had plans to go to the Christmas potluck. You can call him and cancel, or postpone your date."

"No, I want to go with him tonight."

"All right. You are an adult. It's your choice if you want to disappoint all our friends, the people who have been like a family to us all of your life."

"They'll understand, Daddy. People grow up."

"But people don't outgrow their families. The deaf community knows you and loves you. They are your family."

"And I love Sammy!" Sara signed without thinking. She grabbed her purse and dress and hurried to her room before she could see her dad tell her anything else.

Sara expected him to come to her room and try to make her feel guilty, but she made up her mind that it wouldn't work. She heard him finish in the kitchen, and to her surprise, he went into his study. She didn't want to talk to him, because she didn't want to submit to him. She wanted to stand her ground and do what she wanted to do tonight, for the first time in her life, instead of going along with her dad's plans.

In the early evening, her dad did come to her door, just to tell her he was leaving, and to be careful, and that he loved her. She was a little frustrated, because she had created a whole defense, and she didn't need to use it. He didn't try again to convince her to go with him to the potluck. He just calmly left the house with his big roaster full of chicken. Sara didn't expect him to come home until after she left to go with Sammy, since the Christmas potluck at the deaf social club always lasted until at least midnight. She and her dad never stayed that late; they left at about 10 o'clock, when some of the men started drinking.

Sara soaked in a luxurious bubble bath and then began to get ready for her date with Sammy. She put on her new dress and brushed her long hair, deciding not to braid it, but to let it fall down her back tonight. Sammy had never seen her hair out of her braid, and she thought he might like it this way. She pushed the uneasy thoughts of the discussion she had had with her dad out of her mind and focused on the evening ahead of her.

The doorbell rang just after 9:00 and Sara opened the door to see Sammy, stunning in his formal attire, with his long hair meticulously groomed. They stared at each other for a moment before Sammy finally spoke. Sara leaned against the door for support.

"You look gorgeous, my Darling," he said.

"Thank you, and so do you."

"Your hair is so beautiful."

"Thank you."

"The dress looks like it was made for you; yet you make it come alive with your beauty."

Sara was floating among the clouds when they got into the back seat of Hassan's car. He was dressed in a nice suit and he greeted Sara with a huge smile.

"Which way to your friend's house?" he asked.

"Oh, it's not far from here. Just go to the end of the block and turn left. Then go about eight blocks and turn right. Janet lives in one of those big, old houses with her folks."

They drove to Janet's house and Sara went to the door to get her. Sara introduced Janet to Hassan, and they drove downtown. Seattle had never looked so lovely, so sparkling, as it did tonight. Hassan and Janet both seemed shy, so Sammy offered light conversation to help break the ice between them. Sara cuddled under Sammy's arm as Hassan parked in the parking garage. Sammy held Sara firmly close to him.

"Darling, I want you to stay by my side all evening," he said. "No matter what happens or what anybody says, you stay with me."

"I wouldn't feel comfortable any place else," she said, speculating as to why he had said that.

"There's the elevator," Sammy said, pointing the way. The two couples got into the elevator and rode to the top floor. Sara's heart was beating wildly, and one glance at Janet told her she was as excited as Sara was. Nobody spoke in the elevator, and Sara thought perhaps Sammy was feeling a little nervous. He seemed to be extremely distracted.

The elevator doors opened to reveal a lavishly decorated restaurant that had been transformed into a winter wonderland, with millions of Christmas lights, a huge tree, and artificial snow all over the place.

"It's astonishing how just a moment in an elevator can transport us from a parking garage to the top of the world," Hassan remarked.

People crowded the room, dressed in their holiday best, some milling around an endless table of food. Sara had a smile frozen on her face, as seemingly hundreds of flash bulbs exploded, blinding her, as they entered the room. Sammy had his arm around Sara, while Hassan and Janet stayed a few feet behind them.

All of a sudden Sammy came to life, at home in this element. He glided through the crowd, guiding Sara, greeting reporters and photographers, beautiful women and handsome men. Everybody knew Sammy. The men shook his hand, congratulating him, and the women hugged and kissed him. He kept a firm grip on Sara, as if she may escape or get lost. Sara saw Dale and Luke across the room with ladies on their arms. Two official-looking men approached Sammy, each with a huge smile revealing large teeth.

"Sammy, we're so glad you're here," one man said, without moving his lips. "We've been waiting for you. Come on over to the rest of the band. We've got to get some publicity shots of you four together."

"Sara, I'd like you to meet the managers of our band, Jerry

and Jimmy Sharque," Sammy said. "They are brothers."

"Very nice to meet you," Sara said, noting the resemblance between them.

"Sharks, this is Sara Lewis, my girlfriend," Sammy announced. Sara realized it was now official: she was being introduced as Sammy's girlfriend! She was glad he was holding her, because her knees felt very weak.

"Sara, charmed, I'm sure," one of the brothers said, leading them to the rest of the band members. The other brother just nodded, still grinning widely. Jake Jacobi seemed to be hiding in a corner with a beautiful lady in a very pretty black dress. Luke was quite noticeable in his red sequin vest.

"Boys, boys, let's all come together for a group photo," one of the managers said. All eyes were on the members of Grand as they assembled near the Christmas tree. Sara glanced out the window and saw that from up here, they had a breathtaking view of Seattle and Puget Sound. Sammy reluctantly let Sara out of his grip so he could join the band members, but he kept his eyes locked on her. She couldn't look away from him; she didn't want to look away from him; she knew it wouldn't be possible if she tried. A huge group of photographers took photos nonstop for the next ten minutes while Grand displayed a variety of poses and the crowd watched.

The managers moved toward the band, each holding one side of a big package.

"Boys, we would like to congratulate you," they said together, their smiles plastered on their faces. "You are not only at the top of Seattle tonight, but you are also at the top of the U.S. charts!" They handed the package to Sammy and Dale. Flashbulbs were popping continuously as they opened the wrapping paper to reveal a large golden album in a frame.

"You did it! '100 Grand' went gold within the first month of its release!" Cheers exploded among the crowd as the band members patted each other on the back.

"I guess the record stores found a place for titles that start with a number," Luke remarked, glaring at the managers.

"Boys, you were right all along," one of the Mr. Sharques said, "about the album title, I mean."

"You Sharks take care of the business end, we'll do the creating," Dale told him.

"That seems to be the winning combination," the other Mr. Sharque said, stepping out of photo range so pictures could be taken of just the band with their gold album.

"Hi Sammy," said a girl in a slinky, short black dress which looked like bedroom attire. "I had a dream about you. Do you want to make my dream come true?" she asked, leaning towards him, trying to kiss him.

"Young lady, if you'll excuse us," Mr. Sharque said, "Sammy is otherwise engaged at the moment."

"You're engaged?" the girl asked, astonished. "Then what were you doing in my dream?"

The Sharque brothers guided the band members to their seats. The head table, loaded with a variety of fruits, vegetables, meats, cheeses and crackers, had been reserved for Grand and their guests. Sara didn't know where Janet and Hassan were; she just knew she was with Sammy in the middle of the pressing crowd.

"Sara, this is Bambi," Luke said, introducing the girl who joined him at the table. Bambi had short blonde hair, big brown eyes surrounded by thick eye makeup, and she was wearing very red lipstick. "Bambi, meet Sammy's girlfriend, Sara." Luke turned to Jake. "Jake, who is this lovely lady with you?"

"Luke, Sammy, Dale, meet Giselle," Jake said, smiling from ear to ear, "my fiancée. We're getting married next week." Giselle had long, smooth, auburn hair and a beautiful smile.

"Congratulations, man!" Dale said, reaching across the table to shake his hand. Then he turned to a dark-haired young lady sitting beside him. "This is Isabella, my girlfriend. We have known each other since high school, but we just reconnected a couple of months ago. Isabella, meet Sammy, Luke, Jake, um... Sara, Bambi, and Giselle."

"Don't you just love to say 'Bambi'?" Luke asked. "It's

like Bamba. I wrote a song called 'Bamba,' you know. Bamba! Bamba!"

"I know, it's on the album," Bambi shrieked. "I love that song! Don't you love it, Sara?"

"I haven't heard it yet," Sara confessed.

"Bamba! Baaaaam-baaaa," Luke said.

"Your boyfriend is Sammy Samson of Grand, and you haven't heard his new album?" Bambi asked, her eyes wide. "I've listened to it, like, a million times already."

"I don't have a record player," Sara said.

"You don't have a record player?" Bambi repeated. "Why don't you listen to Sammy's?"

"She will have the opportunity to listen to it very soon," Sammy said, saving Sara from this embarrassing conversation.

"Hi, Sammy, I'm Carolyn Higgenbottom, Lakeshore Press. Can you answer a few questions for me?" a reporter asked, pulling up a chair beside him.

"I believe we have prepared statements for the press," Sammy told her. "You can ask one of the gentlemen over there for a copy."

"Yeah, I have that, but I want to ask about this lovely lady beside you and your relationship with her."

"This is Sara, my girlfriend, and that is all I would care to say at this time."

"So, are you exclusive? I mean, are you not available? If you say you're not, you are going to break the hearts of girls all over the world."

"This is my girl," Sammy said, pulling Sara close to him.

"Where did you meet her?" Carolyn asked.

"In Seattle," Sammy said.

"I mean, how long have you known her? Do you live together? Are you engaged?"

"Miss Higgenbottom, I don't know how you made it to the

top tonight, but you are really scraping the bottom," Sammy said.

"So, you do live together?"

"The story is over here," Luke said. "This is my girlfriend, Bambi."

"Bambi who?"

"Bambi, my girlfriend."

"And does Bambi live with you?"

"Sammy and I share an apartment," Luke said.

"All four of you live together?"

"I didn't say that."

"You didn't say it, but is it true? Come on, you've got to give me something."

"I don't have enough to go around tonight," Luke said, putting his arm around Bambi.

"You may be excused, Miss Higgenbottom," Sammy said.

"You're not saying much about anything, are you?"

"Further remarks are in the prepared statement," Sammy insisted.

"Hey, you can print this: I'm getting married next week," Jake said, "to the most beautiful woman in the world. She's right here."

"And who are you? Are you with the band?" Carolyn asked.

"Jacob Jacobi, our bass player," Dale said. "Who put you on this story, anyway? You don't even know who we are."

"I'm new to Seattle, and I'm just trying to do my job. I know who Sammy is, and Luke too," Carolyn said defensively. "And you are Dale?"

"The facts are in our prepared statement," Sammy told her.

"I want something a little more personal, you know, a human interest story."

"You can talk to our managers, right over there, the Shark brothers, but we don't have anything more personal for you tonight," Sammy said.

"How did you make that strange sound on 'Heartbroken Hill?' Did you use a synthesizer?" Carolyn asked.

"No way! No synths!" Dale said.

"We don't use synthesizers. We're musicians, not elevator operators," Luke said.

"Elevator operators?" Carolyn asked.

"Yeah, we don't stand around pushing buttons all day," Luke explained. "We play music."

"Then how did you do it?"

"Part of it is Dale on the guitar," Luke said.

"What's the other part?"

"Ah, that's a trade secret," Sammy said.

Luke put his hands to his mouth and made a very unusual sound. Everyone at the table recognized it as the mysterious sound on 'Heartbroken Hill.'

"How did you DO that?" Carolyn asked, astonished.

"Heartbroken *Sam* Hill," Luke said, as if that explained it.

"Sammy!" yelled a beautiful woman in a skimpy red dress, as she stumbled over to the table. She tried to sit on Sammy's lap, but he scooted his chair under the table and she slid to the floor. Sara thought she might be drunk.

Sammy smiled sweetly as she pulled herself to her feet. "Hi, Theresa," he said.

"It's Ther-ESS-a, not Theresa, Sammy. You know that," she said as she brushed her hands across her dress.

"Of course, Ther-ESS-a," he said. "Ther-ESS-a, this is my girlfriend, Sara. Sara, meet Ther-ESS-a, the lead singer for Silver Geese, another Seattle band."

"Nice to meet you," Sara said. Theressa ignored her.

"Sammy, we had a good time together, didn't we?" Theressa asked, trying to touch his hair.

"Ther-ESS-a, back off, please," Sammy said, pushing her hand away.

"We've had a few drinks tonight, haven't we, Ther-ESS-a?" Luke asked her.

"I'm not talking to you," Theressa said to Luke.

"You're not? You sure fooled me," Luke said.

"I'm talking to Sammy, not to you," she insisted.

"Jake, doesn't it sound like Ther-ESS-a is talking to me?" Luke asked.

"I'm NOT!"

"Yes, Luke, it does sound like she is talking to you."

"I'm not speaking to you, Luke!"

"Oh, yes, you are. We can all hear you speaking to me. Listen to yourself."

"You never called me back!" she said loudly.

"No, I always called you Ther-ESS-a."

"You... you... you!"

"It does sound like she is talking to me, don't you agree, Dale?"

"Sounds like it to me."

"What's she talking about?" Bambi asked. "Why would you call her back?"

"I only called her Ther-ESS-a, " Luke said. "She's right, I never called her 'back,' not to her face, and not behind her back."

"Luke, stop it!" Theressa shouted. "I'm trying to talk to Sammy."

"Well, you're not doing a very good job, are you?"

"Luke, would you stop?"

"You didn't want me to stop before."

"You...you user!"

"At least I'm not a loser, you Silly Goose."

"It's 'Silver Geese,' you know that."

"It might be, but you aren't."

"You are so childish!"

"And a child shall lead them."

"What's that suppose to mean?"

"Look it up."

"Luke, are you flirting with her?" Bambi asked.

"No, can't you tell? She's not talking to me."

"Yes, she is."

"Aren't you listening? She said she's not talking to me."

"But she is arguing with you."

"Hey, Silly Goose, is talking the same as arguing?" Luke asked Theressa.

"I told you, I'm not talking to you."

"See, Bambi? She's not talking to me."

Carolyn seemed to be transcribing everything they were saying.

"Did you two used to date?" she asked.

"Who's she?" Theressa asked.

"Some reporter," Bambi answered. Sara noticed that Sammy seemed to be amused by the whole conversation, as long as Theressa wasn't talking to him.

"I didn't ask you," Theressa said.

"Well, I didn't ask you to join our table," Bambi said.

"Your table? Who are you?"

"I'm Luke's girlfriend," Bambi said defensively.

"Oh, you're the Special of the Week?" Theressa asked.

"We have been seeing each other for three and a half weeks!" Bambi said.

"Oh, that long? Well, he'll have a new one by Christmas," Theressa said.

"Ther-ESS-a, let it go," Luke said.

"Don't you tell me what to do," Theressa warned him, then she turned back to Sammy. "Come on, Sammy, let's get out of here. We can get a room."

"Ther-ESS-a, I have other plans for tonight, and, if you hadn't noticed, I'm here with my girl," Sammy said, not losing his composure.

"You are settling for THAT?" Theressa said. "She's so... PLAIN!"

"I would appreciate if you would not speak about my lady in this manner."

"Stop being so high and mighty," Theressa said. "You know you want me. Let's have a drink to celebrate." She reached across the table and grabbed a bottle of wine.

"Goodbye, Ther-ESS-a," Sammy said.

"See ya later, Silly Goose," Luke added. "Or better yet, let's not see you later."

"I'm not going anywhere without Sammy," Theressa insisted, again trying to sit on his lap. He slid his chair closer to Sara and put his arm around her.

"Ther-ESS-a, Darling, I'm not going anywhere WITH you," Sammy said.

"We don't have to go anywhere! We can get a room here. Look at me. LOOK at me!"

"Security!" Sammy called, looking around the room.

"That trick won't work with me," Theressa said. "I was invited! You can't have me thrown out!"

"Would you kindly leave our table?" Sammy asked.

"That's what I've been saying! Let's go!" She tried to grab his arm, but he pulled it away from her.

"Security!" Sammy called again, raising his hand. He said something that sounded like Arabic, and Hassan appeared at their table.

"Is somebody bothering you, Sammy?" Hassan asked, using a thick Arabic accent.

"Yes, please escort this young lady to the elevator. She has had a little too much to drink."

Hassan gently grabbed Theressa's arm and guided her away from the table.

"What are YOU doing tonight?" she asked Hassan. "Do you want to get a room?"

"Go somewhere and sober up, young lady," Hassan told her as they disappeared into the crowd.

"Hey, wasn't that your cousin?" Dale asked Sammy.

"My cousin, who doubles as my chauffer and bodyguard," Sammy said, smiling.

"Cool," Jake said.

"Thanks for getting rid of Silly Goose," Luke said. "She was really getting on my nerves."

"She wanted to get on something," Dale said. "She just won't leave you alone, Sammy."

"Oh, she'll leave me alone."

"Didn't she write a song about you?" Jake asked.

"If she did, I haven't heard it," Sammy said.

"Yeah, I heard it on the radio."

"It must be about someone else," Sammy said, turning to Sara "I don't want anything to do with her. I am otherwise occupied."

"This is great," Carolyn said, writing frantically in her note pad.

"Are you still here?" Luke asked. "This is a private table, you know."

"You guys are SO funny," Carolyn said. "So, have you all dated Theressa before?"

"She wishes," Dale said.

"What do you mean by that?"

"Only Luke dated her, but that's ancient history," Dale said.

"Sounds like she wants to make it a current event," Carolyn said.

"Sara," Sammy said suddenly, "give me some paper and a pen."

Sara got paper and a pen out of her purse and handed them to Sammy. He began to write as fast as he could.

"Is he writing a song?" Carolyn asked. "This could be history in the making! What's it called? Is this going to be your next hit?"

"He can't hear you," Luke said.

"Why not?"

"He has that look. He's gone, into his music. He'll come back when he's finished."

"This is SO far-out!" Carolyn said, taking more notes. "I'm sitting with a famous musician who is composing a song, right here, right now!"

"Would you excuse us, please, Miss Higgenbottom?" Luke asked.

"What do you mean?"

"Get lost!" Luke shouted at her. He curled his lips into a scary grin.

Carolyn Higgenbottom stood and timidly backed away from the table, as if she were afraid of what Luke might do to her. Sammy continued writing for several more minutes while the other band members had private conversations with their girlfriends.

"Hey, Jacobi," Dale said, "when's the wedding? Are we invited?"

"It's going to be next Saturday at 2:00, just a small ceremony at our church. You guys can come if you want," Jake said.

"Hey, aren't we in the studio that day?" Dale asked.

"Oh, yeah," Jake said, "I was planning to lay down my tracks in the morning, before Sammy gets there, and then I can finish the first songs on Monday or Tuesday. We have it all week, right?

"Yeah, that'll work. Sammy has his vocal and piano tracks to do, we don't all need to be there the whole time. We can work around your schedule."

"I suppose getting married is a good enough excuse to miss a session or two," Luke agreed. He lowered his voice. "Really, Jake, should you be getting married this soon? I mean, you haven't really dated anyone before, you know, try them until you find what you like."

"Giselle is the only woman for me," Jake said, wrapping his arms around her.

"Are you sure?" Luke asked. "I mean, married? For life?"

"For life," Jake said, "for better or worse, for richer or for poorer."

"At this point, we're going for richer," Luke said.

"I've got it," Sammy said, slamming the pen down on the table.

"It?" Dale asked. "By George, I think he's got IT! What have you got, Dude?"

"The next album, the fourth one, a concept album. 'Roman Empire,' that's what we'll call it."

"Yeah, sure. 'Roman Empire?' And...?" Dale asked.

"It's ancient history," Sammy said. He handed the pages to Dale, who looked at them and nodded approvingly. "We won't have Side 1 and Side 2, we'll have 'Rise' and 'Fall.' I have just written the grand finale, 'Rise and Fall.' It's all about the passion of the common people at that time, how they suffered and were tortured as loved ones were elevated and then destroyed. The rulers lead the whole country into degradation and destruction from the inside, and the population just followed their lead, thinking that they were doing the right thing, the acceptable thing. Luke, you can put that now drum solo you've been practicing in the third segment. This is going to be the best album ever."

"You say that about every album," Jake said.

"And so far, he's been right," Dale said.

"Third segment?" Luke asked.

"The emotion in this album is going to blast listeners off the face of the earth. Wait until you hear it," Sammy said. "Hey, wanna split and go to Dale's? I can play it there."

"Uh, I think the Sharks want us to stay another hour or so," Dale said. "Something about another presentation or something."

"The Sharks want us to be eaten alive," Luke said, filling a plate with food and placing it in front of Bambi.

"Yeah, they said something really great, or something," Jake said, also taking some food. Sara noticed that Sammy didn't show any interest in the food.

"Something or something," Dale said.

"What could be better than a gold album?" Sammy said.

"Another gold album?" Bambi asked.

"A platinum album?" Jake said.

"No, we couldn't have a gold album presentation on the same night as a platinum presentation, could we?" Dale said.

"No, the Sharks don't work that way. They'll want another party when it goes platinum," Sammy said.

"Hey, isn't that Randy Fortier, the DJ?" Dale asked.

"Where?" Luke asked.

"Over there, yeah, it is. Remember, he interviewed us last year?" Dale said. "He has a beard now."

Randy Fortier made his way to the head table.

"Sammy, Dale, Luke, Jake," he said, shaking their hands.

"Hey, Randy," Dale said.

"Fortier, how's it going?" Luke said.

"We are going to go live from here in about 5 minutes," Randy said.

"Wow, can you do that?" Bambi asked.

"What's going on?" Dale asked.

"Just stay cool," Randy said, looking around the room. Men were setting up equipment and a guy wearing headphones with a long cord that went clear across the room brought a microphone and gave it to Randy.

"Give us a sound check, Randy," one man said.

"Okay, I'm here at the top of the Hilton, live with the band Grand, the Grand band. How's that?"

"Perfect! Okay, here we go, in 10... five, four, three..."

"Good evening Seattle-ites! Randy Fortier at the top of the Hilton, live, with the members of the hottest group in America, Grand! Sammy Samson, lead singer, say something to Seattle."

"Greetings, everyone, and thank you so much for joining us on this special occasion. We appreciate each of you and your support," Sammy said.

"Thank you, Sammy," Randy said, "and Dale, about your latest song, 'Cool Heat,' it's certainly getting its share of airplay, isn't it?"

"So I've heard," Dale said. "It does seem to be playing every time I turn on the radio."

"Did you think it would be this popular?"

"Well, I've always liked it, Randy."

"It's the hottest song in the country right now, and that's why we're here with you right now. You out there in Radioland, you are hearing this at the same time as the members of Grand... they are just learning as you are, 'Cool Heat' has been selected as Song of the Year for 1970!"

"You're kidding!" Luke said.

"I'm not kidding," Randy said.

"You're not kidding?" Luke asked.

"I'm as serious as a flat tire in the desert."

"That's serious!" Luke said.

"Far-out," Dale said.

"Dale, tell us a little about this song. Following the delicate piano intro with that intense guitar segment was a stroke of pure genius!"

"Well, Randy, we all work together on our songs," Dale said. "I wrote the basic melody of this song, and the lyrics, and then while we were in the studio, Sammy had the idea to add the piano at the beginning. Then that drum and bass combo just after the guitar solo were added by Luke and Jake."

"That is fantastic. That was Dale, who plays guitar for Grand, and he's undoubtedly the greatest guitar player in the world. Do any of you have anything else you'd like to tell our listening audience?" Randy asked.

Luke grabbed the microphone. "Go out and buy the album. If you already have it, buy one for someone else. It'll make an excellent Christmas gift, one that will be treasured forever."

"Thank you, Luke Maybee, drummer for Grand, the hottest band on the radio right now," Randy said. "I want to thank you all, Sammy, Dale, Luke and Jake, for allowing us to join you, live, at the top of the Hilton tonight."

"Thank you, Randy," Sammy said.

"I'm sure Grand wishes to extend their thanks to all the listeners out there who have bought their records. You are the ones who have made this band who they are today. Thank you, Seattle! This is Randy Fortier, saying, good night and good music. Let's hear a spin of 'Cool Heat' right now!"

Cheers exploded from the crowd in the room. Everyone had gathered around the table to listen to the live broadcast. The Sharque brothers navigated to the front of the mob to congratulate the band members and to have more publicity photos taken. Sammy seemed so natural in this environment that he caused Sara to be at ease in what could have been a very uncomfortable situation, with everybody crowding so close and asking who she was, and the photographers taking picture after picture.

"Champagne all around!" a Sharque brother shouted. Waiters materialized with bottles and glasses for everyone, and they began popping corks and pouring frantically.

"A toast!" Randy Fortier announced, lifting his glass. "To

Grand, the hottest band in Seattle, the hottest band in America, the hottest band in the world!"

Someone handed a glass to Sara. Sammy touched his glass to hers, and she followed his lead of just barely touching the bubbly, bitter liquid to her lips. The taste made her shudder, and Sammy held her tightly. She relaxed as she leaned against him. She saw Janet and Hassan standing in the midst of the crowd, talking and laughing. Sara became aware that her cheeks hurt – she had been smiling ever since they arrived, hours earlier.

"Hey, everyone, give me your glasses," Luke said.

"What for?" Bambi asked.

"Just hand them over, right here, line them up," he said, clearing a space in front of Sammy and setting eight glasses in a row. "Jake, hand me that pitcher of water, the one without the ice."

Luke took the pitcher and began to pour water into the glasses. Sara noticed that each glass had just a little more than the glass beside it. Sammy examined the glasses closely, and lifted one to pour a tiny bit of water into the next glass. Luke handed Sammy a spoon.

"Quiet, everyone!" Luke said loudly. The room grew silent. "Sammy Samson is about to perform for us! One, two, three, four!"

Sammy began to tap each glass in a specific order. They sounded like little bells, and it soon became obvious that he was playing the melody to one of Grand's songs. Luke took two spoons and tapped a rhythm on the table. Sara wondered how Sammy could get such perfect pitch from glasses of water. When he came to the end of the chorus, the room erupted in applause.

"He does that all the time at home," Luke said, as if it were nothing special.

Christmas music began to play over the sound system, and people started dancing. As the crowd dispersed, the Sharque brothers, seemingly glued together, glided across the room, coming back to the head table.

"They are up to something," Jake observed.

"I guess a gold album and the Song of the Year aren't enough," Dale said.

"Boys, boys, we have an idea," one brother said.

"Congratulations," Luke said. "Is this your first?"

"A Christmas album," the other brother said.

"I beg your pardon?" Dale asked.

"A Christmas album!" the first brother said. They both had ridiculous smiles pasted to their faces as they stood, staring expectantly.

"Well done, Sharks, you have just identified the type of music playing, and for that you win – nothing," Dale said.

"This is the Christmas season," Sammy said. "People tend to play Christmas music at this time of year, or hadn't you noticed?"

"Exactly!" one Sharque said.

"That's the point!" the other said excitedly.

"Exactly Christmas music?" Luke asked. "Or pointed Christmas music?"

"Yes! Yes!"

"Yes, what?" Dale asked. "Have you two been celebrating a little too much?"

"No! Yes!"

"A Christmas album!"

"You don't mean..." Dale said.

"Yes!"

"No, we're not," Luke agreed.

"Yes!"

"No way!" Dale insisted.

"You boys need to do a Christmas album!"

"We don't play other people's music," Sammy said. "We're strictly original."

"Come on, don't be so strict," a Sharque said. "Loosen up."

"Yeah, you can write your own Christmas songs," the other Sharque added.

"Haven't they all been written already?" Luke asked. "I mean, all the Christmas songs are hundreds of years old."

"Come on, you're creative. Make up some new ones."

"No way," Dale repeated.

"We're a rock band, not a religious group," Luke said.

"Which is exactly why you should do a Christmas album."

"Which is...why?" Luke asked.

"Because all your fans will buy it."

"You may have something there," Sammy said.

"Are you serious, man?" Dale asked.

"Are you saying the Sharks have a GOOD idea?" Luke asked. "I mean, their first idea is a good one? I highly doubt it."

"No, really, think about it," Sammy said.

"I want to think about rock music, not Christmas music," Dale said.

"Listen," Sammy said, "we write a few songs for the Christmas season–"

"A Christmas album," a Sharque added, "a whole album of your own Christmas songs."

"Okay, a Christmas album," Sammy said, "and we record it when we go in the studio in the summer. Next year at this time, we release it. We still do our next two albums as planned, we just add this one."

"So what's that suppose to accomplish?" Luke asked. "Besides wearing us out and bombarding the public with our music?"

"Don't you get it?" Sammy asked. "Next Christmas, people will be adding our Christmas album to their Christmas music collection."

"Ah, yes, I get what you're getting at," Dale said. "Then the next year, it's re-released at Christmas time, and the next Christmas, and the next Christmas, and every year at Christmas, people will want to buy it."

"And your Christmas album joins Elvis and Bing and Perry, as one of the classic Christmas albums," a Sharque said.

"What do you say, boys?" the other Sharque asked.

"Excuse me for being religious," Jake said, "but doesn't Christmas music have to be inspired? I mean, it's not just any kind of music."

"Come on, have a few drinks, look at the lights of the city, you'll be inspired," a Sharque answered.

"No, I mean, inspired by God," Jake said. "I go to church, you know."

"We all go to church," Sammy said. "Well, how about if we ask God for some inspiration? Wouldn't that be appropriate, Sara?"

Sara froze. She had been an observer all evening, and now all eyes were upon her, awaiting her answer. She had to say the right thing.

"Prayer is always appropriate," she answered nervously, hoping it didn't show.

"We'll seek the Lord on this one, Sharks," Sammy said, "and get back to you."

"Yeah, we do have our principles," Luke said. "We wouldn't want to do something like this strictly for its potential commercial value. We're serious musicians."

Jake and Dale snickered.

"Baaaamba," Dale said.

"You boys think about it," a Sharque said, "and think about the bonus it could bring to all of us. Luke, aren't you getting a new car?"

"Thou shalt not tempt me," Luke said.

"We'll talk about it after the first of the year," the other Sharque said.

"Let's get out of here," Sammy said.

"Hey, man, aren't you going to eat anything?" Dale asked.

"Do you want something to eat, Sara?" Sammy asked.

Sara's stomach was one huge knot. "No, thanks, I'm fine," she answered, trying not to think about the little sausages and cheese on the tray in front of her, which would surely give her all kinds of stomach cramps if she were to eat some now.

"Me neither," Sammy said. "I'm ready to go."

"Hey, Sammy, wanna dance?" a chubby lady called, crossing the room to meet him as he stood.

"Thanks, Pepper, but we're leaving now."

"Come on, Sammy, just one dance," she begged, sliding up next to him. Her dress looked several sizes too small for her, squeezing her in all the wrong places and causing a cascade of bulges down her middle. She reminded Sara of a caterpillar.

"Pepper, I'm with my girlfriend," Sammy said.

"Come on," she said, pulling him. "Look at me! I have everything you need."

"No, you don't," Sammy said.

"Look at what I've got," she said, stepping back from him.

"We're trying NOT to look," Luke said.

"Be quiet, you meanie," Pepper said.

"Don't talk to my man like that," Bambi said.

"Your man? He's every lady's man," Pepper spouted.

"You watch it," Bambi said.

"I am not even looking in his direction," Pepper said. "I want Sammy."

"Darling, Sammy doesn't want you," Sammy said. "Can I be any more precise?"

"Am I too much woman for you?" she asked.

"Yes, too much woman, not enough lady," he said.

"Come ON, Sammy," she said, pulling him towards the dance floor.

"Do you know what the word 'no' means?" Sammy asked, escaping her grip.

"Sammy, she's an obedience school dropout," Luke said. "She didn't learn that one."

"Come on, Sammy, it's a slow dance. You can put your arms around me," she pleaded, grabbing him again.

"Fat chance," Dale said, and everyone at the table laughed. "He's not Plastic-man, you know."

"Or Stretch Armstrong," Luke added. "Pepper, I think you're falling out of your dress."

"Sammy, we don't have to go to the dance floor, we can dance right here," Pepper suggested, pawing at Sammy.

"Why are you so salty tonight, Pepper?" Dale asked.

"I'm just here to dance with Sammy. That's the only reason I came, to see Sammy. Look at those muscles," she said, reaching for his arm.

"We are not dancing together," Sammy said, moving out of her reach.

"You are SOOOO sexy! Come on! I just want to dance with you," she said, trying to get closer to him.

"And I just don't want to dance with you."

"Yes, you do."

"No, I don't."

"Why not?" Pepper pouted.

"I'm dancing with my girlfriend," Sammy said, gently pulling Sara from her chair and guiding her to the dance floor. "Come on, Sara."

"You'd rather dance with HER? What's wrong with you?" Pepper asked loudly.

"I think you're the one with the defect, Pepper," Luke said.

"I'm more woman than she'll EVER be!" Pepper shouted.

Sara kept her focus on Sammy. She didn't know how to dance. She had never been to a dance; she had never even seen people dance. She looked at the couples who were dancing so she could get a clue. Since a slow dance was playing, most of the couples were wrapped around each other, moving slowly, some engaging in extended kisses. Sara watched Sammy, who was gazing deeply into her eyes as he pulled her close to him and began to move her slowly to the music. She felt tingly all over her body. She put her head on his shoulder, letting him lead her with small, rhythmic steps. He didn't dance with slick, smooth moves, but with tenderness and care.

When the song ended, Sammy took Sara's hand and started to go back to the table. A young girl who looked to be about 15 pushed her way through the crowd and grabbed Sammy's other hand.

"Sammy, I've been wanting to dance with you all night," she said.

"Do I know you?" he asked.

"You can get to know me," she said.

"I'm finished dancing for the night," he told her politely.

"Well, then, we can get right down to business," she said, trying to rub against him.

"Excuse me, miss," he said, stepping away from her. "You'll have to go somewhere else right now."

"But Sammy, don't you want me?" she pouted.

Sammy ignored her question and led Sara back to the table. She was shocked at the way the women were so forward, and she was impressed at how Sammy handled them with poise.

"We're getting out of here," Sammy said to the band members.

"Getting tired of the leeches?" Luke asked.

"What's with them tonight?" Dale asked. "They won't leave you alone, Sammy."

"I know what it is," Isabella said, smiling slyly.

"What?" Luke asked. "He forgot his pest repellent tonight?"

"No, it's your new album," she said.

"So? We're all on the album," Luke said.

"Yeah, and I wrote as many songs on this one as Sammy," Dale said.

"So why are they all attracted to Sammy tonight?" Luke asked. "Usually they are all over me. I know, it's my boyish smile and beautiful blond hair. It's true, blondes do have more fun. So why are they after Sammy all of a sudden?"

"It's that song on side two," Isabella said.

"Oh, yeah!" Bambi shrieked. "The one where Sammy says, 'you're the girl of my dreams, and I'll make all your dreams come true,' and his voice is so sexy."

"Sexier than mine?" Luke asked, turning toward her.

"That's not possible, Luke," Bambi said. "You know you're the sexiest man alive."

"So I've been told," he said, leaning back in his chair, "more than once."

"I know! I've told you that, like, hundreds of times!" She started to lean over to kiss him, but he held up his hands to stop her.

"Save it for later," he said teasingly.

"You just tell me when you want it," she said.

"So, just because of that song, that's why every woman wants Sammy tonight?" Dale asked.

"The song is beautiful," Isabella said. "The piano, the guitar, the bass, oh, that bass, and then the voice just gets you. And then, you can hear him take a breath. The girls I work with are all in love with that part."

"And you wanted to cut that part," Dale said to Sammy.

"I don't like the way it sounds," Sammy said. "If we had just had another hour in the studio, I would have re-recorded it."

"Everybody loves that song because of that part," Isabella said.

"That song wasn't even released as a single," Luke said.

"Ah, but this is one way to know who bought the album," Jake said.

"We're going to have to come up with another type of indicator," Sammy said. "I mean, fans are one thing, but these women are going too far."

"You wrote the song," Dale said.

"I wrote it for the one I love, not to invite everyone in the world to love me."

"You wrote it for Sara?" Bambi asked. "Or for another girl?"

"There is no other girl in my life," Sammy said. "Goodnight, all. Enjoy yourselves. Eat, drink, dance. Dale, see you in the afternoon. We've got to work on your song."

"Sure, Sammy, see ya," Dale said. "Nice to see you, Sara. Take good care of Sammy. I need his voice tomorrow."

"It was nice seeing you too," Sara said, "all of you."

"Sammy and Sara are leaving," Luke announced.

"Goodnight, Sammy and Sara," the whole group chanted.

"Sammy, leaving so soon?" a Sharque asked.

"It's late. We've got to go," Sammy said.

"I understand," the Sharque said, glancing at Sara, then flickering his eyebrows at Sammy and smiling lecherously.

"Goodnight, Shark," Sammy said, taking Sara's hand and winding around clusters of people until they found Hassan and Janet.

"*Yalla?*" Sammy said to Hassan. "That means 'let's go,'" he explained to Sara.

"Ready?" Hassan asked.

"We're ready," Sammy said.

"Ready for what?" Janet asked.

"Let's get your coat," Hassan said. "It's time for us to go."

"I am so glad you are the one who is leaving with me," Sammy whispered in Sara's ear. Sara was glad, too.

114

CHAPTER 13

The four of them made it to the elevator without any interruptions. They left the top of the world to return to the parking garage. As Hassan drove onto the street, he asked, "Which way?"

"Is anyone else hungry?" Sammy asked.

"A little," Janet said.

"Sure, I'm hungry," Hassan said.

"What about you, Sara?" Sammy asked. "Are you hungry?"

"No, not really," she answered, even though she hadn't eaten all day.

"Are you okay? Are you feeling all right?" Sammy asked, examining her face and putting his hand on her forehead.

"Yes, I feel fine. I'm just not hungry right now."

"Let's go to your house and eat, *Abu-shabob*," Sammy said.

"Why didn't you eat there, at the party?" Sara asked. "They had all kinds of food."

"I don't eat all kinds of food," Sammy said. "What you eat today determines how you will feel tomorrow."

"Are you on a special diet?" Janet asked.

"No, but I have specific foods on my meal plan."

"Your meal plan?" Sara asked.

"Yeah, he plans to eat a meal at our house every night," Hassan said, laughing.

"Home-cooked meals, in the old country style," Sammy said, "like we make at Hassan's house. What did we make tonight?"

"We just made *kibbe* and *tabbouleh*. The nephews were going out to see a movie, and I didn't really have time to eat before I came to get you," Hassan said. "I'm not sure if any is left."

"So, we'll fix something," Sammy said.

After they arrived at the house, Sara was surprised that Imad and Essom got out of bed to come to the kitchen to cook for them.

"Guys, this is Janet. She accompanied me to the gala event tonight," Hassan said. "Janet, these are my nephews, Imad and Essom."

"Nice to meet you," Janet said.

"Hi, Janet, hi, Sara," Imad said.

"It's very nice to meet you, Janet," Essom said.

"What movie did you guys go see?" Hassan asked.

"A really weird movie called '2001, A Space Odyssey,' you know?" Imad said, as he began to make some bread. The dough was already prepared in the refrigerator, so he flattened it and put it on baking pans and put them in the oven.

"Yeah, I didn't really get it," Essom said. "It was really weird. I wouldn't recommend it."

"Thanks, I won't waste my time," Hassan said. "Have you seen it, Janet?"

"No, but I read about it in a magazine. That science fiction stuff isn't really up my alley," she said. "Have you seen it, Sara?"

"No, I very rarely go to movies," Sara said.

"Hey, Sammy, congratulations, man!" Imad said. "We heard you on the radio. Wow, Song of the Year! You're famous now!"

"I'm just doing what I love to do," Sammy said.

"You are so lucky," Essom said.

"Luck has nothing to do with it," Hassan said. "Sammy has superb talent."

"Thanks, *Abu-shabob*, but really, it's a blessing from God," Sammy said. "Being a perfectionist is just how He made me. What are you fixing?"

"Here, have some *hummus bi-tahini* and these vegetables while you're waiting," Essom said. "We're fixing pizza."

"Pizza? You know how to make Italian food?" Janet asked.

"This is Arabic pizza, it's a little different," Imad said. He took the flat loaves from the oven and brushed a light coating of olive oil on them, then he topped each one with crushed garlic, parsley, and chopped tomatoes. Then he sprinkled salt and pepper on each one and put them back into the oven. "Did you know pizza was invented in the Middle East?"

"Really?" Janet asked. "I didn't know that."

"Those look really good," Sara said, as Imad started making another tray of them. Now she was beginning to get an appetite.

Essom set the table. They all ate the vegetables with the *hummus*, and a few minutes later, Imad took the pizzas from the oven and put them on plates on the table.

"These are small enough, you can eat a whole one," Imad said.

"Or two," Hassan said.

"I'm sure one will be enough for me," Sara said. "Or maybe half."

"So, the movie," Sammy said, as they were eating, "was it called '2001' because it's set in the year 2001?"

"Yeah, that's the idea," Essom said.

"I smell food," Jihad said, coming into the kitchen in his pajamas. "Oh, excuse me, I didn't realize we had ladies here," he said, tying the belt on his robe.

"What did you think about the movie, Jihad?" Hassan asked.

"I loved it! It was so cool!" Jihad said excitedly. "Someone is really thinking ahead! Can you imagine what life will be like in 2001?"

"Yeah, we'll be old, man. We'll all be in our 50's," Hassan said.

"No, I mean, like, we'll be able to take a vacation to the moon," Jihad said.

"Yeah, and we'll all have jet packs on our backs and be able to just fly around the city, where ever we want to go," Imad added.

"You know how more and more people are moving to this area? I think by 2001, it will be totally filled in from Seattle to Tacoma, one big city," Essom said.

"No, it will be filled in all the way from Seattle to Portland, no breaks, just city," Hassan said.

"Picture this: I-5 City," Sammy said, "all the way from Vancouver, B.C. to San Diego, one long city, going five miles in both directions from I-5. I-5 City."

"I can see it, man!" Imad said.

"Wow," Jihad said. "That could happen."

"By 2001, they will have a machine they hook up to your head to record your dreams," Sammy said. "Wouldn't that be cool? You wouldn't lose any ideas. You could just rewind it and watch your dreams. All the songs you compose in your sleep, the paintings you make, they'll all be recorded."

"Oooo, that would be scary," Janet said. "I don't want to watch my dreams again. Sometimes once is too much!"

"Or you can just think something and it will be recorded," Sammy said. "Just visualize a painting and it will be there."

"There goes the need for artistic talent, Sammy," Hassan said.

"Well, not everyone can even visualize a good painting," Jihad said.

"What do you think, Sara? What will life be like in 2001?" Sammy asked.

"You are all Christians, right?" Sara asked. The others nodded. "What does the Bible say? Jesus will come and take all the Christians to live with Him. If He has or has not come by 2001, the condition of society will get worse and worse. People will turn away from God, and they will become lovers of pleasure more than lovers of God."

"You sound like a preacher," Janet said.

"She's a preacher's daughter," Sammy said.

"We see that happening already," Jihad said. "Who goes to church any more, anyway? Everyone would rather watch football on Sundays, or sleep in, or go skiing, or do anything but go to church."

"Well, it's going to get a lot worse," Sara said.

"You know what we'll have by 2001?" Imad said. "Like on 'Star Trek,' we'll have communicators, walkie-talkies, so we can just be anywhere and talk to anyone."

"Yeah, on our watches," Essom said.

"I think half of us will be living on the moon by then," Jihad said, "in giant climate-controlled atmospheric pressurized domes."

"No, it will be like the book '1984.' Everyone will have big TV screens in their houses, two-way screens, and Big Brother will be watching everyone," Hassan said.

"Don't they already have that?" Jihad said. "You know, they can watch us when we're watching TV, through the TV."

"I'm not sure about that," Sammy said.

"I think by 2001 they will implant contacts into eyes so people who wear glasses will have perfect vision," Janet said. "My mother would love that."

"We will probably have a miniature camera, like a contact lens, so we can just look at things and take a picture," Essom said.

"Or a movie camera like that, and you can start and stop it by a remote control you hold in your hand," Jihad said.

"What I would like to have is a machine to record TV programs," Janet said. "That way, if you miss your favorite show, you can watch it later."

"What's your favorite show?" Hassan asked her.

"I love 'Here Come the Brides,'" Janet said. "Sara, don't you love it? Bobby Sherman is so cute!"

"I haven't seen it," Sara confessed. "We don't have a TV."

"Oh, yeah, I forgot," Janet said.

"Did you say Bobby Sherman or Bobby Brady?" Jihad asked,

and the others all laughed. Sara looked to Sammy for clarification, but he just shrugged.

"I don't watch much TV either," Sammy admitted.

"Oh, you know what I think they will have in 2001?" Jihad said. "A TV channel that will be all science-fiction. They will show 'Star Trek' and all the science fiction movies all the time, with no commercials."

"That would be cool," Essom said.

"Well, that's about as far-fetched as you can get," Imad said. "They couldn't support a channel like that. Not enough people would watch it."

"I think the cars in 2001 will have big, thick, rubber bumpers all around, so when they hit something, they won't get dented," Janet said, "and they'll be round, and the wheels will be able to go in any direction, so it will be easy to turn around anywhere."

"No, the cars will be like on 'The Jetsons,' you know?" Jihad said. "They will be able to fly, and they will be made of an indestructible material so if they get in an wreck, they won't be wrecked."

"The cars of the future won't hit anything, because they'll be programmed to just go to a certain place. Only one car can be programmed to be in each place at a specific time," Hassan said, "and since all cars will be programmed, we won't have to drive, we can just go along for the ride."

"You just lost your job, Uncle," Essom said.

"By then, he'll be so rich, he won't have to work anymore," Sammy said. "We'll all be rich. None of us will have to work. Isn't life Grand? Pun intended."

"You know what else they'll have in 2001?" Imad said. "Automatic houses, you know, so when you go in a room, the lights will come on, when you leave the room, the lights will go off, and the heat too, like, the room will warm up when you enter."

"What if you want don't want the lights on, like when you want to sleep?" Sara asked.

"Well, you can set it on a timer, or have it automatically know that, you know, be connected to your brain or something."

"Seattle will have a weather machine," Essom said. "Since it's cloudy and raining most of the time, they will put a big machine, like a big fan or something, that will blow a huge hole in the clouds to let the sun shine through."

"Won't that mess up the climate?" Jihad asked.

"No, they can turn it off at night, and let it rain all night, but just turn it on during the day so it will be sunny," Essom explained.

"What I hope they'll have is a different sound for when the phone rings," Sammy said. "I can't stand that loud, shrill sound. When I'm home, I put the phone under a pillow so it won't ring so loud. I would love the phone to make some nice music, like an orchestra playing, when somebody calls, instead of interrupting our lives with that hideous noise."

"It has to sound like that," Hassan said, "so we will think it's urgent to answer the phone. We can't ignore it. That's part of Ma Bell's plan."

"We have a light that flashes when somebody calls," Sara said. "The phone also rings, but maybe by 2001 we will have the option to turn off the sound."

"That would be great," Sammy said. "I can live with a flashing light."

"Hey, do you guys have any Christmas records?" Janet asked. "It was fun listening to all those Christmas songs tonight."

"No, I don't think we have any Christmas records, do we, *Shabob*?" Hassan asked.

"No, we only have rock music," Essom said.

"We don't buy Christmas records," Jihad said.

"We would buy one if your group made one, Sammy," Hassan said.

"Well, that's an idea," Sammy said.

"We have Lebanese music," Essom said. "We have four 'Fairuz' records."

"Hey, I heard she might be touring the United States next

year," Sammy said.

"Oh, man, we should go see her," Hassan said.

"Who?" Janet asked.

"Fairuz, a famous Lebanese singer," Imad said. "She has a really beautiful voice."

"I haven't heard of her," Janet said.

"She's famous in the Middle East," Hassan explained. "All her records are in Arabic."

"So do you want me to put on an album?" Jihad asked. "Which one?"

"I know one record you do have," Sammy said, "the Song of the Year!"

"Yeah, put on '100 Grand,' Jihad," Essom said, as Jihad went to the record player.

"I haven't even heard it yet," Imad said.

"Me neither," Sammy said, "or, I haven't listened to it since we recorded it."

The record began to play, and everyone was quiet for a minute while they listened to the first song. Beautiful music from the four large speakers filled the room.

"Oh, man!" Jihad said.

"What, man?" Imad asked.

"I feel sorry for anyone who has never heard this record."

"Yeah, it is really outasite."

"Really. I LOVE this part!"

"It's so beautiful…"

"Shhh! Just listen!"

"Who is that with the low voice?" Sara asked.

"That's me," Sammy said.

"I thought yours was the high voice on side two," Janet said, "on that song everyone is talking about."

"Yes, it is," Sammy said.

"Yep, Sammy has quite a range," Hassan said.

"Shhh! Here comes the Song of the Year!" Jihad said.

Sara heard the song that had been played so often on the radio, and they all sang with the familiar lyrics. As the record continued, Sammy told them details about each song, who wrote it, odd things that happened in the studio while recording it, and how it always came out better than they had originally planned, with all four band members working together to revise and refine it.

Jihad turned the album to side two, and soon Sara heard why all the girls were in love with Sammy's song: his voice was amazing, and he seemed to be singing directly to her. Probably every girl who heard it felt the same way. Sara thought about the dream love being her, and she instantly fell in love with the song and the singer.

"Oh, man," Imad said, after the record ended.

"What, man?" Essom asked.

"Look out the window."

They all looked out the window.

"What is it, *Abu-shabob*?" Sammy asked. "I don't see anything."

"It's getting light already, and I have to go to work!"

Sara hadn't thought about the time all night. She looked around the room for a clock and saw that it was nearly 7:00 a.m.

"I am going to be in big trouble," Janet said. "I need to get home."

"Yeah, me too," Sara said.

"Do you live with your parents?" Essom asked.

"Yes," both girls said together.

"But you are both over 18," Hassan said.

"It's just that I didn't tell them I would be out this late," Janet said.

"I will explain to your father what happened," Hassan offered.

"Somehow, I don't think that will help," Janet said. "Can you take me home now?"

"Thank you so much for everything," Sara said to their hosts, as they all stood.

"No problem," Imad said. "You are like family. You are welcome in our home any time. Both of you."

"Yeah, any time of the day or night," Essom added.

"It was nice meeting all of you," Janet said.

"We hope you will visit us again," Jihad said.

"I hope so, too," Hassan said, giving Sara an indication that he liked Janet. Maybe they would double-date with her and Sammy some time.

CHAPTER 14

Hassan drove to Janet's house and walked her to the door. He shook her hand, then he made sure she was safely inside before leaving. Sara was surprised that she wasn't even tired. The night had passed so quickly, it seemed now as if she had dreamed it. Sammy made small talk as Hassan drove to Sara's house.

When she saw the lights inside her house, Sara knew she was in trouble. She had never stayed out all night. Her dad either waited all night for her, or he was already awake so he could greet her. She was anxious to get out of the car to receive her lecture; yet she wished she could go somewhere else and not have to face her dad. Sammy pulled her close to himself.

"Did you have a good time tonight?" he asked quietly, his face just inches from hers. She felt an overwhelming affection for him, drawing her heart even closer to him.

"It was really wonderful, amazing," she said quietly.

"Sara..." Sammy stopped, glanced away from her, then turned her face to him so they were directly facing each other. "Sara, I..."

She waited for him to finish his sentence. He swallowed, searched her eyes, licked his lips.

"Sara, I love you," he said, then he pulled her close and kissed her, slowly, tenderly. She knew at that moment that she could never love any man besides him. She wanted to tell him that she loved him, but she had lost the ability to speak. She moved her lips slightly, thinking that words might make their way to her voice and out of her mouth, but no words were there. Sammy kissed her again, then he gently helped her get out of the car. He put his arm around her and they began to walk toward the door.

"Sara, my love, look," he said quietly, stopping her on the sidewalk.

Sara gasped as she saw the sun just beginning to rise, the most beautiful sight she had ever witnessed. They stood still for several moments and watched the huge orange ball as it appeared over the hill. They walked slowly to the porch.

"Are you cold?" Sammy asked.

"No, not at all," she said, feeling a warmth flood her entire body.

"You are shivering."

"It must be the excitement."

"This has been one exciting night."

"It really has."

"Would you like for me to speak to your father?"

"What for?"

"To explain that it was all my fault."

"It wasn't your fault. I'm an adult. I'm responsible for my actions. Besides, he's probably asleep."

"The lights are on in your house."

"He left them on for me. You better go now."

"I wish you were coming with me."

"I need to go inside."

"It's hard to leave you, even for a moment."

"We have plenty of time," she reminded him.

"My whole life is yours," Sammy said. "You can have my next 100 years."

"You plan to live to be 124?"

"As long as you live to be 120."

"I hadn't thought about it."

"Think about it," Sammy said, then he was quiet for a minute. "You know, I wasn't completely truthful with you."

"What do you mean?" she asked, wondering to what he was referring. Her first thought was that there must have been – or there must be – another woman in his life.

"Remember when I told you I'm not afraid of anything?"

"Yeah, when we were at the Space Needle, on our first date."

"There is one thing," he confessed. He paused, looking into her eyes.

"What?"

His brown eyes seemed to be looking into her soul. He took both of her hands in his.

"I'm afraid of being alone," he said, so faintly that she could barely hear him. "I couldn't bear to be left all alone."

"When you have Jesus, you are never alone," Sara said.

"I know, but remember when you said that fear isn't always rational?"

"I said that?"

"At the Space Needle."

"Oh, yeah." She must have been paying more attention to what Sammy was saying than what she was saying that day.

"I am afraid that one day I will be all alone, and I won't be able to function."

"Where is your faith? Jesus will always be with you. He won't leave you alone, and He will always give you what you need. He knows you need people. That's why He didn't put you on a desert island by yourself."

"Promise me you will never leave me alone," he whispered.

"I promise," Sara said. "I will be with you as long as you want me."

"There will never be another girl – or woman – for me. Promise you will never leave me alone," he repeated.

"I promise I will never leave you alone."

"Thank you."

Sara smiled at Sammy. He looked so vulnerable.

"You need to go inside," he said.

"Good night, Sammy."

"Good morning, my sweet Sara."

Sara turned toward the door to open it, to avoid permitting Sammy to give her a kiss. She knew eyes were everywhere. She stepped inside the house and looked around for her dad. When she didn't see him, she walked toward her room. She was startled when he suddenly appeared in front of her.

"You were out all night," he signed, with no expression on his face. Sara tried to read him, but he was blank.

"We went to a promotional party for the band, and the time just got away from us," she explained.

"This is no way for a Christian lady to behave."

"I didn't do anything wrong."

"You were out all night with a man."

"But nothing happened between us," she said, aware that that was not entirely true. Sammy had told her he loved her and she had fallen completely in love with him.

"The Bible tells us to abstain from the very *appearance* of evil."

"Daddy, we didn't do anything wrong."

"You have always been a good girl. I've never had to give you a curfew, but now you have gone too far."

"But nothing happened!"

"You were with a man all night, and that is not acceptable behavior. What are his intentions? Does he plan to marry you? If you are married, you can be with him 24 hours a day, but as long as you live under my roof, you have to live by Christian standards."

"We didn't do anything wrong!"

"The world might say you have done nothing wrong, but you have to call sin 'sin!' Don't sugar-coat it or say that everyone is doing it! It is still sin! God's standards have not changed! The road to destruction is a broad way, and many are following that broad path!"

"He told me he loves me!" she said, without wanting to tell him that.

"So that makes it all right? Boys will tell girls anything to get what they want! Why do you think we have so many unwed mothers these days?"

"Daddy, he doesn't want anything! He loves me!"

He looked at her without saying anything. Somehow, this was harder than his lecture, because she had no idea what he was thinking, and she didn't know what else to tell him. She stood there waiting to see what was coming.

"You better get some sleep," he said finally.

CHAPTER 15

The next day, Sunday, Sara went with her dad to church, as she always did. They arrived early and Sara went to the altar to pray. Her dad had been polite with her yesterday, but not entirely loving. As she was praying, she realized what it would be like to be out of fellowship with God: something would be between them, barring them from communicating, making her feel uncomfortable so she would not want to be around Him. She felt this way about her dad, and she asked God to forgive her. She couldn't bring herself to ask her dad to forgive her, because she knew she hadn't done anything wrong. Her dad was just being unreasonable.

When people began coming into the church, Sara had a feeling they were talking about her. They were keeping their signs small and private, and nobody would look directly at her. Before service started, her dad motioned for her to come into his office.

"Look at this," he said, pointing to the Sunday edition entertainment section of the Seattle Times.

Sara followed his finger to a giant color photo of Sammy and her stepping off the elevator at the party they had attended. At first, she didn't recognize herself because the photo made her look so glamorous. Before she could say anything, her dad pulled out the entertainment section of the other Seattle newspaper, the Post-Intelligencer. This one had a picture of her dancing with Sammy.

"You told me nothing happened that night," her dad signed, disappointment visible on his face.

"Nothing happened," she insisted.

"Except you opened the door to sin," he said. "Once the door is open, even just a crack, all kinds of sin can sneak inside, and you won't even be aware that it is there."

"I didn't do anything that would make you ashamed of me."

"Going to this kind of party, dancing like this, being put on display for the whole city to see in that flimsy dress, staying out all night with a man... what's not to be ashamed of? Is this the very appearance of evil?"

"Daddy—"

"I had to get this news from members of our congregation. You couldn't even tell me the truth. Come on, it's time for church."

He dismissed her without letting her respond. Sara followed him out of the office and people really were staring at her, and talking about her. She found the service extremely hard to follow; she couldn't concentrate on the signing at all. Scripture readings, prayers and testimonies were all just blurs of the fingers as her frustration burned inside of her. What could she say to her dad? He had made up his mind and nothing she said could change it... and nothing he said could change her mind either. Sara and her dad had never before had a barrier between them. She wanted him to understand her point of view.

That evening at dinner, her dad told her, "As long as you live under this roof, you follow my rules and that includes exemplary Christian standards. End of discussion."

Sara didn't say anything to him at all that evening. She stayed in her room listening to the radio after dinner, hoping to hear one of Grand's songs. Her dad made no effort to reconcile, and neither did she.

The next day when Sara arrived at work, Janet was already there, packing T-shirts to be mailed to fans.

"Did Sammy design these new T-shirts?" Janet asked. "They are sooo cool! Look at this design!"

"Yeah, that's his design. He was just doodling one day and he came up with that logo," Sara said. "By the way, he said we each can have one to wear at work. His plan is that we'll move to bigger fan club headquarters and fans will be stopping by sometimes."

"That's a good idea!" Janet said. "Good advertising."

"So, were your parents mad when you came home Saturday morning?" Sara asked.

"They were asleep, but my little brother told them I came home at 7:00 in the morning, and they really blew up. I told them I'm an adult, and they told me I need to set a good example for my brother and sister, come in at a decent hour, all that jazz. My sister's 17, and she's really wild. So anyway, I got to thinking, um, what have you been doing with the money you've been making here, if you don't mind me asking?"

"Putting it in the bank," Sara said, "except for what we spent on Friday."

"Me, too! So, I was thinking, we should get an apartment!"

"You and me?"

"Yeah, we're old enough. Hey, great picture of you in the paper, by the way."

"Which one?"

"Was there more than one?"

"One in each paper."

"Oh, we get the P-I. You are so lucky! Now the whole town knows you are Sammy Samson's girlfriend! You are the envy of every girl in King County! So, anyway, I found some great possibilities for apartments in the U District. Look," she said, shuffling some newspaper clippings, "here's one for just $75. a month, for two bedrooms! What do you say we close up and go look at it?"

"I haven't really thought about moving out," Sara said.

"Well, what did your dad say? Did he notice how late you came home?"

"Yeah, he wasn't too happy about it."

"Are you grounded?"

"No, he's never grounded me."

"Have you ever been out all night before?"

"No."

"Don't you think, with your boyfriend's lifestyle, you might want to be out all night again?"

Sara was still stunned when she heard Sammy being referred to as her boyfriend. She didn't know what to say.

"We're adults. We need to have our own lives," Janet said. "We need to be able to make our own decisions about when to go out, who to date, what time to come home."

"I agree with that," Sara said.

"So, let's get an apartment! Come on, I just cashed my check. Let's at least go look."

Sara wasn't in a hurry to move away from home and be on her own, but what Janet was saying did make sense. Her dad wasn't likely to accept Sammy at all any more, and she couldn't live in her dad's house with the current wall between them. Maybe Janet's idea was a good one. Sara had plenty of money now; all she needed was her freedom.

"Let's take these packages to the post office, and then go look," Sara said.

"Ya-hoo! This is going to be great!" Janet said.

They rode the bus to look at the apartment, which had two bedrooms, was furnished and very clean. Mary Vernon, a matronly lady with kind eyes, was the owner. She liked Sara and Janet from the moment she met them, and she encouraged them to take the apartment. They signed the papers and Janet gave her a $25. deposit. Miss Vernon gave them each a set of keys.

"It'll be nice having two sweet young Christian girls living here," Miss Vernon remarked.

"We did it!" Janet said, jumping up and down, after Miss Vernon left them alone in their new apartment. "When are you going to move in, Sara?"

"Oh, I hadn't thought about that," Sara said. "I need to talk to my dad about it."

"Well, we've signed the papers, you can't back out now."

"No, I don't want to back out, but I can't just move out without telling him."

"Of course not! Look, I'm going to see if I can get my cousin to drive his truck this afternoon and help me move my stuff. We could come by and get your stuff."

"What are your parents going to say?"

"I don't care. I'm moving out. We have an apartment!"

"I'll have to let you know," Sara said, wondering how she was going to tell her dad.

When Sara got home, her dad wasn't there. She considered that to be very unusual, because Monday was his day off, and he rarely went anywhere on a Monday. He hadn't written her a note or left any indication of where he had gone. Sara's mind raced with her heartbeat. She didn't have very many things: a few clothes, some books, the radio Sammy had given her, and a hope chest full of nostalgic items. She didn't have any towels or linens or dishes – but she did have plenty of money in the bank to make a new start. She called Janet and asked her if she and her cousin could bring the truck to pick up her things that afternoon.

Sara rehearsed a hundred times what she was going to tell her dad, but he didn't come home before Janet and her cousin arrived. They loaded the truck and Sara wrote a note for her dad and left it on the refrigerator. Sara rode with Janet and her cousin to the new apartment and they unloaded their belongings. Sara got the bigger bedroom because Janet wanted to be closer to the bathroom.

"Oh, I called the phone company from my house, or, from my mom's house," Janet said, "and I ordered a phone for us. The only thing is, because of the holidays and so many people being on vacation this week, they can't hook it up until after Christmas. But that's only a few days. Hey, we could get a Christmas tree! Let's go shopping! I need some towels and some toothpaste, and we have to get some food for the fridge."

Sara was overwhelmed, with everything happening so fast. She realized she hadn't told her dad the address of her apartment in her note; he had no way of contacting her. Well, she thought, the deaf grapevine would keep him informed. He probably already knew where she lived.

Sara walked two blocks to a pay phone to call Sammy, but no one answered at his apartment. She tried calling his cousins' house, but no one was there either. She wanted to let Sammy know where he could find her. She went shopping with Janet so they could put something in their refrigerator.

The next day, Janet wanted to pick up more items they needed for their apartment, so Sara went to work alone. Shortly after she arrived, she felt that familiar tingle and she knew Sammy was getting close to her. He opened the office door.

"Good morning, Beautiful," he said, reaching out to touch her hair. "Your hair looks very nice like this." A look of concern crossed his face. "What is it? Is something the matter?"

"I moved into an apartment with Janet," Sara said.

"Why did you do this, all of a sudden?"

"It was time for me to move out on my own."

"What did your father say about this? Does he agree?"

"I don't know. He wasn't home when I moved my things."

"But you discussed it with him earlier, right?"

"No, I just decided to move yesterday, then when I went home, he wasn't there, so I wrote him a note."

"Sara, was that wise? What is he going to do without you?"

"What? Do you think because he's deaf, he can't take care of himself?"

"No, because he's a man, he needs you to help him."

"Well, I have my own life now. I want to help you now."

"You are a big help to me. You do so much for me. Look at this place. You have kept it going all these months, and you have done a great job with my finances, which is why I'm here. I need to talk business. Where is Janet?"

"She took the day off so she could get some things for the apartment."

"Great! Because my finances are not her business.

"I know that. I haven't mentioned anything about them to her."

"I know. I trust you with everything I have, including my personal business. I know it will stay personal. By the way, I want you to take off until after the first of the year. You need a vacation. You can get your apartment together. Janet too. The fan club can wait. Anyway, back to business, I need you to put Hassan on my payroll. Pay him half as much as I'm paying you. You have a lot of mailing to do, so I want to put Jihad on the payroll too, and pay him $200 a week. He'll be taking care of the mail a couple times a week."

"Isn't that a lot, for just doing the mail a couple of times a week?"

"He really needs a job and you really need the help."

"Should all this be coming out of your personal account? Or should I set up a business account?"

"You know what to do. Take care of it however's best. I have no interest in that side of things. One more order of business: I need you to write four checks today, and I want you to go buy fancy little boxes to put them in, so I can give them as a Christmas bonus. Three checks for five hundred dollars and one for a thousand."

"For who?"

"For my employees, Hassan, Jihad, and Janet, five hundred each. The thousand is for you."

"Sammy, that's too much."

"Haven't you ever had a Christmas bonus?"

"Well, yeah, one time I got a turkey."

"Wouldn't you rather have a thousand dollars?"

"I guess."

"Anyone would rather have a thousand dollars than a turkey.

It's just my way of thanking you for being such a faithful employee. You all have been great."

"Sammy, working here isn't even like work, it's so fun."

"Well, having you take care of my finances is a treasure I can't pay enough for, because I could never do it myself and I wouldn't trust my money in anyone else's hands. That is your real job. Anyone could take over the fan club, and some day they will. When it gets really busy here, hire someone else, because you will be busier taking care of my needs."

Sammy took both of Sara's hands in his and he pulled her close to him so he could look into her eyes. "Sara, there is no one like you." He closed his eyes and kissed her so gently, then he said quietly, "Christmas is Friday."

"I know."

"What are you doing for Christmas?"

"I think Janet is getting a Christmas tree for our apartment."

"Do you go to church on Christmas?"

"Not unless it falls on a Sunday."

"Will you be spending Christmas day with your dad?"

"I'm not sure."

"I would like for you to spend Christmas Eve with me. You can meet my family. They have invited us for dinner."

"You told them about me?"

"Not yet. They just got back from Lebanon and I haven't seen them yet. But they know you're coming with me."

"How do they know I'm coming?"

"I told them about you years ago."

CHAPTER 16

Sara avoided her dad all week. She bought a Christmas gift to give him, but she just couldn't face him. She knew he would be mad at her. She kept busy with her new apartment and with her new lifestyle, talking to Janet all hours of the day and night, cooking the foods she liked without thinking about her dad's limited food desires, and watching TV. Janet had bought a TV, and that opened a whole new world to Sara. She liked having the background noise. She liked hearing the news instead of always reading it. She liked seeing the fashions of New York and Hollywood. She liked the idea that Sammy could come to her apartment at any time, without restriction, and without a lecture about the dangers of letting sin in her door.

On Christmas Eve, the doorbell rang and Janet ran to answer the door.

"Our first visitors!" she said, as she opened the door to see Sammy and Hassan standing on the porch.

"What a lovely place," Sammy said, looking around the room. "You can see the woman's touch. Those curtains are lovely. Where did you get them?"

"I made them," Janet said, "with the new sewing machine I bought."

"Sara, you look lovely this afternoon, as usual," Sammy said.

"Hi, Sammy, thank you. Hi, Hassan."

"You did all this in a week?" Hassan asked, examining the furniture and decorations.

"Four days," Janet corrected.

"I have some paintings you can hang on your wall," Sammy said, "if you want to fill the empty spaces."

"Really?" Sara said. "We would love that!"

"Janet, would you like to join us this evening?" Sammy asked. "We're going to my father's house."

"Oh, no, I don't want to intrude on your family Christmas dinner," Janet said.

"You won't be intruding. You can be Hassan's guest."

"No, I don't think I should."

"Will you just ride with me to drop them off?" Hassan asked. "My nephews are making Christmas dinner at our house, and I would love for you to join us. Don't worry, you won't be the only girl. Imad's girlfriend will be there. Actually, she's fixing a turkey, but the guys are making other things to go with it. We can take Sammy and Sara to his father's house, we'll go back to our place to eat, then we'll go pick up Sammy and Sara later."

"Well..."

"Come on, it's a long drive to Bothell. Won't you just keep me company? Or do you have something better to do?"

"No, not me. Just let me put on something warmer," she said, hurrying to her room.

The drive to Bothell passed in a moment for Sara. On one hand, she was nervous about meeting Sammy's parents, but on the other hand, she was so happy to be in Sammy's arms again. Although they hadn't spent a lot of time together in the nine months since they met, every moment with Sammy was full and precious, forever engraved in her mind. Sara faintly heard Hassan and Janet talking, but her focus was on Sammy, warm and tender beside her.

"Here we are," Hassan said, pulling into a huge circular driveway. The house was enormous, decorated with thousands of Christmas lights. Sara suddenly felt extremely under-dressed in this fancy neighborhood.

"Is that a lake?" she asked, pointing between the houses.

"Yeah, that's Lake Washington," Sammy said nonchalantly. "Thanks, *Abu-shabob*. Give us a couple of hours, but not too long."

"Yes, sir, you're the boss," Hassan said. Janet was staring at the house, and Sara could almost read her mind: Janet was glad she was not the one going in there.

"Come on, my Dear," Sammy said, helping Sara out of the car. He had to nudge her to the front door; her legs were not working properly.

"You didn't tell me your parents are so rich," she whispered, aware that the car was pulling out of the driveway, leaving her with no escape vehicle.

"They're not," Sammy said, "compared to what I will be when Grand really launches. You, my Darling, are holding onto a shooting star, so you better hold on tight. I need you to be with me all the way."

"What do I say to them?" she asked, trying to delay the inevitable.

"Just be yourself. With my family talking, you won't need to say much." He gave her a kiss on the cheek, presumably to give her courage, as he touched the doorknob.

"Master Sammy," a butler said, opening the door. He was dressed in formal wear, causing Sara to wish she were invisible. "Ah, you have brought a guest."

"Riley, this is my girlfriend, Sara," Sammy said. "Sara, this is Riley."

"Lovely to meet you, Miss Sara," Riley said, extending his hand to welcome her into the home. Sammy and Sara stepped into a huge foyer with a wide staircase leading to up to a landing. On each side of the foyer was a huge room, reminding Sara of old Victorian houses that had drawing rooms. Another door directly in front of them, under the landing, led to the back of the house. A maid stood in that doorway.

"Sammy!" a little girl shouted, running down the stairs. "Mom, Sammy's home!"

Another girl, a teenager, came around a corner. She looked like a bigger version of the first girl. Both had huge brown eyes and dark brown, flowing hair. "Sammy!" she shouted.

"Merry Christmas, my angels," Sammy said, hugging them both at the same time.

"Sara, these are my sisters, Lena and Layla. This is Sara."

They stopped hugging Sammy and stared at Sara. Lena's mouth dropped to her chest.

"Where are your manners?" Sammy asked.

"Where did you find her?" Layla asked, her eyes wide.

"How did you make your painting come to life?" Lena asked, walking around Sara, to be sure she was real.

"Sara is my girlfriend."

"Wow," Layla said.

"Sammy, Sammy," an elegantly dressed lady said, coming from one of the drawing rooms. She gave him a hug. "Are you eating enough? You have lost weight."

"Mother, I want you to meet Sara Lewis," Sammy said. "Sara, this is my mother, Helen Nader."

"Sara, welcome to our home. I hope you are a good cook. Sammy needs to put on some weight."

"Mother, please," Sammy said.

"Come in, come in and sit down," Mrs. Nader said, directing them into one of the large rooms. Sara carefully sat beside Sammy on a sofa that looked more like a decoration than a piece of furniture. The girls followed them into the room and sat across from them on chairs that matched the sofa. The floor was covered with a huge, beautiful ornamental rug.

"How was your flight?" Sammy asked.

"It was really neat! We got to watch a movie!" Lena said.

"Really? They have movies on airplanes now?" Sammy asked.

"Yeah! You should go back to Lebanon with us, so you can watch one."

"Sammy, what have you been doing?" his mother asked.

"I've been busy, Mother."

A tall, good-looking man came into the room through another door. Sammy stood, so Sara did too.

"My Father, I would like you to meet Sara Lewis," Sammy said. "Sara, this is my father, Yussef Nader."

"Very nice to meet you, Sara," Mr. Nader said politely, then he turned to Sammy and said something in Arabic.

"My Father, please, Sara does not know Arabic. I ask you, please, let's keep our conversation in English."

"Very well, Sameer. Did you get a job yet?"

"I've been working with the band."

"No wonder you can't get a real job, with that long hair of yours."

"We are doing quite well," Sammy said.

"You need to do a man's work, get a real job. Look, I was talking to Bill at the State Department, and they have an opening there –"

"Father, we had the record of the year."

"That doesn't mean anything! It's not real work!"

"Our latest album went gold in less than one month!"

"You need to get a real job!"

"That means it has sold more than a million copies already!"

"Wow!" said Layla.

"So, you think you can make a living playing around on a stage and singing those fairy tale love songs you write?"

"Yes! We are doing very well!"

"Come on, now," Mrs. Nader said. "It's Christmas. Let's not have this argument now."

"Yeah, we want to hear some of Sammy's songs!" Layla said.

"Yeah, play one on the piano for us, Sammy!" Lena begged.

They all followed Sammy to the other large room, where he sat at the grand piano. He began to play 'Dream Love,' filling in the guitar portions with the piano. Then he played several other songs that Sara had never heard. His sisters were entranced by Sammy's flawless performance, and even his father smiled. Sara knew he must be proud of his son. A woman in an apron came to the door and Mrs. Nader nodded to her.

"I think dinner is about ready," Mrs. Nader said, when Sammy finished playing. "Let's go into the dining room."

"We have to wash our hands first!" Lena said.

"Of course. Girls, show Sara where she can wash her hands," Mrs. Nader said. The two girls each took one of Sara's hands and walked her to the largest bathroom she had ever seen, with finely painted porcelain, hand-painted tiles and gold fixtures. Sara washed her hands with soap that smelled of fresh wild flowers and she dried her hands on a pink towel that was so soft, she didn't think it could absorb water – but it did.

The girls took Sara through a maze of hallways and rooms, finally arriving in a huge dining room that had a wall of windows overlooking the lake. The dining room table must have been at least twenty feet long. Sammy held out a chair for Sara to sit and he sat beside her. His sisters sat across the table from them. The table was beautifully set with fine china and gold eating utensils.

"I hope you like lamb, Sara," Mrs. Nader said.

"It smells wonderful," Sara said, although her stomach felt tightly closed. She tried to take a deep breath but she didn't want to get dizzy.

"Where's Nadim?" Sammy asked.

"Oh, he stayed with your grandmother," Mrs. Nader said. "She needs extra help, so he volunteered to stay with her. I think he's liking a girl who lives near her."

"Nadim is my brother," Sammy told Sara. "He's 19. Layla is 13, and Lena is 9."

"I WILL be 9," Lena corrected, "in two days."

"She WILL be 9," Sammy repeated, smiling at his sisters.

"Where are you from, Sara?" Mr. Nader asked.

"I was born here in Seattle," Sara said, "at Virginia Mason hospital."

"I was born in Seattle, too!" Lena said.

"Why are you not with your family tonight?" Mr. Nader asked.

"Father! That is not your business!" Sammy said.

"Family is the most important thing in life, and you should be with them during the holidays," Mr. Nader said.

"I only have my dad," Sara said. "I'll probably see him tomorrow."

"Probably?" Mr. Nader asked furiously.

"No, I mean, I'll be spending tomorrow, Christmas day, with him," she decided. Now that she had said it, she had to follow through with her promise. She actually felt a little better, having made that commitment. Her stomach relaxed a little bit and she thought she might be able to eat.

"Let us bless the table," Mr. Nader said, closing his eyes. Sammy took Sara's hand. "Father, thank You for family and friends, for bringing us together once again to enjoy this feast, and for traveling mercies for us to get here safely. Thank You especially for the gift that You sent more than 1900 years ago, Your Son, Jesus. Bless this food and the hands that prepared it. Amen."

The maid and butler served the food and drinks, and the conversation changed to Lena's and Layla's school work. When everybody finished eating, the family and Sara retired into another room to relax. Sammy left the room for a moment. He returned with a big bag of gifts, which he distributed to his family members.

"Now, you can't open them until tomorrow," he said.

"What is it?" Lena asked, shaking hers.

"You'll know in the morning," Sammy said.

"Are you staying tonight?" Mrs. Nader asked. "Sara, we have plenty of room. We can have one of the guest rooms made up for you."

"No, Mother, Hassan is coming back to take us home," Sammy said.

"You're not living in sin with this girl, are you?" Mr. Nader asked accusingly.

"No, of course not, Father!" Sammy said. "I'm still living in the apartment with Luke, and Sara lives in a different apartment with her friend, Janet."

"I don't want you bringing disgrace on our family name," Mr. Nader said.

"Don't worry, my Father, I won't. People don't even know I'm a Nader."

"You're still going by that ridiculous name, Samson?"

"It's legally my name now."

"You are ashamed of your family heritage."

"It's not that! Our managers just thought–"

"Your managers, my foot!" Mr. Nader said. "You picked that name."

"Mother, Father, it is time for us to be going," Sammy said, as he stood to his feet.

"No, Sammy! Stay!" Lena said. "We want to give you your presents!"

"I'll come back tomorrow and get them, my littlest angel. I need to take Sara home now. Remember, no peeking at your presents!"

"Thank you so much for having me," Sara said. "The food was delicious, and I'm so glad I met all of you."

"Sara, are you going to marry Sammy?" Lena asked.

"Lena!" Layla said. "You can't ask her that."

"But I want her to be part of our family and come back."

"She'll be back," Sammy said. "I promise to bring her again."

"Sammy never breaks his promise!" Lena said, beaming.

The doorbell rang and Riley showed Hassan into the room.

He and hugged his aunt and uncle and exchanged Christmas blessings with them. Sammy and Sara followed Hassan to the car where Janet was waiting. As they stepped into the night air, Sara noticed the temperature had dropped considerably.

"So, what's it like in the mansion?" Janet asked.

"It is not a mansion," Sammy said.

"It is!" Janet insisted. "Look at it! How many bathrooms does it have?"

"Seven," Sammy said. "No, eight."

"Only mansions have that many bathrooms."

"How was the turkey?" Sammy asked.

"Pamela did a great job. She made stuffing and gravy and everything," Hassan said.

"I feel like a stuffed turkey," Janet said. "Did you guys have turkey?"

"Lamb," Sara said.

"Eew, lamb?" Janet said.

"It was really good," Sara said.

"*Abu-shabob*, take us to my place for a few minutes," Sammy said, then to Sara, "Excuse me, Darling." He said a few words in Arabic.

"What?" Sara asked.

"You'll see," Sammy said.

When they arrived at Sammy and Luke's apartment, Hassan and Janet stayed in the car.

"Where's Luke?" Sara asked, stepping into the dark apartment.

"I guess he went out with his new girlfriend."

"He has a new girlfriend already? What happened to Bambi?" she said, waiting for Sammy to turn on a light.

"She went the way of the disposable girlfriends of Luke. She was tossed aside like a used Kleenex."

146

"That is awful."

"When Luke meets a girl, he lets her know he's just in it for fun, and that it probably won't last long. They like it, for the thrill of dating a guy in a band."

"I can't believe it."

"Don't move. I want to turn on the Christmas lights."

"What's going on?" Sara asked, as strings of colored lights began to glimmer around the room.

"Everything has to be perfect," Sammy said. "I want to give you your Christmas present."

"Oh, I left yours back at my apartment."

"We can get it later. Yours is here."

Sammy led her by the hand to a huge box the size of a washing machine, wrapped in Christmas paper.

"What is it?"

"Open it."

"Don't I have to wait until tomorrow?"

"It is tomorrow. It's 12:02 a.m. Merry Christmas, my Love." He kissed her, soft and sweet, before she could say anything. She treasured the moment, then she approached the huge package.

"Our first Christmas together," Sammy said.

"How am I suppose to open it?"

"Just rip the paper. I'm not saving it for anything."

Sara tore the paper and opened the box. Inside was another box, also wrapped in Christmas paper. With difficulty, she lifted it out of the bigger box and tore off the paper and opened the box, which revealed another box inside of it. She looked at Sammy, who was grinning from ear to ear.

"What?" he asked.

"What is this?"

"Just open it."

Sara kept opening boxes – nine in all – until she came to a

very small box. When she opened it, she saw a small, red velvet box from a jewelry store. She felt almost ashamed that her gift for Sammy was a tie with the Space Needle on it. She slowly opened the box to reveal a gold bracelet with her name beautifully engraved on it, and a small heart charm dangling from one link.

"Oh, Sammy," she gasped.

"Do you like it?" he asked quietly.

"It is so beautiful."

"I know, but do you like it?"

"I love it! Thank you!" She jumped up and threw her arms around him, surprising him. He held her for a minute, then he guided her to the sofa.

"Try it on, let's see how it looks on your arm." He fastened it for her, then rotated her arm so they could admire it.

"This is 24 carat gold," he said. "You can't buy gold like this in the United States."

"Where did you get it?"

"When I went overseas, I got it for you."

"When did you go overseas?"

"Last Christmas."

"You didn't even know me then."

"I was preparing to meet you."

"But this has my name on it."

"I know a good jeweler who engraved it."

"Sammy, you shouldn't have."

"Yes, I should have, and I should do more for you. You don't know how much you mean to me. I wish I could just wrap you up and keep you as my Christmas present."

Sara was thinking the same thing. She knew Sammy was the only man for her, and her love for him multiplied every minute.

"We should get out to the car," Sara said. "Janet and Hassan must be freezing out there."

"They went to get some gas. When they come back, we'll take you home."

"They must have gone to a gas station in Tacoma."

"I wonder what's taking them so long?" Sammy asked. "They should be back by now. You must be getting sleepy."

"No, are you?"

"I'm wide awake. How can I be sleepy when I'm with you?"

"I am a little cold, though."

"Oh, your hands are freezing," Sammy said, covering them with his warm hands. "I'll go get a blanket."

"That would be nice."

On his way to the bedroom, he stopped near the window. "Darling, look," he said, pulling back the curtain.

She joined him and he put his arm around her as she looked out the window. "It's snowing," Sara said softly.

"That's why they didn't come back yet," Sammy said. "Hassan can't drive in the snow."

They stood at the window, watching the snow fall for a few minutes, as it began to make the whole neighborhood bright and beautiful. They didn't often get snow in Seattle, so this was like a magical Christmas gift from God. Sammy got a blanket and they cuddled together on the couch. Sara was satisfied just being close to Sammy. He respected her. He didn't even kiss her. Sara was afraid that if they started kissing, alone together for the first time, they might not be able to stop themselves; but Sammy remained the gentleman, gently stroking her hair as she leaned her head on his chest. She listened to the rhythmic beating of his heart.

"Ho-ho-ho! Merry Christmas!" Luke's voice awakened Sara, and she had to think of where she was; oh, yes, she was in Sammy's apartment with him. She must have fallen asleep in his arms, for now it was morning.

"Wake up, young lovers, it's Christmas morning, and Seattle is one huge skating rink!" Luke said. "It snowed, it rained, it froze, and now we have an ice glaze over the whole city! Are you planning to spend Christmas day with us, Sara? I can give you a ride, if you need one. It's a sheet of ice out there, but I love to drive in it, you know, slip and slide. I just got new tires and they really grip the ice."

"I think it would be best for us to stay here until it warms up out there," Sammy said. "We don't need to go anywhere, do we, Darling?"

Sara thought about her dad. She had planned to see him today, and now it looked like that wasn't going to be possible. She couldn't call him because Sammy didn't have a TTY. She only knew a couple of hearing people she could call who did have a TTY and could relay a message to him, but she didn't have their phone numbers with her.

Sara smiled at Sammy. "We'll just have to spend Christmas together," she said, secretly happy about the circumstances. She thought about how everything happened for a reason, how God was in control of everything. She knew He was the One responsible for her being here with Sammy today.

"Anyone hungry?" Luke asked. "I can make some pancakes."

"I can't eat this early," Sammy said. "What time is it, anyway?"

"It's almost 8:00," Luke said.

"Sara, are you hungry?" Sammy asked. "I think I need to lie down for a few minutes."

"No, not really," she said.

"I'll make some pancakes and you can eat whenever you get up," Luke said. "Hey, sleep in! It's Christmas! What better gift to give than yourself, to the one you love?" Luke opened and closed a few cupboards, then he started banging pots and pans in the kitchen area.

"Let's go lie down in the bedroom," Sammy said. When he saw Sara hesitate for a moment, he added, "so we can get a little sleep."

They spent all of Christmas morning sleeping. When they

awakened at noon, Luke was gone and the pancakes were cold. Sammy fixed scrambled eggs and toast.

"Not exactly what you were planning for Christmas dinner, huh?"

"It looks and smells delicious," Sara said, joining him at the table.

"Let me see your hand," Sammy said, holding it gently. "Father, for these gifts we are about to receive, we thank You. And thank You for letting Sara be here with me on this beautiful Christmas day."

After they ate, they peeked out the door to see the frightful weather, now a layer of snow over the ice. Icicles hung from every branch of every tree, and from the fence. Sammy pulled Sara back into the warmth of the apartment.

"Sara," Sammy said, "you are so beautiful. When I look at you, I want you so badly."

Sara's heart skipped a beat, then it began pounding so loudly she almost couldn't hear what Sammy was saying. She wanted Sammy more than she wanted anything, but she wanted him the right way, the way she had always been taught: she wanted to be his wife. She didn't know what to say. She felt that any word or voice fluctuation would betray her true feelings. She really did want to be with him, and every moment with him was building up a tension inside of her that she wanted him to release, with a kiss or maybe something else.

"I need you forever, Sara," Sammy said. Maybe he was talking about marriage, Sara thought, so she just continued to listen. "I can't live without you, but right now, we are too close. I don't want to do anything we will regret. All night, I was watching you sleep. You look like an angel when you are sleeping, but you are also an inviting young woman, the woman I love, and in order for me to be locked up alone with you all day and still practice restraint, it's a real challenge for me. I have been waiting for you all my life, and now you are here, but I can't have you now. You're a Christian. You know what I mean."

"Lead us not into temptation…"

"That is exactly what I mean. I would love nothing more than to carry you into the bedroom and hold you in my arms all day and night..."

"I think I'll wash the dishes," Sara suggested, since the sink was full and dirty dishes were piled all over the counters.

"Oh, my Love, how do you know just what to do? I'll just have to do something besides watch you, because even watching you is really getting to me. I think I'll go take a shower, a nice, cold shower. We'll have plenty of time in the future to indulge in each other."

Sara washed and dried all the dishes and pots and pans and put them in the cupboards. She cleaned the stove and wiped the table and the counters. The kitchen was now spotless, so she looked for something else to do. Sammy hadn't come out of the other room, so she sat on the sofa and wrapped up in the blanket. She felt so warm and comfortable, she soon fell asleep. She awakened to a gentle touch on her face.

"You looked so peaceful, Darling, I didn't want to wake you," Sammy said quietly. "Hassan is here, and the roads are okay for driving now. Are you ready to go home?"

Sara nodded. She noticed it was already dark. Sammy helped her stand, then he walked her to the car where Hassan was waiting. They took her home to her apartment, and Sammy kissed her gently on the cheek before he left.

"Merry Christmas, Sara!" Janet said, as soon as she opened the door.

"Is it still Christmas?" Sara asked.

"Yes it is! Did you have the most wonderful Christmas with Sammy?" Janet asked, being exceedingly cheerful.

"It was very unusual," Sara said.

"What did Sammy give you for Christmas?"

"Oh, I forgot to give him his present! He gave me this bracelet." She held out her wrist to show Janet.

"Wow, that's beautiful," Janet said, examining the bracelet. "It looks really expensive. Guess what! Hassan gave me a ring!

We're going together." She held out her hand so Sara could see her ring.

"Congratulations, Janet!" Sara said, hugging her and feeling a little envious. She felt Janet's tension and stepped away from her friend. "What's wrong?"

"Nothing, really... well..."

"What is it? Are you alright? Tell me!"

"Yeah, I'm fine, wonderful. Well, Hassan is really my first boyfriend since high school, and, um, you know..."

"No, what?"

"After we took you over to Sammy's, Hassan said he had a Christmas present for me, so we came back here, so he could give it to me in private. Anyway, he gave me the ring and then he asked me to be his girlfriend, and you know, I like him, so, anyway..."

"Anyway, what? What's wrong?"

"Anyway, I was so happy, I kissed him and he kissed me and one thing led to another, well, you know ... you've spent the night with Sammy."

"What are you saying?"

"Well, we were kissing and stuff, and then we were going to leave to go get you, but it was snowing and icy outside and he said he couldn't drive in the snow, so I asked him if he wanted to stay, and he was going to sleep on the couch, but we just kept kissing and stuff, and anyway, we went to bed together. There, I said it."

Sara saw a tear running down her cheek.

"Janet, are you okay?"

"I wanted to! He was trying to be polite and stay on the couch, and I invited him to join me. At first, I thought we would just sleep in the same bed together, holding each other, but we couldn't be that close and not do anything. I really love him and he loves me, too. You know what I mean. You and Sammy have slept together, haven't you?"

"No, we haven't."

"Come on, you can tell me. I told you."

"No, we fell asleep on the couch waiting for you to come back to get us, but we didn't do anything. We didn't even kiss until he brought me home this evening."

"Wow, he must have a will of iron," Janet remarked. "Anyway, that's not the problem."

"What do you mean?"

"I mean, Hassan and I getting together, that's not the problem."

"Problem? What is the problem?"

"The problem is, this morning, we got up and Hassan went to the bathroom. Then someone knocked on the door, and I thought it was you, maybe you forgot your key or something, so I opened it, and it was your dad."

"My dad? What did he say? What did you tell him?"

"I couldn't tell him anything, I don't know sign language. He read my lips when I told him you weren't here. Then Hassan came out of the bathroom in his underwear, and your dad saw him. I think he was really mad. He left."

"Oh, no," Sara said, sinking down into a chair. She knew that even though she hadn't done anything wrong, to her dad, her independent life displayed the appearance of evil. She couldn't contact her dad now; he would never understand.

CHAPTER 17
APRIL 1971

Sara admitted to herself that she was a coward. Springtime had come to Seattle, and she still hadn't made contact with her dad since she moved out of his house. She had intended to go to see him the day after Christmas, but she was afraid to face him. She thought she would make amends at church, but on Sunday she decided not to go to church. Three days after Christmas, Grand began a cross-country tour, on the road for four months. Sara kept busy with Janet and with work while Sammy was out of town. Sammy called Sara frequently, and they confessed their love to each other over the phone. Each evening when he called her, he asked her to look out the window at the moon, so that they may be looking at it together, as if they could see each other's reflection. Sara thought less and less about her dad as she focused more and more on Sammy.

"It's April 9," Sara told Janet one day at the fan club headquarters. Janet was buried under a truckload of new T-shirts and Sara was working on the fan club newsletter.

"It's Friday, that's all I know," Janet said, "and we have WAAAYYY too many T-shirts in here."

"We could get someone else to help us," Sara suggested. "Sammy doesn't want us to work too hard."

"Really? You can hire someone else?"

"Sure, do you have someone in mind?"

"How about my sister? She loves Grand and she needs a job."

"Isn't she still in high school?"

"She's a senior. She only goes to school half-day because she's suppose to be getting some work experience in the afternoons."

"Is she a good worker?"

"I guess. She would love this! This is the best job."

"Tell her to come Monday afternoon. She can start part-time."

"So, you were going to say something."

"I was?"

"About today being April 9?"

"Oh, yeah! Exactly one year ago today was the day I met Sammy. He came with his cousins to Nordstrom to pick up their suits for a wedding."

"Really? One year ago? Were you attracted to him right away?"

"Oh, for sure. Just remembering that day makes me believe in love at first sight."

"Really? That is sooo cool! It's just too bad you guys can't be together more," Janet said. She spent lots of time with Hassan. Sara was aware that they often spent the night together, but she chose to ignore that fact. She didn't really see anything happening in their apartment; she usually stayed in her own room when Hassan was there.

"Absence makes the heart grow fonder," Sara said.

"Does it really? Or do people just say that to help them get through the times they are apart from each other?"

"All I know is that I love Sammy more and more, whether or not we are together. Our hearts are always together."

"You must really trust him, I mean, he's all over the country, with all kinds of girls throwing themselves at him. Do you really think he's being faithful to you?"

"Yes, I do. I trust him. I believe in him."

"But he could have any girl he wants."

"He only wants me."

"All those girls want him. They'll do just about anything for him."

"He told me he wouldn't go out for a hamburger at McDonald's since he knows he has a steak waiting for him at home."

"Huh?"

"Sammy has really high standards. He's not going to settle for some girl, just because she's there."

"Wow, he must be a saint."

"No, he just doesn't have any interest in other girls. I mean, they might be trying every night to entice him, but he doesn't even notice them. When he's performing, he's concentrating on the music, not the audience. He's really a perfectionist. He won't let himself get distracted."

"What about after the concert? I've heard about the kinds of parties rock bands have."

"He knows I am here for him, and if he wants to go out with someone, he can go out with me. I could meet him anywhere."

"Why don't you?"

"I don't want him to think I'm trying to spy on him. I mean, if he invites me, I'll be on the next plane. Hmm, even though tomorrow IS his birthday..."

"You could surprise him!"

"Where is one of those concert schedules? Where are they going to be tomorrow?"

Janet dug through a pile of fan mail and pulled out a schedule. "They have tonight and tomorrow night off," she said.

"That's strange, a Friday and Saturday off?" Sara asked, suddenly feeling tingly all down her head and back. "He's here!"

"No, they were just in St. Louis last night," Janet said, "and they're going to play in Indianapolis next."

The door opened and Sammy and Luke came into the office. Sammy wrapped his arms around Sara without saying anything.

She hugged him tightly.

"Do you know what time it is?" Luke asked, wading through the new mail and pushing aside a mound of T-shirts.

"Almost 2:00," Janet said.

"It's time to get new headquarters for our fan club. This place is way too small for all this stuff."

Sammy took Sara's hand and led her to the hallway. When the office door had closed, Sammy turned so he was directly facing Sara. His brown eyes were full of love for her.

"Sara, my Sara," he said, stroking her hair, "I missed you so much. I just had to come back so I could see you."

"I missed you too," she said.

"I wish I could pack you up and take you with me everywhere I go. You know, when we finish this tour, we are spending three months in L.A. to record our new album."

"I thought you were going to record it here, in Seattle."

"The Sharks got a great deal at a studio in L.A., some promotional package. We are going to be on a couple of TV shows."

"That's great! Congratulations!"

"But it means more time away from you."

"Like you said, we have plenty of time. This is your big chance. You have to do it. I'll still be here when you get back."

"Oh, Sara," Sammy said. He looked deeply into her eyes, then he closed his eyes as he gently kissed her. He tenderly held her shoulders, then he kissed her again. "My sweet Sara."

"Tomorrow is your birthday."

"Yes! I want to spend today with you – since you refused to spend my last birthday with me."

"We had just met!"

"To you, we had just met. I have known you all my life."

"I want to make your birthday special. What do you want to do?"

"Just being with you makes it special."

"We could ride the ferry to one of the islands."

"Whatever you want to do, all I want is to be with you."

"We could go to the Space Needle again."

"You know, today is our anniversary, of the day we met."

"I was thinking about that earlier."

"Let's do something now."

"Like what?"

"Do you want to go to a movie?"

"Do you?"

"Not really, but I will if you do. I've been hearing a lot about a movie called 'Love Story.' I heard it's really good."

"I read the book and it is good, but it's really sad."

"Really? Then you already know the story. Is it a very romantic love story?"

"Yeah, a couple meets and they fall deeply in love. The guy is really rich and the girl is poor, kinda like us."

"You are not poor. So, do they live happily ever after?"

"I don't want to spoil the end for you."

"Well, I'm not going to read the book, and I won't be going to the movie without you. So, is it an ideal love story, like ours?"

"No, she dies at the end."

"Oh, forget it. He's left all alone? No, I know I don't want to see it now. Our love story is going to last forever. We are going to grow old together, and have our great-grand children come and stay with us at Queen Anne Castle. I know! Let's go look at our future home."

"Queen Anne Castle?"

"Yeah, let's go look and see what it's like inside."

"Will they let us?"

"Sure they will."

"Do you know the owners?"

"Not the current owners. I know the future owners." He opened the door to the office and they saw Luke getting ready to kiss Janet. She looked at Sara with a startled expression. Luke smiled at them sheepishly.

"Hey, man, let's go," Sammy said. "You too, Janet. It's time to close up for the day."

"Where are we going?" Luke asked.

"To our future home," Sammy said, "Queen Anne Castle."

"Queen Anne Castle?" Janet asked. "What's that?"

"The place Sammy is going to buy when we really hit the big time," Luke said.

Luke drove to Queen Anne Hill and parked the car in front of the huge gate of the massive estate, which was surrounded by a high stone wall and towering evergreen hedges. The house couldn't be seen from the street.

"How do we get in?" Janet asked.

"Ring the bell," Sammy said.

Luke got out of the car and boldly rang the bell. He spoke into the intercom and then returned to the car.

"They won't let us in," he said.

"What did you tell them?" Sammy asked.

"I said we had an appointment to meet with the owner."

"Let me out, I'll get us in," Sammy said. He climbed out of the car and rang the bell. He said something into the intercom and the gate began to slowly roll to one side. Sammy jumped back in the car and Luke drove up the long driveway.

They passed several beautiful gardens, three houses made of stone, and two large fountains before coming to the enormous stone house that looked like a castle. A man came out to greet them as they piled out of the car.

"Sammy Samson, it's so nice to meet you," he said, shaking Sammy's hand.

"This is Luke Maybee, the drummer for Grand, and this is Janet. This is my girlfriend, Sara."

"So nice to meet all of you," the man said. "I'm Kurt. Come in, let me give you the grand tour – no pun intended," he said, laughing at his own joke. Sammy laughed politely as they stepped into the house.

"First, a little history," Kurt said. "This house was built in 1900 for a family who was planning to move here from England. It has a total of 27 rooms, with two complete kitchens. Five smaller houses were built on the grounds to house the servants, three of which you passed on the drive, and the other two are on the back side of the estate. The house was not yet finished when the owner's wife became sick, and then she died. The owner could not bear to bring his seven children across the ocean to a new home without her. He had the house finished, with the intention of selling it, then he became ill and was incapable of taking care of his business. After he died, the children had no reason to sell it until 1950 when a very rich family – I am not at liberty to disclose their name – bought it, and they still own it now. They are not living here. No one lives here, well, except the hired help. We keep up the houses and the grounds."

"Is it for sale?" Sammy asked.

"No, they have no plans to sell it, but I am happy to show it to you." Kurt led them through several very large, sparsely furnished rooms on the main floor. Sara saw several stairways leading to floors upstairs and downstairs. After weaving around all over the first floor, Kurt led them up the main stairway. "The master bedroom is right through here," he said, taking them across a huge landing that overlooked both of the largest rooms on the main floor.

The master bedroom was at least twice as big as Sara's entire apartment, with two bathrooms and four large closets.

"This will be our room," Sammy whispered in Sara's ear. A huge window with a window sear overlooked a beautiful garden, and a glass door led to a private balcony off the master bedroom.

They followed Kurt down a hall to see six more bedrooms

and another staircase that led up to the third floor. Sara noticed that each of the rooms had a huge fireplace and she thought that it must be very expensive to keep the house warm. As they toured the rooms on the third level, Sammy noted which rooms would be best as art studios and guest rooms. Kurt took them to a balcony on top of the house which revealed a breathtaking view of downtown Seattle and Puget Sound. Sara looked at the Space Needle and remembered how this place had looked from there. They went down a back stairway to a large kitchen and a very large formal dining room. Double glass doors opened to a beautiful covered patio which was surrounded by picturesque gardens, blooming with spring flowers.

"This path leads to the other houses," Kurt said. "You can't see them from here. One is over that way, and the other one is at the back of the property, down there. Do you want to go see them?"

"I think we've seen what we came to see," Sammy said. "So, is the estate for sale?" he asked again.

"No, the owners don't seem to care about it, but they don't want to sell it either."

"How much do you think they would want?"

"They are not interested in selling."

"A million? Two million?"

"I can ask them, but they are not interested in selling."

"That's okay, we're not in a hurry," Sammy said.

They followed Kurt through the house to the front driveway.

"Oh, the six-car garage is over here," Kurt said. He took the men to look at it while Sara and Janet waited by the car. Janet seemed desperate to talk to Sara.

"I wasn't going to kiss him," Janet explained, "but he just kind of talked me into it. I wasn't thinking. I don't know how he charmed me. You know I love Hassan. I'm so glad you guys opened the door right when you did."

"You don't have to explain anything to me," Sara said.

"I'm not that kind of girl."

"I know."

"Really?"

"Sure, I've seen how Luke is with girls. It's like he's trying to collect them or something, you know?"

"I'm so thankful that he didn't get me! What would I tell Hassan?"

"I don't know."

"Has Luke ever tried anything with you?"

"No, but he knows I'm with Sammy."

"Yeah, that's true. But you better watch out for him anyway. He's tricky."

The men came back to the car and they all said goodbye to Kurt, thanking him for the tour.

"Does anyone want to get something to eat?" Luke asked. "We could go to that new pizza place."

Sara thought it would be rather thrilling to go to a restaurant with two members of Grand, but Sammy had another idea.

"Just take us to my cousins' place," he said.

"Yeah, sure," Luke said. "Well, I need to call Barbara anyway."

"Barbara?" Sammy asked.

"Yeah, I met her on the plane."

Luke drove them to Hassan's house, then he left. Sammy, Sara and Janet went to the door and Essom answered. He greeted them, giving Sammy a hug, then he invited them to the kitchen where they were getting ready to eat.

"Hey, Sammy!" Imad said, standing to hug him. "When did you get home?"

"I'm not really home. I'm just here for today, then I'm back on the road, to Indianapolis, Indiana," Sammy said, as Hassan embraced Janet. She led him to the living room while the rest of the group began to fill their plates with a variety of Lebanese food.

163

"Tomorrow is your birthday," Essom remarked. "What are you going to do?"

"I'm getting on a plane," Sammy said, "but I had to come home to see Sara."

Sara blushed.

"You came all this way just to see Sara?" Jihad asked.

"And you, *Shabob*, of course," Sammy added.

"Of course!" Essom agreed.

After they ate, Hassan and Janet were busy in the other room, so Imad offered to drive Sara home.

"Sara," Sammy said, on the way to her apartment, "I wish I could spend every moment with you."

"Me too."

"But we must remain strong. Can you wait for me?"

"You know I can. I told you that before."

"Most of this year we will be apart, but you know I love you."

"Yes." They arrived and Sammy walked her to her door. She wanted to invite him to come into her apartment, but she knew that would not be proper. She felt that if they were alone together, they would be tempted to go farther than they wanted to go. Even though society was saying it was okay for unmarried couples to sleep together, she didn't feel like it was okay. She was so thankful that Sammy shared her point of view. They were standing together, so she didn't have to take a stand against him. She knew she was weak, and that she would most likely give in to him if he indicated he wanted to go further. She whispered, "I love you too."

"How much?"

"I love you forever."

Sammy closed his eyes and Sara thought he might start to cry. He bit his lip, then he opened his eyes and looked at her. He seemed to change his mind about what he was going to say.

"How's your father?" he asked.

She looked at the floor, not wanting to tell him.

"Is he well?" Sammy asked with concern in his voice. He lifted her chin so he could look into her eyes.

"I don't know," she said.

"What do you mean?"

"I haven't seen him in awhile."

"How long?"

"Since I moved here."

"What?"

She told him what Janet had told her about her dad coming to the apartment on Christmas day.

"You haven't seen him since then?"

"I know he's mad at me," she concluded.

"But he's your father!"

"I know, but I just can't face him now. He doesn't approve of my lifestyle."

"What's wrong with your lifestyle?"

"Nothing, that's the point."

"You need to talk to him."

"I can't."

"He's your father and he loves you."

"I just can't."

"My father and I have our differences, but I still go to visit him."

"I have my own life now."

"He needs to be a part of your life. Your mother is in heaven. Your father doesn't have anybody else. Doesn't the Bible tell you to honor your father and your mother?"

"Yes, but..."

"But what? A father never stops loving his daughter, no matter what she does."

"I haven't done anything!"

"So, let him know that."

Sara knew he was right. "I'll go see him."

"When?"

"Tomorrow or Monday." She didn't want to see him at church.

"Do you promise?"

"It's that important to you?"

"Yes, it is."

"I promise I will go see my dad either tomorrow or Monday."

"Thank you." Sammy kissed her gently. "I need to go."

"I didn't get you a birthday present yet. I didn't know I was going to see you before your birthday."

"You are my birthday present."

CHAPTER 18

Sara summoned her courage and went to visit her dad on Saturday. As she rang the doorbell, she noticed lots of flowers blooming in the front garden, flowers that hadn't been there last spring. A woman answered the door. Sara didn't know her, so she didn't know if she were deaf or hearing. Sara signed as she spoke.

"I'm looking for Pastor Lewis."

"He's not here," the woman signed, without speaking.

"Can you tell me when he will be home?"

"Who wants to know?"

"I'm his daughter."

"Oh, come in, come in," she said, ushering Sara into the house. The house was completely redecorated, with new carpet in the living room, new curtains, a new sofa, and everything was very clean. "What brings you here?"

"I want to talk to my dad." Sara wanted to know who this lady was, but she didn't want to appear rude.

"I can give him a message. What do you want to tell him?"

Sara didn't want to approach her dad through another person, a woman she didn't even know. "When will he be home? I want to talk to him about a personal matter."

"You can tell me. We share everything."

"What time will he be home?"

"Don't be afraid to tell me. I'll tell him when he gets home."

"I can wait for him. I'm not in a hurry."

"He probably won't be home until late."

Sara thought that was rather odd, because her dad was always home early on Saturday to prepare his sermon for Sunday. She didn't want to argue with this woman.

"Why don't you just tell me what your problem is?" the woman said.

"I don't have a problem. I just want to talk to my dad."

"Are you in trouble?"

"No! I'm not in any trouble! I just want to talk to my dad."

"Of course you do. I'll tell him you came by."

"I can wait for him."

"I don't think that's a good idea."

"Why not?"

"You run along now, and I'll tell your father you were here."

For some reason, Sara didn't trust this woman, this nosy woman who wanted to know her business but wouldn't even tell Sara who she was. "I'll write him a note," Sara said.

"Okay, that's fine," the woman said, as Sara pulled a pen and note pad out of her purse. The woman watched her write the note, then she held out her hand. "I'll give it to him."

Sara reluctantly handed her the note. She decided to come back and talk to her dad on Monday.

"Thank you," Sara said, as she was leaving.

"You're welcome. I'll make sure he gets the note."

On Monday, Janet's sister, Jennifer, came to work at the fan club office after she got out of school. She was so excited to be working for a rock band, and she was absolutely giddy at the prospect of one day meeting the band members. She proved to be an enthusiastic and fastidious worker, like her sister, and Sara was glad she hired her. Just as Sara was about to tell Janet and Jennifer she was leaving for the day, so she could go visit her dad, Jennifer pulled a magazine out of her purse.

"Did you see 'Tiger Beat' this month?" Jennifer asked.

"No, I never read those magazines," Sara said.

"Me neither," Janet said. "They're for teenagers."

"This one has a good picture of Sammy," Jennifer said. "Did you know he has a new girlfriend?"

"What?" shrieked Janet. "Let me see that!" she said, snatching the magazine from Jennifer's hand.

"Yeah, Anna Caramba, that Mexican movie actress," Jennifer said. "It says they danced the whole night at the premier party of her new movie."

"I don't believe it," Sara said.

"You have to believe it, it's right here in black and white," Jennifer said. "The picture is in living color."

"I don't care. I know Sammy loves me."

"Are you engaged?" Jennifer asked.

"No."

"Going steady?"

"No, but we love each other."

"Yeah, this is probably just a publicity stunt," Janet said, as if she were trying to convince herself that's what it was.

"You can't believe everything you read," Sara said.

"Hey, weren't you going to leave early?" Janet asked.

"Yes, I am," Sara said.

"You better go now. In a few minutes it will be too late to leave early."

Sara left the fan club office and wandered down to the pier. She passed Pike Place Market and thought about the booth Sammy and Luke had last year, before Grand made enough money so they didn't need to sell clothing and art any more. She was troubled by the magazine article, and tried to recapture the feeling she had about Sammy. He must have known about this article when they were together on Friday, but he hadn't said anything to her about it. She loved him and she had trusted him; now she was hurt by him. She stared at the water, feeling the mist coming off Puget Sound and the warmth of the spring sunshine.

She loved Sammy but he hadn't made any type of commitment to her. She trusted him but he was obviously dating another woman. She needed him and she thought he needed her. She wanted to be with him. She wanted to give him the opportunity to explain the situation to her. Magazine articles were printed to sell magazines, whether or not the information was accurate. Her dad had jumped to conclusions about her and Sammy; she had to give Sammy the benefit of the doubt. She needed to see him as soon as possible. A plan formed in her mind.

Sara raced back to the fan club office where Janet and Jennifer were packing t-shirts into mailing envelopes.

"Janet, call Hassan and ask him to pick us up," Sara said excitedly. "Jennifer, where is one of Grand's concert schedules?"

"I put one on the wall, by the door."

Sara looked at the schedule. Grand was to perform tomorrow night and the next night at the Stadium Chicago.

"Where are we going?" Janet asked, dialing the phone.

"To Chicago!" Sara said.

This was Sara's first time on a plane. She had called a travel agent to purchase tickets for Janet and Hassan and herself to fly to Chicago, and to book two rooms in the same hotel where Sammy was staying. She and Janet had rushed home and thrown a few things in a bag, then they had stopped at Sears on the way to the airport to purchase suitcases. Hassan was as excited as the girls to be flying to Chicago for a concert, and as they sat in the plane waiting for it to land, Sara felt herself shaking and shivering, all throughout her body. They took a cab to the hotel and checked into their rooms. Hassan tried to find out in which room Sammy was staying, but the desk clerk wouldn't tell him. When they got to their rooms on the fourth floor, Hassan and Janet went to one room and Sara went to the other. Sara dialed the front desk.

"May I help you?"

"Yes, Sammy Samson's room, please."

"I'm sorry, we don't have anyone registered under that name."

Sara's mind raced. "What about Sameer Nader?" she asked.

"One moment please."

The phone rang and a man answered.

"Can I please speak to Sammy?"

"Who's calling?"

"Sara."

"Sammy, some chick named Sara is on the line."

"Hello, my Darling!" Sammy said. "What a pleasant surprise! Is anything the matter?"

"No... but, surprise!" Sara said nervously. Suddenly she wasn't sure this was a good idea. "We're here!"

"Who's where?" Sammy asked.

"Janet and Hassan and I flew to Chicago. We're here at the hotel!"

"Well, come on upstairs. We have a whole suite of rooms. I'm sure we can find room for you."

"Oh, we have rooms already. We're going to your concert tomorrow night!"

"It will be nice to see some familiar faces in the audience," Sammy said. "What are you doing now?"

"We just got here."

"I want to see you. Come up to the 18th floor. I'll meet you at the elevator."

Sara knocked on Janet and Hassan's door, but they didn't answer, so she went up to the 18th floor by herself. When the elevator doors opened, Sammy was waiting with his arms outstretched. Sara felt tingles go from her head down to her feet as he swept her into his arms and lifted her off the floor.

"Come, come," he said, leading her to a huge suite. Several

171

men were standing or sitting in the room. Some were drinking. Sara didn't see any other women.

"Everyone, this is my girlfriend, Sara," Sammy announced.

"Hi, Sara," they said in unison.

"Hey, want something to drink?" one man asked. Sara didn't see anybody she recognized.

"No, thank you," Sara said. She sat beside Sammy on the sofa.

"What brings you to Chicago?" Sammy asked.

Sara felt foolish. "You. We came to see you."

"Did everything go well with your father?"

Sara had forgotten about him again, when her imagined troubles began. "He wasn't home when I went to his house," she said, trying to justify her actions.

"Did you go back?"

"No, there was this lady there—"

"A lady at your father's house? Who was she?"

"I don't know, she didn't say."

"Was she in the house?"

"Yes. I think she's deaf."

"Your father's girlfriend?"

"He's never had a girlfriend."

"But you haven't seen him in, what, four months?"

"Yeah."

"Maybe it's his housekeeper."

"He's never had a housekeeper."

"He didn't need one when you lived there."

"That's true."

"So why didn't you go back?"

Sara couldn't tell Sammy the real reason: that she had been planning to go today, then she had heard a rumor about him, and her jealousy had driven her to impulsively jump on a plane.

"I will. I just didn't have a chance, because we decided to come to Chicago."

"I appreciate that, but you are not off the hook with your father."

"I know."

"Do you have tickets for the concert tomorrow?"

"Not yet. I hope some are still available."

"Double N!" Sammy shouted. A tall, thin, stylishly dressed man with blond hair glided across the large room in three strides.

"Sara, this is Nicholas Napolean Tundra. We just call him Double N. Double N, get Sara three backstage passes for tomorrow's show."

"Sure, no problem, Sammy." N. N. Tundra opened a big briefcase and handed three passes to Sara.

"Come with me," Sammy said, pulling Sara by the hand. He led her into a large bedroom. "Sit over there," he said, indicating a small sofa. He sat on a bench at a grand piano and began to play a beautiful song.

"Those guys are ready to party, but I have a couple of songs ready to be born."

Sara listened to the most beautiful piano music she had ever heard for the next 45 minutes, then Sammy abruptly left the room. About fifteen spiral notebooks were piled beside her and she opened the one on top of the stack. It was filled with musical notations and lyrics to songs, written in Sammy's handwriting. She glanced through the stack and saw that all the books were similarly filled. According to the dates written on the front of each book, they had all been written within the last month. Sara realized Sammy wasn't only an artist and musician, he was a musical genius.

Sammy opened the door to the bedroom and a waiter brought in a tray full of food on a rolling table. He removed the covers, Sammy gave him a handful of money, and the waiter left the room.

"I thought you might be hungry, so I ordered room service," Sammy said.

"Thank you," Sara said. "You are so thoughtful."

"Full of thought, that's me."

While Sara ate, Sammy wrote in one of the notebooks. "I wrote several more songs for you, Sara," Sammy said.

"You did?"

"You are the inspiration of my love songs. You are my love."

Sara didn't know what to say. Any doubt she had had about Sammy was gone now. She was ashamed of herself for doubting him.

"You'll always be the only girl for me," Sammy said. Sara just smiled as she ate her dessert.

"You know, I know you don't read teen magazines, but it has been brought to my attention that the media is trying to make something out of nothing," Sammy said, reading Sara's mind. Sara didn't say anything.

"The Sharks thought it was a good idea, good for publicity, for us to attend a premier party when we were in Hollywood last month, and some photographers took pictures of us escorting the stars of the movie. If you EVER hear or read anything about me and another woman, I hope you will immediately dismiss it as ridiculous, as I would if I heard a rumor about you and another man. There is no other woman on earth for me. I will never love another woman but you. I need you. I will always need you. By the way, you are doing an excellent job with my finances. Give yourself a raise."

"Sammy, I can't do that."

"Why not? You deserve it and I can afford it, can't I?"

"Well, yes, but..."

"But nothing. And I have discussed this with the other band members, we want you to find new headquarters for the fan club. Move to a bigger place."

"Okay, we can do that."

"Good. That's settled. Now, do you want to spend the night here with me?"

Sara's heart leaped at this unexpected invitation. She wanted so badly to say yes.

"I can't," she forced her mouth to say, against her body's wishes.

"I understand completely," Sammy said. "So you must leave now, or you may not be able to leave at a later time."

"I understand completely," Sara said, smiling. Sammy gave her one chaste kiss, then walked her to the elevator.

"Where's Hassan?"

"With Janet."

"He's going to have to marry her, you know."

"Why do you say that?"

"His father would not approve of their relationship. They are going too far, for an unmarried couple."

"I agree, but I guess they think they are just doing what everyone else is doing."

"Not everyone else is doing it! Look at us! We are able to abstain." Sammy seemed to be proud of that fact. "No, just because everyone SEEMS to be doing something, that doesn't mean everyone IS doing it, and that doesn't make it right. You are a Bible scholar, aren't you?"

"A Bible student, maybe, I wouldn't say I'm a Bible scholar."

"Remember Sodom and Gomorrah?"

"Yes."

"Everyone in those cities agreed that what they were doing was acceptable. Their lack of standards didn't make it right. As a matter of fact, God could not find one righteous man besides Lot in either city. Look what God did. He rescued Lot, then He destroyed two entire cities. Everybody in both cities was destroyed. No, a consensus among people does not make a wrong right."

"You're right."

"In what room are Hassan and Janet?"

"Room 412."

"And your room?"

"I'm in 410."

"Of course, my birthday."

"Yeah, I'm sure that's why they gave it to me."

"Be downstairs tomorrow night at 5:00. I'll have a limo take the three of you to the stadium. They'll take you to the stage door, then we'll get you seats for the concert." Sammy held Sara's shoulders as he kissed her. "You need to go now, or I won't be able to let you go at all." He reached over her shoulder to push the elevator button and kissed her until the elevator arrived.

"I'll see you tomorrow evening," Sammy said.

"Tomorrow evening," Sara repeated.

Sara had just arrived at her room when a knock came on the door. She opened it and a waiter brought a huge tray of food into her room.

"Compliments of the 18th floor," he said, leaving before Sara could offer him a tip.

Two minutes later was another knock on Sara's door. When she opened it, she was surprised to see an enormous pot of flowers on the mat. The delivery person was not in sight. She brought in the flowers and pulled out the little card.

"To the girl of my dreams. Thank you for coming to me in Chicago. Love, Sammy."

Sara had just set the flowers on a table when she heard another knock. This time, Janet and Hassan were standing at her door.

"Come in, come in," Sara said.

"We were going to invite you over for something to eat," Janet said, "but I see you got a tray too."

"You got one too?" Sara asked. "I already ate. I was going to give this to you."

"I guess Sammy doesn't want us to starve," Hassan said.

The next evening, a limousine took Sara, Janet and Hassan to the Chicago Stadium. They were all so thrilled to be backstage. They arrived before the band, while the road crew was finishing setting up the equipment. They learned that the band had been there earlier in the day for the sound check and would be arriving shortly. They were given three seats in the third row and were the first ones to be seated.

When the doors opened, the seats filled quickly with noisy, excited Grand fans. Many of them were wearing the T-shirts that had been designed by Sammy, and Sara was suddenly overwhelmed when she realized the popularity of Grand. The hundreds of T-shirts and fan club packets they had mailed had been such a repetitive process, it had become automatic: she had failed to realize that each item had gone to a living person who loved Grand.

The room was darkened. The crowd hushed. The music of Grand exploded, colored lights flooded the stage and the fans began to scream and shout, as Sammy, Dale, Luke and Jake took their places on stage. The concert was a magical experience, with the songs and movements more polished than the last time Sara had seen Grand perform. Sammy moved across the stage with poise and confidence. His voice was heavenly. Dale played a captivating guitar solo that caused the entire audience to cheer, and every song was greeted with thunderous applause.

When the concert ended, some of the audience headed toward the backstage door. A guard refused to let them enter. Sara, Janet and Hassan stood at their seats, wondering what to do, when a member of the road crew came to escort them. They pushed their way through the group trying to get backstage, and as they were let through the door, they heard shouts and cursing from those who were not allowed backstage. They walked down a long hall and were told to wait for Sammy.

Sara heard Sammy's voice, shouting and yelling, from one of the dressing rooms. She heard another muffled voice and more shouting.

"Sammy likes everything to be perfect," Hassan said.

"I thought it was perfect," Sara said.

"Me too! It was amazingly awesome!" Janet said.

"Apparently, something was wrong," Hassan said, "but you can bet it will be corrected by tomorrow's show."

About an hour later, Sammy came out of the dressing room. He had showered and changed, and he was smiling.

"I feel so alive!" he said. "We're having a party at the suites. Come on, let's go to the limo."

As soon as they stepped out the side door, they were mobbed by fans who were waiting for Sammy. He graciously signed autographs for the next hour, then the limousine took the four of them back to the hotel.

The party lasted all night. The whole band was there. The room was packed with people drinking and smoking. Sammy was all over the place, a ball of energy, making sure everyone was happy and had what they needed. The smoke bothered Sara's eyes, and Sammy took her out onto the balcony every half hour for fresh air – he couldn't stand still. He was constantly moving. Finally at about 7:30 in the morning, Sara had to call it a night and she returned to her room. She instantly fell asleep.

At noon, Sara and Janet and Hassan went to check out of the hotel. They had a flight back to Seattle scheduled for 4:00. Sara was surprised to discover that Sammy had paid for their rooms. Just before they caught the taxi to the airport, Sara went upstairs to say goodbye to Sammy. The door to the suite was open. She didn't see anyone in the main room, so she tapped on Sammy's door.

Double N answered and he told her Sammy was asleep. He opened the door and Sara peeked in to see Sammy sprawled across the bed. Sara stepped softly and kissed Sammy on the cheek. He didn't move, so she asked Double N to tell him goodbye for her. As she approached the elevator, she was tackled, and she fell to the floor with Sammy on top of her.

"I appreciate you coming all this way to see me," Sammy

said, kissing her cheek, rolling her, so they were facing each other, side by side.

"I had a wonderful time," Sara said.

"Every moment spent with you is wonderful, my Love. Tell me, how do you said 'I love you' in sign language?"

"Make your hand like this," she said, holding up her forefinger and pinky, with her thumb extended. "This is an 'I,' this is an 'L' and this is a 'Y.' All together, it means 'I love you.'" She helped Sammy position his fingers correctly.

"That's nice," Sammy said.

"How do you say 'I love you' in Arabic?"

"It depends if you are saying it to a man or woman," Sammy said. "To you, I would say, '*ana bahybik*' but to me, you would say, '*ana bahabek*.'"

"*Ana bahabek*," Sara said.

"*Ana bahybik inti*," Sammy replied.

CHAPTER 19
APRIL 1976

During the next five years, Sara saw Sammy daily when he was in Seattle, which, unfortunately, was only a few times each year. Grand was becoming increasingly popular. They recorded two albums in Los Angeles each year, then they went on tour to promote each album. Grand became a regular feature on Wolfman Jack's late night musical showcase program, "Midnight Special." Sammy kept in touch with Sara nightly by phone, and he sent her postcards from each city he visited.

Sammy took Sara to visit his family each Christmas. They accepted her as part of their family. Sara met Sammy's brother, Nadim, and she really loved Sammy's family. Although they hinted that she would become a member of their family soon, Sammy still didn't mention anything about marriage to Sara.

Grand's fan club had grown to more than four million members, generating more than $50 million per year through fan club dues and merchandise sales. Jennifer proved to be a great worker, and she and Janet completely handled the fan club. Sara had found a house for the new fan club headquarters in Seattle's University District. She had a large office in the house where she took care of Sammy's finances, which had become a much larger job now that he had more people on his payroll. Jihad moved to the top floor of the house and he did all the yard work and maintenance on the house.

Imad and Pamela got married in the spring of 1972 and moved into an apartment of their own. Hassan and Janet got married that autumn. Sara was the maid of honor, and Sammy was the best man. Sara hoped this would give Sammy some ideas, but then, she realized they would have a very difficult marriage if they couldn't spend any time together. Janet moved into the house with Hassan, where Essom still lived in the basement.

Sara's dad married Kate, his housekeeper, in 1973. Sara didn't hear about it until after the wedding, through the deaf grapevine. A woman from her dad's church sought Sara to inform her of her dad's affairs. Sara's prolonged avoidance of her dad made it progressively harder to make contact with him. How could she tell her dad she hadn't gone to church in years, when she had been raised to know that church should be a foundation of her life? Each time she talked with Sammy, he encouraged her to go see her father; each time he said that, she felt angry with Sammy for reminding her that she was not the perfect daughter she had always been before she met Sammy. Now that her dad was married, Sara couldn't bring herself to go visit him. She had moved on with her life, and she figured he had the right to move on with his life too, without any interference from her.

Sara was organizing Sammy's financial records when she felt that familiar chill, from head to toe. The door to her office opened and Sammy entered.

"Sammy!" Sara said, dropping an armload of files. "Why didn't you tell me you were coming?"

"I wanted to surprise you," he said, stepping across the room to her to give her a hug.

"I missed you so much," she said.

"And I you."

They hugged and kissed for several minutes.

"What brings you to Seattle?"

"You. I have a few days off, and I needed to take care of some business and see you."

"Congratulations on 'Central Station.' It's really soaring up the charts."

"Thank you. We really had something on that album."

"Every one of your albums has been fantastic."

"Each one is selling more than the last. Oh, by the way, look for a big deposit coming into the account next week. 'Roman Empire' went double-platinum and 'Rise and Fall' was best-selling song of the year, three years in a row, world-wide."

"I've never heard of that happening before."

"It hasn't ever happened before. They will be sending quarterly royalty checks to my account, because I wrote 'Rise and Fall.' I want you to give everyone on the payroll a thousand dollar bonus, and give yourself five thousand."

"Sammy!"

"I can't do all I do without all of you supporting me."

"That's too much."

"Wait until you see the royalty checks," Sammy said. "Oh, one other thing. Can I move my things to Janet's old bedroom? Luke is moving to L.A. and we're getting rid of the apartment. We're not here enough to even use it at all. Don't worry, I won't be living with you. We won't do anything that is not proper."

"Well, that will be one check I'll be glad to stop writing," Sara said, wishing that Sammy would be moving in with her. After loving him for so many years, she wanted to be closer to him and spend more time with him: she wanted to be his wife.

"I have something for you," Sammy said, reaching into his pocket.

"What is it?"

"For you."

Sara opened a small red velvet box to reveal a gold ring with a huge, flawless opal. She took it out of the box and Sammy put it on the ring finger of her right hand. It fit perfectly.

"It's your birthstone," Sammy said.

"Thank you, it's so beautiful," Sara said, concealing her disappointment that it wasn't his birthstone, a diamond. The ring did look stunning on her finger.

"Sara..." Sammy said, then he stopped.

"What? What is it?"

"You know how much I love you, and I appreciate you so much. You know that, right?"

Sara nodded, so her voice would not betray her true feelings. She knew something unpleasant must be coming.

"I feel that we are already married, in our hearts," Sammy said, "but I can't propose actual marriage to you."

Sara waited for more, but Sammy didn't explain. He looked longingly at her, as if willing her to understand. She just shook her head; she didn't understand.

"I love you and I need you," he said finally, "but a marriage requires one hundred percent from both partners. I can't give that to you because I am dedicated to my music, my art, my career. I just don't have the time to give you more of myself, as much as you deserve."

"I don't care," Sara said.

"I care," Sammy said. "I care about you and you don't deserve a fraction of a man. You deserve a whole man."

"You're all I need. I love you. *Ana bahabek*."

"I love you, too, Darling. I'm not saying that I will never be able to dedicate all of me to you. I'm just saying I can't do it now. You are my girl, but I can't even propose an engagement at this time, because I want to be fair to you."

"Are you saying that if I get a better offer, I should take it?"

"If that is what will make you happy."

"Only you make me happy!"

"If you choose to wait, it could be years."

"I have already waited years, and they have flown by, because I love you."

"The choice is yours. I am leaving your options open."

"I'm closing them. I don't want anyone but you, Sammy. You said it years ago. You told me God made us for each other."

"I am leaving it up to you."

"So, does that mean, if you get a better offer, you will take it?"

"That's not possible. There is no one like you. I just want to be fair to you."

"So, you just don't want to make a commitment to me."

"I already have, in my heart. If that is not enough, you are free to make another choice."

"My heart has made a choice, and it chose you. I didn't have a choice."

"I want you to keep the door open."

"That's not what I have learned about love, just to love someone until something better comes along. Love is patient and kind, honest and true, dedicated, and always thinking the best about the one you love."

"Oh, Sara, my Darling, my Love." Sammy put his arms around Sara and wept.

"What's the matter?"

"I write songs about love, but you are the one who knows love. I just don't want to hurt you. I don't want you to feel I'm putting my career over love. It's just that this has always been my goal, my dream, and this may be my only chance, in an arena such as this."

"You can't let your career pass you by. Love is strong. Love is long. Love will abide. I can wait."

"I always knew I would find you. I just didn't expect to find you so early in my career."

"I'll wait."

"Any time you want out, you are free."

"I'll wait."

"If you get tired of waiting, I'll understand."

"You are the one I love. We still have another 94 years together, remember? We don't need to be in a hurry."

"Sara, you are the only girl for me, now and forever."

"And you are—"

"Don't say it. You might not be able to live up to it."

"Do you expect me to fail? Love never fails."

"The day may come when you change your mind."

"I can't change my heart."

"I love you."

"I love you forever."

CHAPTER 20
DECEMBER 24, 1980

Grand was now the most popular band in the world, with 18 best-selling albums, 15 of them having gone platinum and the other three gold. Their Christmas album sold nearly a million copies every year. The band was touring in countries where rock bands had never been, with more than eight million fans from all over the world. The International Grand Fan Club, with Janet as the president, now had branches in Brazil, England and Japan. Sara was in charge of millions of dollars, and 14 full-time employees on Sammy's payroll. Even when Sammy wasn't home for Christmas, Sara spent Christmas Eve with his family. His sisters and brother were all married now, and Sammy's mother kept hinting that soon Sammy would be ready to settle down with Sara. Sara wished that were true – she had loved Sammy for more than ten years now – but she knew Sammy, and his motivation was his work.

On Christmas eve, Sara was getting ready to call Hassan to ask him to take her to Sammy's parents' house – one of Hassan's duties was to drive Sara anywhere she needed to go in the limousine Sammy had purchased – when the doorbell rang. She had been thinking of moving to a larger apartment, she definitely could afford it; but there was something endearing about having Sammy's old things in the spare bedroom, and she couldn't bear to move them.

She opened the door and was astonished to see Sammy. She hadn't felt the tingling. She became worried; something was wrong.

"Sara," he said. "May I come in?"

"Sammy! Yes, come in! I was just going to call Hassan. Your parents have invited me for dinner."

"I came to go with you."

"I thought you were in Paris."

"I was. I came home for Christmas."

"I'm not quite ready to go."

"Take your time, I have plenty of it."

"What's wrong?"

"Nothing."

"Something is wrong. I can feel it."

"Things are happening fast."

"What do you mean?"

"I know we haven't seen each other in nearly a year..."

"I know! I missed you."

"I missed you, too. Darling, I just bought Queen Anne Castle."

"You what?"

"I said, I just—"

"I know, I heard you, you just bought Queen Anne Castle?"

"They gave me a good deal."

"Why did you buy it if you are never here, in Seattle?"

"I'm having some renovations done, so by the time I'm ready to spend some time in Seattle, it will be ready. I'm having some redecorating done also. You know, some of those rooms were just hideous, and others were lacking in furniture, to say the least. Hassan and Janet can move into the apartment over the garage. It's bigger than the house they have now. I suppose you know that Janet is expecting?"

Sara's heart leaped in her chest. She nodded. Maybe this was the proposal finally coming... but no, something was wrong. She waited for Sammy to tell her what it was, searching his eyes unsuccessfully for a clue. He avoided her eyes.

"There's something else." He paused.

"What?"

"I bought a house for you."

"You WHAT?"

"It's just four blocks away from Queen Anne Castle, and I'll be able to see it from my bedroom."

Sara was puzzled. Why did Sammy buy a house for her? If he was planning to be spending more time in Seattle, what did this mean?

"Sara, can we sit down for a minute?"

"Sure, let's sit on the sofa."

"Sara... I think..."

Sammy looked around the room, as if seeing it for the first time. He wouldn't look at Sara. He seemed uncomfortable. He looked at the wall of postcards he had sent her. She waited. This was obviously difficult for him. What was he trying to say?

"Sara, I'm not sure how to say this."

"Just say it."

"You have been so wonderful."

"And what? Tell me!"

"I hope you will understand."

"Understand what?"

"I think I may be gay."

"What?"

"Do I have to say it again?"

"No, I heard you. I just want to be sure I understand what you said."

"You understand. Promise you won't tell anybody."

"Sammy, how can this be? You said you loved me."

"I do love you. I love you so much. But I find myself attracted to men."

"Men?"

"One man, actually. I knew him in school, and now he has come back into my life. I have feelings for him."

Sara couldn't believe what she was hearing. Tears began flowing from her eyes. She had been confident that she wouldn't lose Sammy to another woman; she had never considered that she might lose him to a man.

"I still need you, Sara. You are the only one I can talk to. You are the one who shares my secrets. I still need you to manage my accounts. I don't trust anyone but you. I want to give you a raise, double your salary."

"All the money in the world won't replace you," she choked.

"I need you. I love you. I know now why I couldn't marry you."

"You have kept me hanging on for ten years to tell me this?"

"I didn't know. I just found out. I knew it wasn't right for us to get married. I just didn't know why."

"I need you to leave now."

"What about Christmas Eve dinner?"

Sara had forgotten. Was Sammy expecting her to go with him and act as if everything were fine?

"Hassan is waiting for us in the car."

"Does he know?"

"Nobody knows. We can't tell anybody."

"This is too much."

"I know it's a lot, but you told me you love me. Can you accept me as I am?"

"What made you change?"

"I don't know. Maybe I was always like this, I don't know. I just know this is how I am now."

"Are you saying God made a mistake?"

"No, I am saying I made a mistake."

"How long do you think you can keep it a secret?"

"We can't ever tell. Look, if it were just my career, I wouldn't care. But this is for the band. We're at the top now, and this would be a total blow to all of them."

"Do they know?"

"I haven't told anyone, not even Antonio."

"Antonio?"

"My old friend."

Sara hated Antonio immediately, for transforming the man she loved into some kind of pervert. She hated Antonio for dashing her hopes for the future, for taking away the man she loved. The real problem was, she still loved Sammy, even though he was slipping away from her. The name 'Antonio' gave her an instant headache.

Sara was still tied to Sammy because of her occupation. She wanted to run out the door and just keep running, but she knew she couldn't do that. She had to go with Sammy to Christmas Eve dinner and pretend that he hadn't just told her the most devastating news of her life.

Sara dried her tears, pasted a smile on her face and hoped she wouldn't be required to speak this evening. Hassan and Janet were waiting in the limousine. Sammy and Sara climbed in the back seat and Sammy opened the privacy window and carried on a superficial conversation with Hassan and Janet. They were so excited because they had been hoping for years to have a child, and now their dreams for starting a family were finally coming true.

Sammy told them about the purchase of Queen Anne Castle, and the apartment over the six-car garage where Hassan and Janet could live. He told them he would pay for furnishing it and decorating it to their liking. They thanked and thanked him, nobody mentioning that Sara hadn't said a word. When they arrived at Sammy's parents' house, everybody (but Sara) was pleasantly surprised to see that both of Sammy's sisters were also expecting. Sara's heart was breaking, her world was collapsing, but she couldn't let anyone know. She was just thankful that everybody else had so much to say, they didn't seem to notice her silence. She pushed the food around her plate; her stomach was filled with a boulder. Sammy acted as if nothing had changed, as if he hadn't pulled the world out from under her and then let her fall.

Sara decided not to move into the house Sammy had bought her. That decision changed the next day when he took her to see it. It had four bedrooms and was beautifully furnished. Sammy had purchased it two months ago and had hired decorators to complete it for her. When Sara saw it, she couldn't deny that Sammy had impeccable taste and a flair for style. She loved it and didn't want to change a thing. Every bit of it was created by Sammy's love for her. She prayed for a miracle, that Sammy would realize that she was the one he loved, that he would return to her. Then she realized that she had neglected God for so long, she didn't deserve a miracle. She needed to visit her dad. She hadn't seen him in ten years.

Part 2

Sammy

CHAPTER 21
JULY 1983

Sammy saw faces before his eyes, hundreds of faces, thousands of faces. This wasn't just an image of being on stage burned into his memory: these were faces that came out of the woodwork. For as long as he could remember, he had been seeing faces in everything: in the patterns of the carpet and the linoleum, on the ceilings, in textured painted surfaces, in leaves of trees. Rarely did he see happy, friendly faces. Usually they were hideous, angry, frightening, judging, condemning faces. When he was young and naïve, he had created a painting of a tree in autumn with more than a thousand red, orange and yellow leaves, each leaf with a face that could be seen when closely examined. The scene was typical of his reality. The painting was beautiful from a distance, but terrifying at close range. Sammy hid the painting in the attic and never showed it to anyone. It depicted his reality, but not a reality he wanted anyone else to see.

Sammy sent everyone from the suite as he paced angrily back and forth across the room, in a rage. How could Antonio have done this to him? Sammy was a big star and Antonio was nothing! He was nothing but a cheater and a liar and a user. Sammy had taken a huge risk by getting into this relationship, and now it was finished! Antonio's sneaky ways had taken him too far. How long had Antonio been planning to use him? Sammy felt like breaking something, but he restrained himself. He refused to tarnish his reputation for self-control by trashing a hotel suite.

A knock sounded softly on the door.

"Not now!" Sammy shouted. He continued to pace, fuming. Here he was, in Brazil, with an audience of nearly 600,000 to be present at the show tonight, and he was fuming. Antonio had seduced him, lured him, tricked him, until Sammy finally submitted to him last night. The moment he did, Sammy knew he had made a mistake. How could he have ever listened to Antonio? How could he have fallen for such a deception? Everything was all wrong.

"Sammy, it's time to go," Hassan said through the door. He was now Sammy's personal assistant.

"Not now!" Sammy shouted. He caught sight of himself in the mirror, his dark, angry eyes and his full lips pulled tightly together. He felt faint. He tried to control his breathing. He leaned against the wall.

"Hassan!" he yelled.

Hassan opened the door and entered the room.

"I need some paper!"

"Coming right up."

"Now!"

"Here it is, Sammy."

Sammy furiously scribbled the song lyrics and musical notations that had just popped into his head, while Hassan patiently waited.

"Get out!" Sammy shouted.

"Sammy, you're going to be late for the show," Hassan said gently.

"Get out!"

Sammy needed space. He felt like a caged animal, enclosed in a tiny corner. He began to pace again, pounding his fist into his palm. He stopped himself, knowing his fingers needed to be ready to dance across the piano keyboard tonight. He had never been so angry in his life, as he was right now. He had been conned, misled, deceived, defiled.

Who was the master of lies, but the devil? Sammy saw it clearly now, how he had been set up to fall. He and Antonio had waited until just the right time when they could be alone. No one else knew about what had happened between them. Sammy paid Antonio a hefty sum to keep their relationship quiet. With one statement, Antonio could ruin his reputation, his popularity, and the career of all the members of Grand. The world would not accept him if it were made known that he had had a gay affair. His family would reject him if they discovered his secret. Sammy had had it all: world-wide fame, immense fortune, supportive friends, a loving family, and whatever he wanted at his fingertips; yet something was missing. Something was terribly wrong with his life.

He couldn't think about it now. He had to pull himself together for the show tonight. He had to get to Morumbi Stadium. He called to Hassan, who instantly appeared and escorted him to the elevator. Sammy's body guards and the rest of his entourage were already waiting in the limousines. He focused completely on the concert ahead. He did not partake of the conversation in the limousine. He was traveling alone through space and time. Forces inside of him were building to the point of explosion.

As Sammy stood on the stage two hours later, the sea of faces, real now, were before him, hundreds of thousands of faces. He gave the best performance of his life, even though his insides were wound tight as a rope. His vocals were executed perfectly, his piano playing was flawless, his movement on stage excellent, as he played with the audience. The applause was deafening, the energy he felt was intoxicating.

After the concert, he stood between his body guards while he was signing autographs. He had never felt so keenly aware of each person, each movement, each sight, each scent, each sound. He memorized every face he saw, as if he were to be tested tomorrow. As soon as he finished signing the last piece of paper, he motioned for Hassan to take him to the limo. The hired driver was waiting for him in the car.

"Get me into my room before the party starts," Sammy said to Hassan.

"Some people are already there."

"Get them out of the suite. Pull the fire alarm if you have to."

"I don't think that will be necessary."

"I don't want to see anyone."

"Sure, Sammy, I'll take care of it."

The sea of faces, which were usually tormenting him through the windows of the limousine, all converged into one face: Sara's. Sammy had pushed the thought of her out of his mind for nearly three years, depending on her to take care of his finances, but not contacting her in any way. He had felt he had to do it that way, to avoid rubbing salt into her wound. Now he realized he had been mistaken; he was the one who was hurting.

When he got into his bedroom in the suite of rooms, he locked the door, something he had never done in a hotel, but he had to do now. He paced the room for about two hours before falling to his knees. He cried out to God.

"Dear Lord, I have sinned against you. I have replaced you as the Most High with my own self and my own selfishness. I have come to love pleasure more than I love You. Forgive me, Lord. I have turned away from the woman you gave me, the woman who loves me. I have turned to a man in an effort to replace her, and I realize that was wrong. Father, I have always loved Sara. Help me, Father. You put Sara in my life. She is the one woman for me. I need her now. I know I don't deserve a second chance, but if there is a way I can still make Sara happy, please, show me. I love You, Lord. Help me, Lord, for I am weak."

Sammy realized he was crying. His strength was gone, his muscles unable to hold him in a kneeling position as he slid to the floor. He kept his eyes closed as he considered how good God had been to him, despite his disobedience. He fell into a deep sleep on the floor, which was out of the ordinary. After a concert, he was always awake all night, full of energy; yet tonight, he was completely at peace.

He dreamed of Sara. She was reaching out to him, but as he tried to catch her hands, she dissolved. He could feel her presence, but he couldn't see or touch her. Sammy awakened and wrote this song:

Your ghost has a hold of me
Why can't you just let me be?
I'm in love with a ghost,
A less than gracious host,
The one who loves me the most,
I can feel but can't see.

He wanted to call Sara. God had given him the answer he needed. Why hadn't he understood this when it could have changed his future, when he could have made Sara so happy, before he had made such a big mistake? Could he describe it in a way that Sara could understand? Would she be able forgive him? She had to forgive him. She loved him completely, he knew that now.

Everything was so clear now in Sammy's mind. All those years when he had loved Sara, he had been able to restrain himself because he was able to control his urges. His friends were describing how they couldn't contain themselves, how they had to have sex with their girlfriends, but for Sammy, the desire wasn't overwhelming. He loved and respected Sara more than anyone, and he had known he loved her before he even met her, but his longing for her wasn't sexual. The more he was with Sara, the more he loved her, but he wasn't driven by a longing to sleep with her. For the first few years, he dismissed it because of his drive to succeed professionally, but then he began to think something was wrong with him. He had just had a hard time thinking of Sara sexually.

When Grand was touring in Europe, Sammy heard a psychologist at a party say that subdued sexual feelings, such as the ones he had, were more like the feelings a woman might have. He began to question his sexuality. Shortly after that, he ran into Antonio. He had been close to Antonio, but he hadn't seen him since he was 13 years old, in boarding school. Antonio had grown to be a very handsome man. He convinced Sammy that their attraction was mutual. Sammy mistook the feelings he had toward Antonio for sexual feelings. They bantered back and forth for nearly four years without getting together, teasing and building sexual tension between each other. Sammy had invested huge sums of money in Antonio's modeling career. Antonio told Sammy he had never loved anyone else, man or woman, and Sammy believed him. When they finally got together, Sammy realized he was making a mistake. Everything within him told him he was doing the wrong thing. What Sammy had thought was a passionate love for Antonio turned into a passionate hate. They argued, they fought with each other. He told Antonio that their relationship had to end immediately. Sammy forced Antonio to leave, not caring that Antonio had taken him for hundreds of thousands of dollars. Antonio had probably just used Sammy for the money from the very beginning.

Now Sammy understood why, in all his years with Sara, he hadn't been driven to go to bed with her: he loved and respected her so much, he couldn't think of her sexually until they were married. It was so obvious to him now. Why hadn't he seen it sooner?

He was ready to ask Sara the question she wanted to hear. He wanted to rush back to Seattle immediately, but Grand still had five more weeks on the road before they had a short break, after which they would go into the studio again. Sammy could fly Sara to South America. They could get married, and she could travel with him. Jake's wife often traveled with the band; Sammy's wife could, too.

Everything would fall into its proper place: Sammy would no longer have a secret to keep from the world, his parents would be pleased, and, best of all, he and Sara would be together and they would both be happy. Wasn't that what they had both wanted, from the first day they met, to be together and to be happy? The answer seemed so simple now.

Sammy called the front desk and got the international operator on the line. He made a person-to-person call to Sara's house. Why wasn't she answering her phone? Where could she be? She worked from her home now. She didn't have to go to an office. What time was it in Seattle now, anyway? He asked the operator to keep trying her number and ring his room when she had Sara on the line.

"Sammy!" Hassan called through the door. Sammy didn't reply.

"Sammy! Do you want something to eat? Sammy? Are you okay?"

"Go away!" Sammy said, needing to talk to Sara and nobody else. He waited in his room the rest of the day, but the operator didn't call him with Sara on the line.

That night, Grand performed to another sold-out venue of more than 600,000. Sammy was as sharp and as agile as ever on stage. He was driven by the hope of seeing Sara. He was a changed man. He felt as if he had just stepped into manhood and he instantly understood everything. The world seemed so logical. Every word he heard seemed predestined, scripted, expected. The pieces of the puzzle were all in place except one: Sara.

After the concert, Sammy retired alone to his suite again, while Hassan reminded him that he needed to eat. Two nights in a row Sammy had expended extreme amounts of energy, but he hadn't eaten a thing in three days. Sammy was not interested in food. He had no physical appetite. As he waited to speak to Sara, he wrote song after song for her, filling sixteen spiral notebooks with lyrics and music. He was emotionally starving for her love.

Sammy was in his room at Queen Anne Castle, asleep, when he heard the screaming. It was the middle of the night – why wasn't somebody taking care of this? Wait, the voice was Sara's, and she was screaming in pain. Sammy got out of bed, wearing only his shorts, and left his room. He couldn't tell from which direction the scream was coming. He looked over the balcony to the first floor but he didn't see her. He raced down the stairs and ran from room to room, looking for her, but she wasn't there. The volume didn't get louder or softer, the screaming just continued. He ran outside to the back garden. He could tell now he was getting closer to her, wondering what she was doing outside at this time of the night. She sounded frantic, hurt. In the dark, he could barely see her through the garden, way across at the edge of the property. She was looking for him, and still screaming in pain. He had to make his way through tangled vegetation to get to her; he couldn't waste time going around by the path. She was in so much pain, she didn't see him. He wanted to call to her, but she couldn't hear him. He wanted to help her. He wanted to relieve her pain. She just kept screaming. He had to get to her. He couldn't reach her.

Sammy awakened in a sweat. He was still in South America, in his hotel suite, but he could still hear Sara screaming... or could he?

He got up and washed his face. What was that screaming sound? It was not quite so loud now, but continuing, as if every time Sara could get another breath, she renewed her scream.

Sammy went to the door of his suite and listened. He opened the door and saw Hassan asleep on the couch, waiting for Sammy to need something. Hassan obviously couldn't hear Sara screaming.

Maybe the screaming was all in his mind, coming to him the same way lyrics and songs usually did. Nobody could hear it but him.

Sammy went back to bed and listened as the screaming faded. He could still hear it as it got more and more faint, as if Sara were getting farther and farther away from him with each scream. He closed his eyes and said a prayer for Sara, then he instantly fell asleep.

During the next few weeks, the fans at Grand's shows were treated to flawless, magnificent performances. Sammy was driven to absolute perfection. He tried to call Sara every day and night with no success. He would not accept the fact that she was not at home; she had to be home, waiting for him. She said she would love him forever. She was the only one he loved, and he needed her. He dared not imagine that he had really driven her away from him with his foolishness. He was sure that she understood him better than he knew himself, and that she must be waiting for him. That thought, that hope alone, kept him focused and sane.

CHAPTER 22
SEPTEMBER 1983

As soon as they arrived in Seattle, Sammy had Hassan drive him to Sara's house. Sammy walked up the long sidewalk to the house, which was completely dark, although the yard was neatly tended. He knocked on the door and peeked in the windows. He knew she wasn't home. He pulled out his key to her house and unlocked the front door. Inside the house, the rooms were dark and quiet. Everything had been left exactly as he had had it decorated. Sammy's heart skipped a beat when he thought he might find her upstairs, sleeping; but no, the house had no scent of life. The air was stale, as if the door hadn't been opened in months.

He returned to the car and instructed Hassan to take him to Sara's father's house. He knew Hassan was anxious to see Janet and their two children, but Sammy's business was extremely urgent right now.

As Sammy approached the parsonage, he wished he had taken the time to learn sign language so he could communicate with Sara's father. He would have to use paper and pen. He pushed the doorbell, which he did not hear ring, but he saw a light flashing through the window. A woman came to the door.

"I'm looking for Pastor Lewis," he said.

The woman pointed to her ears and shook her head.

"Pastor Lewis!" he shouted.

She looked at him blankly.

Sammy took a small notepad and pen from his jacket pocket. He scribbled on the paper, "Is Pastor Lewis home?"

She nodded and retreated, without asking him to come in the house. Sammy waited on the porch.

Pastor Lewis came to the door. He looked quite a bit older than the last time Sammy had seen him.

"I need to see Sara," Sammy said, then he wrote it and showed the note to Pastor Lewis.

Pastor Lewis shook his head, took the pen and wrote, "She is not here."

"Where is she?" Sammy wrote.

"I don't know. I haven't seen her or heard from her in years."

"I need to find her."

"She left home because of you. You took her from me and she never came back. I assumed she was still with you. I hope you are happy," Pastor Lewis wrote.

Sammy shook his head. "I love her," he wrote.

"So do I," Pastor Lewis wrote.

Sammy wanted to leave a message with Sara's father, but he doubted that she would contact him after all this time. Still, he wrote one more thing: "If she comes home, please let her know I'm looking for her." Her father nodded.

Hassan drove Sammy to Queen Anne Castle, where Sammy hadn't yet had a chance to spend much time. His household staff, including Imad, who had become Sammy's chef, Essom, who had become his gardener, Martin Matson, his head housekeeper, and Jihad, who still lived upstairs at Grand fan club headquarters, were all waiting at the castle for them to arrive. Hassan rushed to the apartment above the garage to get Janet and their children to join the homecoming celebration.

"Sammy, how was the tour?" Essom asked. "You have been getting great press, even in Seattle!"

"Your albums are all over the place, and they play your songs on the radio all the time!" Jihad said.

"I made your favorite dinner," Imad said.

"I need to find Sara," Sammy said insistently, disregarding

the small talk.

"Sara?" Martin asked.

"I haven't seen her in a long time," Essom said. "I think she moved."

"No, she still lives in the same house. Jihad still mows her lawn," Imad said.

"Every week!" Jihad said.

"She always gets our paychecks to us on time," Imad said. "She mails them."

"I think she went on vacation," Essom said.

"I haven't seen her in months," Jihad added. "She hasn't been home when I've been there."

"Maybe Janet knows," Imad said, as she and Hassan brought their kids in the room. Sammy didn't even take a moment to look at their children: he had a vital mission to accomplish.

"Janet, where can I find Sara?"

"I don't know. I haven't seen her in a few months."

"Somebody has to know where she is!"

"I might be able to find out."

"Then find out!" Sammy shouted. "I've got to see her!"

"My sister might know." Janet called Jennifer, who told her Dale's wife, Isabella, might have an idea where Sara was, but Jennifer didn't have Isabella's phone number.

Sammy called Dale's number but it had been changed. Sammy recalled Dale had told him they recently moved.

"Hassan!" Sammy shouted to his cousin, who was laughing with his children.

"What is it, Sammy?"

"Take me to Dale's house, now!"

Sammy didn't want to wait for Hassan to get the limo, so Hassan drove his new station wagon to Dale's house, in Edmonds, north of Seattle.

As soon as they arrived, Sammy pounded on Dale's door.

"Sammy! What brings you here?" Dale asked.

"Your wife," Sammy said, pushing his way into Dale's living room.

"What? My wife brings you here?"

"Yes! No! Where is she? I need to ask her something," he said, looking frantically around the house.

"Relax, she's not here. She went to the store. She'll be back in a few minutes. What's up?"

"Does she know where Sara is?"

"Sara?"

"Yes, Sara! I need to find her."

"I don't know. Why would Isabella know where Sara is?"

"The girl that runs the fan club, Jennifer, said she might know."

"I don't know, I just got home a few minutes ago. Did you check Sara's house?"

"Of course I checked her house!"

"Hey, man, take it easy."

"To what store did she go? We'll go find her."

"Just relax, man, she'll be back in a few. What's the hurry, anyway? I thought you guys broke up a couple of years ago."

"I need to find her right away!"

"Why? What's the deal?"

A car pulled into the driveway and Sammy ran out of the house to greet Isabella.

"Hi, Sammy! What are you doing here?"

"Where is Sara?"

"What?"

"Where is Sara? Janet's sister said you know where she is."

"I don't know."

"You don't know?"

"How would I know where she is?"

"Janet's sister said—"

"Oh, wait, is she still gone?"

"Gone? Where? Where did she go?"

"I was talking to her a few months ago, and she said she needed to get away from the dreary weather. We were talking about vacations, and I told her where I used to go, to my uncle's villa, out in the country in Tuscany—"

"Tuscany?"

"Yeah, in Italy—"

"Sara's in Tuscany?"

"That was months ago when we talked about it, about, um, in April, I think. If she decided to go, she would probably be back in Seattle by now."

"Hassan! Let's go to the airport!"

"I doubt that she's still there! I don't even know if she went or not! Hey, don't you want the address?" Isabella called, as the car sped out of the driveway and down the street.

For the first time in years, Sammy was traveling on a plane without his entourage, or even his personal assistant. He had a seat in first class. He was on his way to New York, where he would change planes and fly to London, then to Florence, Italy. He realized that he hadn't asked Isabella for any specifics of the location, and he hoped that Tuscany wasn't so big that Sara could be there without him finding her. Grand had performed in Italy numerous times, but he had never been to Tuscany. Sammy had a good feeling about this: he was going to find Sara.

He didn't sleep at all during his flights, even though he had a long layover in New York and another one in London. He was focused on finding Sara. He was wide awake when the plane landed in Florence 30 hours after he left Seattle. He was able to leave the airport immediately since he hadn't brought any luggage.

As soon as he tried to hail a cab, he realized he needed to hire an interpreter. He went back into the airport and found a booth that offered guides and interpreting services, and he paid a man handsomely to assist him for as long as it would take to find Sara.

He explained to his guide that he was looking for a woman staying in a villa in Tuscany. The man laughed, telling him there were thousands of villas and millions of women in Tuscany. Sammy tried to convey the importance of his search, saying it was extremely urgent that he find her. He described Sara, sorry that he hadn't brought a picture of her. He told the guide that he would pay him triple if they found her within 24 hours. The guide made several phone calls, and then they got in a car and drove for about an hour to a secluded location. He talked to several people there, who then directed them to Pisa. Sammy had no interest in seeing the Leaning Tower of Pisa; his heart was leaning and only Sara could make it upright inside of him.

They left the city and traveled through several small towns where the guide asked questions of the villagers. When it began to get dark, the guide suggested they rest for the night and resume the search in the morning. They each got a room in a small boarding house, and the guide disappeared behind his door.

Sammy felt he was near Sara. He couldn't wait until tomorrow. He stepped into the warm evening air and took a deep breath, asking God to lead him to the woman he loved. His heart was bursting with love for Sara. All he wanted to do was to hold her in his arms and hear her say she still loved him. He began to walk down a narrow path, asking for God's direction every step of the way. He had no idea where he was or where he was going, but he knew he was getting closer to Sara. Oh, how he longed to see her.

After walking for a long time, he came to a villa. The gate was closed. Sammy was sure this was where he would find Sara. He could smell her scent, hear her breathing. For the first time in his life, he didn't know what to do. He leaned against the stone wall, closed his eyes and prayed for direction.

"Sammy?"

He had been too long without sleep, and he was dreaming

while he was awake. His imagination was over-active. He heard Sara's voice, speaking his name in that sweet way that only Sara could say it. He willed himself to hear her voice again.

"Sammy!"

He wasn't imagining! He opened his eyes. Sara was standing in front of him! Her long hair had been smartly cut to her shoulders. She was much thinner than he had remembered, but she was so beautiful, the most beautiful woman in the world.

"Sara," was all he could manage to say, in a whisper. He gently put his arms around her and held her, feeling the missing part of his heart being put back into its place. Sara returned his hug. They stood together, unmoving for a long time; then, like two lovers slow dancing across a room, she led him through the gate into the villa and inside the house.

"Sara, I need you," Sammy said. He could no longer refrain from kissing her. He held her face and became intoxicated by their kisses. They fell onto the sofa and Sammy looked into Sara's eyes, aching to think that he had put the hurt he saw in them.

"Sara, my Sara, I have made so many mistakes. Please tell me you'll forgive me. I don't know how I could have left you. I have never stopped loving you. I love only you. I will always love only you. Sara..."

Sammy pulled a small box from his pocket. He opened it and took out a lovely diamond ring he had purchased for her in Rio. As he placed it on her left ring finger, he asked, "Sara, will you marry me, and be mine forevermore?"

A tear ran down Sara's cheek. She didn't say anything. She took Sammy's hand and led him to the bedroom. Now that she was about to become his wife, Sammy decided that tonight was the night for them to consummate their relationship. He planned to find a chapel and marry her the next day. Sara welcomed Sammy, as if she had been waiting all her life for this night.

In the middle of the night, Sammy awakened with Sara's head on his shoulder. Life was perfect now; Sammy was now complete. Sara was his other half. He stroked her hair, completely satisfied. He fell into a peaceful sleep with a smile on his lips.

With Sara's first movement, Sammy was awake. Sara looked at him as if she thought she were dreaming.

"Good morning, my Darling, my wife," he said.

"How did you find me?"

"The same way I found you in the first place. God led me to you. Why did you come here, all by yourself?"

"I had to."

"Oh, my sweet Sara, you are the one true love of my life. I had to find you and make things right with you. How could I have been so blind as to not see you right there, loving me, the way I needed to be loving you? Ah, but that is all behind us now. I'm not afraid of marriage. I am ready to marry you today. I know now marriage is what you needed from me, while I searched the world looking for something, trying to satisfy my selfish desires. But my search is over. God has revealed His plan for my life, and the first thing I need to do is to marry you right away. Let's go now and find a chapel. It doesn't matter what you wear. I came all the way from Seattle without bringing any luggage! I was in such a hurry to find you. Love conquers all barriers. Sara, can you possibly understand how much I love you?

"Come, let's get ready to go to our wedding. From now on, every night will be like last night. We will be together all night, in each other's arms. Oh, you are so quiet! I don't mean to be overbearing, but I know you love me as much as I love you. I can see it in your eyes. I can feel it... but wait. What is it? Is something wrong? Do you still love me?"

"I told you a long time ago, I love you forever. That hasn't changed."

"Is it because you want a big wedding? We can call all our friends and have them join us here. I'll charter a jet and they can be here by tomorrow, or whatever you want. We can fly to Seattle and get married there. I just want you to be my wife, and I want you to be happy. Darling, why are you crying?"

"Sammy," Sara said, her tears flowing freely, "I can't marry you."

"Isn't this what you have always wanted? Isn't this what is meant to be? Don't you know, this is what God planned for us? Why do you say you can't marry me?"

"I'm already married."

CHAPTER 23

Sammy fell back onto the bed, feeling as if he had been shot in the heart. Sara's voice was so faint, she sounded so defeated; he must not have heard her correctly.

"Pardon?"

Sammy could see by the look on Sara's face that she was unable to repeat her statement. He also saw that she was telling the truth.

"You are married?"

She nodded.

He couldn't fully comprehend the meaning of her statement. "Are you saying, because we are married in our hearts, you are already married to me?"

"No." She seemed so reluctant to talk to him. She began wringing her hands, not making eye contact with him.

"Look at me, my Darling." She looked at him through watery eyes. "You don't mean you are married to someone else?"

"Yes," she mouthed. Sammy couldn't even hear her say it.

"Who is he? Where is he?"

"I don't know."

"You don't know who he is?"

"I don't know where he is."

"How could you..."

"When you left me for a man, I was so confused. I felt like it must have been my fault, somehow, that I wasn't good enough for you."

"No, Darling, it wasn't your fault at all. I was the one who was confused."

"Well, I was a mess. I couldn't face anyone, not even my dad. I became a recluse. I moved into the house you bought for me, which reminded me of you every second of every day, and really, I went into mourning. I felt like you had died. You were gone, with no chance of ever coming back to me. Really, I was mourning because our love had died."

"Love never dies, Darling. We might get it mixed up for something else, but love never dies."

"I know that now, but for more than two years, I mourned. Then I decided I should try to get on with my life. I went out to dinner a few times with a man who worked at the bank. He kept telling me he loved me and I wanted to believe him. It never crossed my mind that he was paying so much attention to me because I managed so much money, your money, but anyway, I guess I thought he could give me some sort of a normal life. When he asked me to marry him, I thought it was the right thing to do... until the day we got married. We went to Reno together and I thought I was just nervous. I thought I would get over it. But then I realized I still loved you, and I couldn't give myself to this man. The worst moment of my life was when I promised to love him forever. I knew I was lying, and I knew I couldn't really marry anyone if I couldn't marry the man I loved... but I said the words anyway. I felt like I was watching myself in a movie and I couldn't stop what was happening." Tears were running down Sara's cheeks, causing a pain in Sammy's heart like nothing he had ever felt.

"On our wedding night, we both realized that he was competing with my memory of you, my love for you. You still had my heart. He left the hotel the next morning and I never saw him again. I went back to Seattle, back to the bank and I found out he had quit his job. I don't know where he is. I felt like I was making a mistake, but I just couldn't stop myself."

"Who could have?"

"What?"

"Who could have stopped you?"

"I don't know, I guess I thought that if I wasn't suppose to marry him, God wouldn't let it happen."

"So, you thought a lightening bolt would come from heaven, or an earthquake, to stop the wedding?"

"Or something."

"I have learned that usually when you have doubts about something important, then you should not do it."

"I shouldn't have done it, I know that now."

"The trick is to know it then."

"I know that now."

"I'll hire a private investigator to find him. You can get divorced, and then we can get married. I don't care about him. I love you. Say you will marry me, Sara."

"There's more."

"More?" Sammy watched her speak with trembling lips.

"About six weeks after he left, I started getting really sick."

"Sick? What's the matter? Are you all right?"

"Just let me finish…I was throwing up all the time, so I went to the doctor and I found out I was pregnant."

"You're going to have a baby?" he asked, gently placing his hand on her stomach. "But you were together just one night?"

"That's all it takes."

Sammy didn't know what to say. He looked at her closely.

Sara began to sob. "I came here as soon as I found out about the baby, because I didn't want anyone to know. I was ashamed to be having a baby that wasn't yours." She searched Sammy's eyes, which were now damp. "I lost him a few weeks ago."

"You lost him?"

"It was a boy."

"Oh, my Dear, Darling Sara. I am so sorry." Sammy tenderly put his arms around Sara as she cried on his shoulder. "Surely you went to the hospital."

"What hospital, way out here? I was out in the yard, and I had really bad cramps, so I came inside to run a hot bath. I felt a little better after soaking for awhile. Just as I stepped out of the tub, he was born, and I caught him. He was tiny and perfect, but he wasn't breathing. He was so small, he fit in one hand."

The image of a tiny baby in Sara's hand broke Sammy's heart. "You were all alone," he said softly.

"God was with me."

"Did anyone come to help you?"

"I don't have anyone... no one but you."

"Where..."

"Way in the back of the yard, beyond the garden, by the back fence, I dug a little grave."

Sammy was crying now, holding Sara, sorry he had caused her so much pain. Everything that had happened to her was his fault, because he had been so selfish and had not seen the opportunity for happiness, for his and her happiness, right in front of him. They held each other for a long time.

"Sara, I'm sorry about last night. I had no idea—"

"Don't be sorry," she said, putting a finger to his lips. "Last night I began to live again."

"It won't happen again, until we get married. I promise."

"I can wait."

"So can I."

Part 3

SARA

CHAPTER 24
JUNE 1985

When Sammy and Sara returned to Seattle together they decided not to tell anyone of their engagement until Sara could get her divorce. They hired a private investigator to locate Sara's husband. Sara was so happy with her life with Sammy. When they were together, he acted as if he couldn't get enough of her; she was his precious gem that had been recovered, the light of his life. His music took a new direction, as Grand was still recording and touring, still the most popular band in the world. Sammy's haunting vocals on 'Who's Holding You Now,' which he had written while he was searching for Sara, made the song an instant world-wide hit. The emotion Sammy poured into his music was well-known and even expected by Grand's audiences. All across the United States and Europe, droves of people were constantly singing and chanting his new number one song: "Who's holding you now? Who can hold you now? Who's holding you now?"

Often Sammy brought Sara to stay at the hotel in the city where Grand was performing, always with her own suite of rooms, so they could avoid temptation. When Sammy was in Seattle, Sara spent most of her time at Queen Anne Castle, where Sammy had given her several rooms to use as an office, a sitting room and a bedroom with an adjoining bathroom. They decided she should keep her house until they got married.

Sara ran all the way from her house to Queen Anne Castle with her divorce papers in her hand. After searching the globe for nearly two years, the private investigator had finally found her husband, who agreed to sign the papers for a price: $150,000. Sara had the money, and it was well-spent, to purchase her freedom so she could marry Sammy.

Sara punched the code into the security box of the gate at Queen Anne Castle and the gate rolled to one side. She ran up the driveway and let herself in the front door. She flew up the steps up to Sammy's room, but he wasn't there. Imad followed her up the stairs.

"Looking for Sammy?"

"Yeah, where is he?"

"Hassan took him somewhere. They should be back shortly."

Sara went into her office and moved some papers from one place to another, excitedly waiting for Sammy to get home. Today they could finally announce their engagement! They were free to get married any time now!

Two hours later, Sammy stepped into her office and closed the door.

"Darling."

"Sammy!" Sara ran to him and threw her arms around his neck, kissing him.

"Imad told me you were here."

"I got the papers!" she said, smiling from ear to ear.

"Your divorce papers?" Sammy didn't seem as happy as she was.

"What's the matter? This is what we've been waiting for! Now we can finally get married!"

"Let's sit down," Sammy said, leading Sara to the sofa. The expression on his face was serious. Could he be having doubts? Didn't he want to marry her?

"What's wrong?" she asked, suddenly very worried.

"I just came from the doctor."

"The doctor? Are you sick?"

"Possibly."

"You look fine."

"I feel fine."

"Why did you go to the doctor?"

"Sara, you are the only one I can tell this to, and I know you won't tell anyone."

"No, of course. What is it? Is it cancer?" She could see it was something very serious.

"It's not cancer."

"What is it?"

"The man I was with…"

"Man? What man?"

"Antonio. I just found out that he died last week."

"So, what does that have to do with you?"

"He died of AIDS."

"AIDS?"

"You've heard of it, right?"

"Yeah, I heard something about it on the news. Isn't that a gay men's disease? But you're not gay!"

"I had a gay affair. I went to the doctor today to see if I have it."

"What did he say?"

"They gave me a bunch of tests. They won't have the results for at least a month or two. We can't announce our engagement until we find out if I have it or not."

"We can still get married."

"I can't do that to you. We couldn't live as husband and wife if I have it."

"I don't care if you have it. I still love you."

"It wouldn't be fair."

"You're not going to die. Look at you!"

"It's deadly."

"Let's just wait and see what the doctor says," Sara said. "I think you are perfectly fine."

"I pray that you are right."

"Is it dangerous for me to touch you?"

"No, it can't be transmitted by touch... only if we make love."

"What about kissing?"

"Kissing is allowed. It's not transmitted by kissing."

"I think we'll be doing a lot of kissing."

"The doctor said as long as I feel well and have no symptoms, I can live a normal life, although I didn't ask him what he considers to be normal."

"You don't feel sick, do you?"

"Not at all."

"You are fine."

"Thank you for believing in me."

"That's what love is."

Six weeks later, on a sunny August afternoon, Sara and Sammy sat on a bench at Seattle Center, holding hands. Sara gazed up at the Space Needle towering above their heads. Sammy spoke quietly, directly into Sara's ear.

"The results of my tests came back. I'm HIV positive."

"Positive... that's good, right?"

"No, in this case, negative is good. Positive means I have the virus."

"You have AIDS?"

"I have the virus that causes AIDS: HIV, human immunodeficiency virus."

"Are you sure?"

"Positive. They tested me twice, just to make sure."

"What does that mean?"

"It means I'm going to die."

"We're all going to die."

"If I don't make some lifestyle changes, HIV could rapidly develop into AIDS."

"What kinds of changes?"

"First of all, no more touring. I'll let the band know we can't go on tour anymore. Who wants to see a 40-year-old man jumping around on stage, anyway? We can still record. This would be a good time for us to work on our solo projects we have in mind. And there is some experimental medicine I'm going to try. If I start taking it now, it could add years to my life."

"How am I going to live without you?"

"We are going to make the most of every moment we have together. You are so precious to me. You have been my best friend, my confidante, my only love."

"Let's get married. I want to be your wife."

"I can't do that to you. It wouldn't be fair. It wouldn't be a real marriage. We can't sleep together. Oh, that's another thing. You need to get tested."

"Why?"

"Because we were together that night in Tuscany."

"But it was only one time."

"That's all it takes."

"Are you sure?"

"Sara... I was only with Antonio one time."

"No," Sara said, leaning back on the bench. This was not happening. Sammy wasn't sick and she couldn't possibly be HIV positive.

"You need to make an appointment, either with your doctor or at a clinic. They'll keep everything confidential."

Sara felt dizzy, hit in the head by reality. Their lives were ending; she could see the end of the road, with not enough time to get to the things she wanted to do. Where were their children? Where was the hope of growing old together?

"God is punishing us," Sara said quietly, looking at a gum wrapper on the ground.

"You don't believe that."

"Sin always has consequences."

"God is a forgiving God, not a punishing God."

"Why is this happening?"

"God has a reason. Come on, my Darling, you have always been the one with so much faith. Where is your faith now?"

"Do you believe in divine healing?"

"Of course. All healing is divine. Only God can heal people."

"God can heal you, us, both of us."

"I believe He can, but that doesn't mean He chooses to do so."

"Let's pray and ask him."

"Wouldn't that be a selfish prayer?"

"You sound like my dad."

"Speaking of your dad, we need to go see him."

CHAPTER 25

Sara's mind was completely unsettled. Where was that peace from God she used to have? Sammy was going with her to visit her dad, whom she hadn't seen in nearly 15 years; she and Sammy couldn't get married now, the only thing she had ever really wanted; Sammy was going to die, and she had to get tested for HIV.

"I can't do this," she whispered to Sammy, as they rode in the back seat of the limousine.

"You have to."

"I can't keep all our secrets from him."

"You have to."

"I'm not ready for this."

"We have to do this now. Life is fragile. We don't know how much time we have."

"Did the doctors tell you how much time you have?"

"If the medicines work for me, I could live another ten years or more. Maybe by then, doctors will find a cure for AIDS. On the other hand, a bus could hit this car today and both of our lives could end."

"Are you ready to go to heaven?"

"I'm not ready to leave this earth, but I'll go when God says it's my time."

"I mean, have you made peace with God?"

"The night I made peace with God was the night I decided to come back to you."

"Do you believe Jesus is the Son of God, He died on the cross for your sins, and God raised Him from the dead?"

"That's the basis of my Christian faith."

"You have always said you were a Christian, but have you lived a life of obedience, a life pleasing to God?"

"If I haven't before, from this day until the day I die, I will behave as a saint."

"I have been terrible."

"No, you have been wonderful. By your faith, your example of a Christian life, you have drawn me closer to God."

"I have wandered so far away from Him."

"How can you say that?"

"I haven't gone to church in 15 years, I haven't read my Bible in ages, and I only pray when I want something from God. Oh, and there's the little fact that I haven't even seen my dad since the day I moved out of his house, 15 years ago."

"You have told me many times, God is a forgiving God."

"He is."

"So, you can start over right now, with a clean slate. Ask Him to forgive you, and to fill you with His Holy Spirit to guide you do the things He wants you to do. You can go back to church. You can read your Bible. What better time than now?"

"You sound like my dad."

"I got it from you and I guess you got it from him. Full circle. Ahh, here we are."

Hassan stopped the car in front of the parsonage. As Sara stepped out of the car, her dad came out of the house to greet her. He looked so old.

"Daddy?" she signed tentatively.

He spread his arms for a hug. The years she and her dad had spent apart from each other closed into one moment. Sara was aware that Sammy was watching as she cried on her dad's shoulder.

"I am so sorry," she said.

"Sara, I am sorry, both to you and to your boyfriend – or is he your husband now?"

Sara realized she needed to voice what he was saying for Sammy's benefit.

"No, we haven't gotten married," she said. "We're just not ready yet."

"Come in, come in," her dad told them.

"Where is your wife?" Sara asked.

"Oh, didn't you hear about it?" her dad asked.

"About what?"

"She died about two months ago. She had cancer."

"I'm so sorry," Sara said, her own mortality becoming a reality. She wanted to tell him everything, but she had promised Sammy she wouldn't tell anyone anything.

"So, when is your wedding?" her dad asked.

"We haven't decided yet," Sammy said. Sara interpreted for him, wishing it were that simple.

"I won't ask why you left home," her dad said, "but why did you decide to come home now?"

"Love," Sammy said, signing one of the few words he knew how to sign.

"I love you, Daddy, and I missed you. Sammy convinced me that I needed to see you today. He wouldn't let me put it off any longer."

"I am so happy to see you. My life hasn't been the same without you here. I know it's a lot to ask, but please, will you consider coming back to church?"

Sara knew that was exactly what she needed.

CHAPTER 26

For the next month, Sara's mind was in turmoil. Attending church one Sunday did not relieve her burdens. She couldn't talk to anybody about her problems. The hardest part was not knowing, one way or another, if she was infected or not. All the time when she had no idea that she might have it, she was fine. Now that she knew she might be infected, she was torn. She tried to tell herself, whatever the results of the test, either way had its positive points. If she were infected, she and Sammy could get married; they could live as husband and wife. If he had already given it to her, she didn't have to be afraid of catching it; however, then she could be nearing the end of her life. She and Sammy would be together in the same boat, floating down the same river, going over the same rapids, hurtling over the same waterfall, plunging into the depths with each other. If her tests came back negative, she would have to get tested again in six months to be sure the results were still negative, and she would stay in the mode of waiting. Then, after six months, if the results were still negative, her health wouldn't be an issue, but her heart would be. She would be so close to Sammy, but they couldn't get married. She would do all she could for him, but, practically speaking, she would have to prepare herself to watch him die. He could die within a year or two, or he could live ten or more years, depending on how he responded to the treatment and how well he followed the doctor's instructions.

Sammy seemed to be so calm about everything, Sara couldn't help but wonder what was happening inside of him, as she sat beside him on a bench in one of the gardens at the Queen Anne Castle estate.

"You look worried," he told her, the day before her birthday. She was expecting to get the results of her tests by the end of next week.

"I am."

"Don't think about it."

"How can I not think about it?"

"There are millions of other things to think about."

"But none are…"

"What? None are as important as this one?"

She didn't answer.

"I thought you trusted God."

"I do."

"Can't He do anything?"

"Yes, but…"

"Is this too hard for Him?"

"No, nothing is too hard for God. Maybe it's not important enough to Him."

"Are any of our matters important to Him?"

"Yes, He cares about us."

"Do you think any of our affairs are too insignificant for Him to be concerned about them, or to do something about them?"

"Probably."

"So if it's a big matter to us, does that make it big to God?"

"Not necessarily."

"Where do you think He draws the line?"

"What do you mean?"

"Which of our problems or concerns is big to God, and which is small to Him?"

"I don't know."

"I think all of our problems are small to God."

"Since when did you start thinking so much about God?"

"When I realized that I not only put my life in danger, but I risked yours too. How can you ever forgive me?"

"Jesus forgave you. So did I."

"I should have controlled myself, that one time, of all times. I should have listened to that voice telling me I was making a mistake."

"You didn't know."

"I was irresponsible."

"I was, too."

"I should have –"

"You can't do that! You can't say what you should have or shouldn't have done. It's in the past, and, to tell the truth, the night we spent together in Tuscany was the best night of my life."

"Don't say that."

"It's true."

"You're saying, no other time we spend together can ever be as precious as that night?"

"I didn't mean it that way."

"Sara, every moment I spend with you is precious to me. Just sitting beside you is as precious to me as the night we made love. Don't look so sad. The doctors have declared death, but isn't God able to give life?"

"Yes, He is."

"Let's not behave as if we have no hope. We always have hope in Christ Jesus, don't we?"

"Yes."

"You know, it's so ironic. I used to feel that I had to be accomplishing something every moment of every day. When I had all the time in the world, I was so busy *doing*. Now that I know my time is limited, just *being* is enough.

"We need to get our priorities in order. My first priority is, I want to spend as much time as possible with you."

"I agree with that."

"We can travel anywhere in the world. Just tell me where you want to go and I'll take you there."

"I want to go where ever you are going."

"Unfortunately, I can't take you to the one place I would love to go, to my home country, Lebanon. It would not be safe for us to go there now. My father is going to bring the rest of his family and my mother's family to the United States. They live in a very dangerous area, just outside Beirut."

"I want to meet all of your family."

"You will. We shall spend the next few years together, or ten years or 100 years, however many years God gives us, and we will live as if we have nothing to worry about. Do we have anything to worry about?"

Sammy made everything seem so logical, so simple. Sara shook her head, but she still had the lump in her throat.

"Are you afraid to kiss me?" Sammy asked.

"No," Sara answered. "I can't catch it by kissing you... and if I already have it, well, then..."

She kissed him gently.

"You are afraid to kiss me."

"I don't want to hurt you."

"Hurt me? As long as you are here with me, you won't hurt me. If you leave me alone, now, that's what will hurt me, Darling."

"I won't ever leave you. I will stay with you as long as you want me."

"Ah, my one true and faithful. I want you to be with me forever."

"I love you forever." She gave him a passionate kiss and felt God lift her burden a little bit.

The next Thursday afternoon, Sara charged into Queen Anne Castle, running from room to room.

"Sammy! Sammy!" she called. She ran into the kitchen. "Where's Sammy?" she asked Imad, who was making bread.

"He's still asleep, I think. He hasn't come out of his room yet."

Sara scampered through the dining room, the front drawing room and foyer, sped up the steps and dashed to Sammy's room.

"Hey! Sammy doesn't like people running in the house!" Hassan called to her, as he was coming in the front door.

Sara gently opened the bedroom door to find Sammy seated at his desk, writing in a spiral notebook.

"Another song?" she asked.

"I just wrote four more. I wrote seven last night. I'm going to use them on my solo album I'm recording next month. Maybe I'll make it a double album, if I can get my musicians to learn – and play perfectly – all the songs in time. What's the matter, Darling?"

"My biggest fear just came true!"

"You got the results back? You're HIV positive?"

"No!"

"You're HIV negative? Don't tell me you wanted the results to be positive! Don't say that!"

"No, I didn't get the results back yet."

"Then what is it?"

"I dropped my keys down the storm drain in the street!"

Sammy smiled as he put his arm around Sara. "Sit down, Darling," he said, guiding her to the window seat that overlooked the back garden. He sat beside her and took both her hands in his. "We have some very important work to do."

"What?"

"I want you to go to your office, get a pen and piece of paper, and make a list."

"A list of what?"

"A list of ten things you want to accomplish before you die.

I'm going to sit in here and do the same thing."

"You've already helped me accomplish so much, Sammy, more than I ever thought I could."

"You can't count anything you've already done. We're starting from here, now, today, and we have until the end of our lives."

"But we don't know when that will be."

"So we better get started, right away." He kissed her on the cheek and returned to his desk. "Run along, Dear. We have no time to waste."

Sara carefully considered her list. She had been thinking for more than three hours, and with great difficulty had finally thought of ten things she wanted to do before she died; actually, before Sammy died, because she wanted to do all of them with him. She took the list with her to Sammy's room.

"Are you finished?" Sammy asked.

"Finally. That was hard."

"Let's make it easy. Sharing time. You go first."

"How about if I tell you one, then you tell me one?"

"No, I want to hear your whole list first."

"Should I start at number 1 or number 10?"

"Which one do you want to do first?"

"I don't know."

"Which one is more important to you?"

"Number 1."

"Start there."

"Okay, number 1, I want to be your wife."

"Scratch that one. We can't get married, Sara, you know that. We have to be realistic. You need to think up another one."

"I know, I just thought I'd give it a try. Okay, I have an alternate number 1. Be here."

"Be here?"

"Be here, with you, stay with you, for better or for worse, in sickness and in health. I'm committed." She couldn't say the final line she had written, 'til death do us part,' because she could see death in their future. She secretly wished she would die before Sammy died, because she didn't know how she could ever live without him; but he had told her how much he needed her, and how he was afraid of being alone, and she didn't want him to ever have to experience that.

"I'll accept that. That is within reason. Number 2?"

"Number 2, I want to buy a video camera so I can preserve our memories on tape, now, while we are both healthy."

"Piece of cake. Number 3?"

"My number 3, really, I guess it should be number 1, but it's to trust God and not worry at all, about any situation. That's going to be kinda hard."

"We can do it together. If you forget, I'll remind you."

"Number 4, I want to go into the studio with you when you record your next album."

"My solo album, or the next Grand album?"

"I don't know, it doesn't matter. Either one, or both."

"That's easy enough. Are you sure these things are what you really want to do, or did you just think of things that you know are possible?"

"No, these are things I really want to do. With you, everything with you."

"What's number 5?"

"Number 5, this might be harder, but I want to see you in concert again. Are you planning to do another concert?"

"I'm sure Grand will make a few more appearances. We're finished touring, though. Fifteen years on the road was enough. I'll make sure you get a front row seat and a backstage pass to every concert."

"Thanks! Okay, number 6, I want to visit every art museum

in Seattle with you. I want to go to every art exhibit, so you can tell me what you see. I want to see art through your eyes."

"Just take a look at my paintings hanging on the walls and in the studio down the hall."

"I know, I've seen them, but I want to go with you so you can tell me what you think about other people's art."

"Hmmm, interesting idea. I'll go for that, as long as we don't have to visit all of them in one day. What's number 7?"

"I want to ride the Princess Marguerite to Victoria with you."

"The Princess Marguerite?"

"Yeah, it's a luxury ferry boat that goes from Seattle to Victoria. We can see all the famous gardens in Victoria and everything."

"That sounds like a marvelous plan. Maybe we can get some ideas for our gardens here; not that there's anything wrong with ours, but I'm all for better gardens. We'll take that video camera you're going to buy, then we can remember what we saw. We can stay a few days – but wait, this is your wish list. Do you want to go and come back the same day? Or do you want to stay longer?"

"Whatever you want."

"Your wish is my desire, Darling."

"As long as we go when the weather is warm. Yeah, we should stay a couple of days. I hear they have tons of gardens up there. Okay, number 8, I want to paint a painting with you. I want you to show me how to paint a painting, a real one, on a canvas."

"Of what?"

"I don't know yet."

"We can go in the studio right now and accomplish that goal."

"No, not now. I don't know what to paint. Anyway, it's not at the top of my list. Besides, I still have to tell you numbers 9 and 10, and you have to tell me your list."

"Fire away."

"Number 9, I want to go with you to Mt. St. Helens."

"Why?"

"I want to look in the crater with you."

"Do you want to hike or rent a helicopter?"

"Can we do both?"

"It depends on when we go."

"What time of year?"

"How soon in life."

"Have you ever been in a helicopter?"

"Yeah, a few times. I don't really like them. Have you?"

"Not yet."

"We'll do it. So, what's number 10 on your list?"

"I want to go back to the top of the Space Needle with you."

"Why is that number 10?"

"Well, it's special, because that was where we had our first date, if you can call it a date, but it's last on my list because we have been there before, so if we don't make that one, that's okay."

"That's quite an impressive list you have there. Not bad for spur of the moment."

"It's not fair, you have probably been thinking of your list for days."

"Or years. That's beside the point. We can do everything on your list. But are you sure about it? I mean, don't you want to do anything for yourself? Every item on your list includes me."

"My whole life includes you. I don't want to do anything without you. Okay, it's your turn. What's your number 1?"

"I'm going to read my list, and I want you to wait until I finish before you make any comments."

"Why?"

"You'll see."

"Okay, number 1?"

"First, send my entire staff on vacation in Tuscany for at least a month, everyone who works for me, and everyone who lives here at Queen Anne Castle."

"That's number 1?"

"Shhh!"

"Oh, sorry, I forgot."

"Number 2, make contact with every one of my family members, to get to know them very well."

"That's a good one."

"No comments, please."

"Ooops."

"Number 3, read the Bible daily."

"Daily? That's good."

"Daily. Number 4, go to church regularly."

"Really?"

"Really. Number 5, exercise daily."

"You, exercise? When are you going to start?"

"Will you let me finish?"

"Go ahead."

"Number 6, sit peacefully in the garden."

"I love that one."

"Me too. Number 7, send a free copy of my solo album to every fan who has ever written to the fan club and mentioned my name. They are keeping all the records, aren't they?"

"I'm suppose to keep quiet until you finish, remember? But yeah, they are. Jennifer is really organized. She probably has every fan letter Grand has ever received filed by date or name or something."

"That's fantastic. Number 8, start a scholarship fund for college students studying music and give one million dollars every year."

"Wow, what a great idea."

"Number 9, donate a million dollars per year to charities of your choice."

"My choice?"

"You know better than I do who is worthy and needy. Can I afford it?"

"Sammy, Grand has generated more than two billion dollars, and you have more than seven hundred million dollars in your personal accounts. Plus, another royalty check is due this month."

"That's fine. So, those all need to be done in that order."

"You forgot number 10."

"I didn't forget it. Number 10, raise children in this house, here, in Queen Anne Castle. That has always been my dream."

"Adopt?"

"I don't mean that."

"What do you mean?"

"Look again at my list."

Sara looked. "You have 11 things listed."

"Read number 11."

"It says, 'Go on without me.' What do you mean by that?"

"Sara, this is a list of things I want you to do."

"Me?"

"After I'm gone. All except the first item on the list. When I get really sick, when you see that I am dying, I want you to send the staff away, out of the country. I don't want anybody here but you when I die. I don't want them to know until after I'm gone. I don't want anyone moping around or trying to do something at the last minute for me. I just want you here with me. We'll do your list while I'm here and I am still able to do these things, and then you can continue on with my list."

"Sammy..."

"Sara, will you promise me that you will do your best, so we can fulfill all 21 wishes, both lists?"

"I promise."

"But for now, Sara, will you just hold me?"

CHAPTER 27
JUNE 1993

Sara walked slowly around Queen Anne Castle, expecting to see Sammy at any moment.

"Sammy, I brought you something."

"What is it?"

"It's something to brighten up this place, to bring some life into your castle."

"Our castle," he corrected. "A kitten? Come here, Baby."

"Isn't he cute?"

"Adorable! What's his name?"

"He doesn't have a name yet. What do you want to call him?"

"Ember."

"Ember?"

"Isn't he the color of embers?"

"Glowing embers, maybe, but not burnt embers."

"His name isn't Burnt Ember. Just Ember."

Sammy was in every piece of furniture, every painting. His exquisite taste had decorated each room. Sara couldn't believe he was gone. She felt as if he would be coming around the corner, or sitting in the garden where they had spent so many afternoons and evenings.

"Darling, put away that paperwork. Come and sit with me in the garden. We don't know how much time we have. Let us not waste a moment we can spend together."

The patio garden was blooming with color and life. Seven cats: Ember, Sim-sim, Shavey Crockett, Albert McNebo, Silo, Cleo Clone and Beauhahnaphish now graced the castle. One of their favorite places was this garden. They were all lazing and stretching in the bright sunshine.

"These gardens are really amazing."

"Do you think we can recreate them back at Queen Anne Castle?"

"Sure, if we can just take that tree with us."

"And that waterfall, and those hanging vines, and how about the gardener?"

"Hold still, you have something in your eye."

"What is it?"

"Hold still, let me see..."

"Do you see it?"

"Oh. It's me."

"What are you doing?"

"Reading fan mail."

"You really get a lot, even now."

"You know, there are a lot of lonely people out there."

"Yeah, and your music touches so many of them. They connected with you, and maybe then they weren't so lonely."

"We are so blessed to have each other."

"I don't think we know how blessed we are."

"I know. We are blessed."

"What is it?"

"Can't you tell?"

"It looks a little abstract."

"It's you."

"That's what I look like to you?"

"No, that's what the paint brush made me paint of you."

"Hold still!"

"Why? That's a video camera. You are the one who has to hold still."

"We were here together exactly 20 years ago."

"It seems like just a few months since we met."

"Yes, but we have shared a lifetime of memories together."

"What is that?"

"A painting."

"I know it's a painting, but what is it suppose to be?"

"A good painting, but really, it's a bad painting."

"I thought art wasn't supposed to be good or bad."

"This one is bad."

"This next song is dedicated to the woman I have always loved, and she's here with us tonight, in the very front row."

"What are you doing?"

"Writing my memoirs."

"Can I see?"

"I haven't started yet."

"Your memoirs are in your songs. You must have written a thousand songs."

"2,642."

"Really? That many?"

"Yeah."

"And you said you weren't good with numbers!"

"That is one of my favorite."

"It's time."

"Time? For what?"

"For you to send the staff on vacation to Tuscany."

"I can't do it."

"Just tell them it's my orders, they all have been working too hard."

"No, I mean, once I tell them and they leave, that means..."

"It's time."

The memorial service had been private, with just Sara and Sammy's family in attendance. Thousands of fans had sent flowers and gifts when the news of Sammy's death had shocked the world. The official cause of death was pneumonia; Sara didn't tell anyone his secret.

"Are you still afraid of heights?"

"No. Yes. I don't know. Are you still afraid of being alone?"

"No. You have managed to cure me of that fear."

Sammy's cousins and the Queen Anne Castle staff returned from Tuscany when they heard about Sammy's death. Hassan mentioned that he thought Sammy was acting strange and spending too much time alone with Sara, but he hoped they were finally going to get married.

"Sara, can you pick up that pen for me? It rolled all the way under the table."

"Sure... I'll get it. Hey, here's the reason your stereo isn't working. The speaker came unplugged. I wonder if one of the cats did that? We couldn't see it from up there."

"It's amazing what you can discover when you get on your knees."

"You sound like my dad."

Maybe someday she would be able to watch the video tapes they had made together.

"I want you to have Queen Anne Castle."

"You should make it into a museum."

"No, I want you to have it. You have to raise children here. This should be a home full of life."

Several of the cats ran up to Sara when she entered the room. Ember jumped up on the counter, waiting for her to pet him. She scratched his back and wondered if he knew that Sammy wasn't coming home.

"I'm leaving everything to you."

"No, you can't do that. You have given me enough already."

"I want you to be able to enjoy life."

"I have enjoyed life, with you." She didn't know how she could enjoy life without him.

242

"I have written my will. My cousins, my parents, my sisters, my brother and all of my staff will each get a generous amount, and everything else goes to you."

"Sammy…"

"You are the one I have trusted, and you promised that you would always trust God."

"I do."

"God will take care of everything. I'm just helping out with your finances."

Sara picked up Sammy's Bible. She had been reading it every day for the past eight years, out loud to Sammy. This was the source of her strength right at this moment. She was not alone in this huge castle of a house; God was with her.

"Who else would show me such love and care and tenderness? I love you, Sara."

"I do it all for you, Sammy, because there's no one like you."

She looked at the two lists, still on Sammy's desk. They had done everything together on her list. Now it was time to work on the list he had made for her. She could feel Sammy's presence in the room.

"They did the tests a third time. I'm not HIV positive. It's been more than four years since our night together. They say since I don't have it now, I won't get it."

"I'm so relieved."

"I'm not. What am I going to do without you?"

"Everything on the list."

Other books by Dana Pride:

Immediate Search (Book 3 of Great Devastation Trilogy)
Hope Continually
The Hidden City (Book 2 of Great Devastation Trilogy)
So How is THAT a Bully?
After the Great Devastation
The Red Cloak
Nightmares of Murder
Existing
All These Things
Kissing a Dead Man
What Really Happened in Mexico
How to Get Fat Without Even Trying
Sayings of the Old Folks
Sayings of the Young Folks
Perceptions of Perfection: 66 Poems for a Rock Star
(written as Dana Fram)

Everlasting Publishing
P.O. Box 1061
Yakima, WA 98907
USA
everlastingpublishing.org